THE BLUE CANTINA:

DOWN THE DARK LADDER

By Paul Blades

I0638699

Dark Visions Publications
darkvisionspub@gmail.com

Other books by Paul Blades:

The Blue Cantina: Anna's Surrender
Klitzman's Isle
Klitzman's Empire
Klitzman's Paradise
Klitzman's Pawn Parts One and Two
Slaver's Dozen- A Tale of Klitzman's Isle
The Taking of Cheryl Part One
The Taking of Cheryl Part Two: Slaver's Bait
Comfort Girl No. 4
Sacrifice to the Emerald God
The Warlord's Concubine, Books 1, 2, 3 and 4
Dreams and Desires, Books 1 and 2
Carmella Condemned
Carmella's Fate

The Maddy Saga:

Vol. I	Maddy becomes a Ponygirl
Vol. II	The Training of a Ponygirl
Vol. III	Ponygirl Champion
Vol. IV	Ponygirl Summer
Vol. V	Ponygirl Love
Vol. VI	Ponygirl Season
Vol. VII	Ponygirl Gambit
Vol. VIII	Ponygirl Pleasures
Vol. IX	Ponygirl Peril
Vol. X	Ponygirl's Choice Part One
Vol. XI	Ponygirls' Choice Part Two

CHAPTER ONE

Anna was standing in front of the full length mirror on the inside of her bedroom closet door. It was a last minute check before she sat down on the bed and waited for the ringing of her doorbell that would signify that her lord and master had arrived. It was Wednesday, and she had officially been his slave for three whole days.

She didn't count the torrid weekend she had spent with Miles Devlin as part of her term of embondment. As harrowing as that had been, it had been merely a dry run. She had still possessed the power to walk away, to say, 'No!' Ever since Monday morning though, when the money that Carol had stolen was placed into her account at the Eastside Bank and Trust, the power to say no had been taken away.

Anna looked at the enticing face and body displayed before her. She had made herself up as Devlin had instructed: bright red lipstick, dark lines around her eyes, pale blue shadow on her eyelids. Her eyebrows had been tweaked just enough to tame their wildness and a very thin application of mascara had been used to darken them. She had powdered her face very lightly, just enough to give contrast to the mild blush she had applied. Her skin was naturally olive. In the summers, it turned a deep copper, a gift from her Italian heritage. Her eyes were soft and brown, set wide apart, a bit large for her face. Her nose was strong and noble, larger than the Anglo-Saxon ideal, but it gave her face a striking personality. Her lips were full and plump and her chin strong. It was not a submissive face. It had an aura of pride and self sufficiency.

Mr. Devlin had called and specified that she wear the short, silvery dress she had purchased on Saturday during her shopping spree rather than the long, green gown he had selected previously. It came down only about six inches from the base of her pudenda. He had specified that she wear no underwear and she was frightened that she would reveal her now hairless loins whenever she sat down.

Her legs were encased in dark, sheer, self supporting stockings. At the tops, around her thighs, there was about six inches of a lacy design, two inches of which were clearly visible even when she stood. On her feet were glittery, silver, four inch heels. They made her sinewy legs seem long and sleek and raised her heavy breasts to presentation position. She was worried about that too. She had long, fat nipples and they could be easily discerned behind the thin fabric of her dress. If they stiffened for one reason or another, they would stand out like points. The neck line of the dress swept low and hung loose, revealing an embarrassing amount of her pulchritude. If she leaned over, anyone looking would be able to see her entire breasts. She knew that any man standing in front of her, if he looked down, would be able to see just about all there was to see. She was only 5'5" tall and there were plenty of men taller than that.

A tuft of her now mid-length, black hair had escaped from behind her ear and she brushed it back. The large diamond post she wore in her earlobe sparkled in the light. She turned her head forward so that she could see them both. She had worn them constantly, except when asleep, since Mr. Devlin had given them to her. They had caused quite a stir at the Center. There were several female staff members whose job it was to serve as regulators for the behavior of the young girls who lived there. They all oohed and ahhed when they saw the bright jewels. They were distinctive. Anna had never owned anything so beautiful or valuable. What the women at the Center didn't know was that they were really Miles Devlin's badges of ownership. Every time she saw them, she remembered that she was his slave now. It made him seem ever present.

Satisfied that she looked her best, as Mr. Devlin had commanded, Anna went back and sat on her bed. She thought back to how she had finally committed, after a long, agonized night, to accept Mr. Devlin's money and save the Center.

When she arrived home that Sunday night, she flung herself on her bed and cried and cried. Partly it was because of the cruel treatment she had received. Her body was covered with the evidence of her beating at the hands of Vincent, Mr. Devlin's butler and major domo. Her rear still burned from where Mr. Devlin had cruelly pierced it with his cock just before she left. The memories of how meanly he had treated her were etched into her brain, how he had used her like she was his property, without regard for her feelings or the pain he caused her. But that was only part of it. She cried because she had enjoyed it.

Deep down inside, it had been the most passionate experience of her life. The feelings of debasement were familiar to her from her childhood, after all that her father had done. It felt like Devlin had discovered her secret shame. Being used like a whore triggered some desperate need inside her. What her father had done had made her feel dirty, sluttish, made her believe that that was who she really was. It had taken years of therapy to convince herself otherwise. Miles Devlin had exploded all of that artifice of deception in three days.

After she finished crying, she took off her clothes and took a long, hot shower. The soothing flow of water was a beneficence. She was careful to wash completely her now hairless mons and her rear aperture. She dried herself off, blow dried and combed her hair, donned a lacy, cotton, pink nightgown, poured herself a couple of ounces of scotch and got into bed. She lay there, propped up against her pillows, sipping at her nightcap, agonizing whether or not to accept Devlin's perfidious deal. Every time her mind went back to the violent, enthralling sexual use that had been made of her, her pussy began to burn and her breasts grew hard and hot.

But every time she thought of the cane with which Vincent had beaten her, the sting of Devlin's sharp words, the humiliations he had forced upon her, her stomach quailed.

Her hand, as if of its own volition, drifted down to her smooth, naked love lips. She idly slipped her fingers over them. A warm feeling suffused her. And then she remembered Devlin's instructions. She had been told to get herself off every night before she went to sleep. It would be a daily reminder of her subservience to him and the nature of their relationship. She was his toy, his fuck thing. His whore. More than a whore, a slave.

Her long finger of her right hand found its way to her sensitive love button. Before she knew what she was doing, it had commenced a gentle, slow circuit around it. She closed her eyes. "I have to do this," she thought, fighting off her own reserve. "I have to do this."

Her legs spread. Her knees raised. Her nightgown had been pushed up around her waist and she slipped her free hand under it, caressing her tummy and then moving up to seize a breast. She squeezed it tenderly and then flicked her finger over her already stiffened nipple.

"But what if I don't do it?" she thought idly as her finger's caresses to her clit became more pronounced. "How will he know?" She slid her finger down into her slit to gather up some moisture and then rubbed it over her hard nubbin. She took a deep intake of breath as the feelings of pleasure coursed through her.

"How could he know?" she repeated in her mind even as her needs began to rise. She thought of his fat cock slipping back and forth in her pussy the time he had fucked her on the floor of his large library. She had had the folds of the green gown he had bought her flipped up over her torso and over her head, closing her in darkness. She was on her elbows and knees. Her legs were spread wide and her back arched, her ass bare. And he had fucked her and fucked her and fucked her.

She moaned at the recollection and her finger's activities became more urgent. "He fucked me. He fucked me," she repeated to herself again and again.

She remembered her orgasm, how it thrilled her whole body, shook her innards. That was what it was going to be like. He would fuck her and fuck her and fuck her, she thought. He would make her come again and again. She slipped her two longest fingers deep into her crevasse and began to work her clit with her thumb. "Ohhhhhhhhhhh," she moaned. She squeezed her breast harder and then the other one. "Oh, god, what am I doing?" she murmured to no one. "Oh, it feels so good! It's good! It's sooooooo good!" Her breathing got deep, her heart started to pound. Her lusts were overflowing. When her climax came, she groaned loudly, "Arrrrrrrrrrrgh! Arrrrrrrrrrrgh! Arrrrrr-rrrrrgh!" Her back arched and her heels dug deep into the mattress. Her knees spread as far apart as they would go. "Arrrrrrrgh! Arrrrrrrrgh!" she groaned.

When her convulsions were done, she lay there for a while, letting the pleasure drift through her. A few moments later, she was asleep.

The next morning, she was still unsure whether she would go through with this devil's bargain, become Devlin's slave for a year in exchange for him replacing the money that Carol stole, right up until the moment that she heard the ringing of her doorbell a little after 8. Her apartment was actually the east wing of an older house that had been converted to three living areas. Anna's apartment was the remotest of the three, sharing only one common wall, in the bathroom. It was almost as if she lived in a detached dwelling as far as privacy went. The other tenants were a single guy who was away on business trips most of the time and an elderly couple, at the far end of the house from Anna, hard of hearing and in bed each night before 10.

She opened the door and it was Devlin's driver, Carlos. His swarthy face exhibited a lascivious grin. Anna had not forgotten the two hours or so she had spent with him in her little prison on the fourth floor of Devlin's mansion. He had fucked her like she had never been fucked before. He had taught her how to deep throat. He had left her hogtied and gagged when they were done, telling her, "That's the way to tie up a whore!" She had no doubt that he was recalling their encounter as well.

He didn't need to tell her what he was there for. She was ready to go, all dressed up in her workaday clothes, a knee length, beige, wool skirt, a long sleeved, vermillion colored, ribbed, pullover top, shiny apricot colored shoes with modest heels. In accordance with Mr. Devlin's orders, she wore no panties. She didn't like it; she felt half naked. But she didn't want to risk him coming by and checking. It was just something he would do. Devlin had ruled them out except for the scanty, lacey underthings she had bought on Saturday when she went shopping with Elaine, his apparent mistress, or one of them anyway. They were all still at the mansion.

She had agonized over whether to wear a bra. She still had her modest, cotton ones. She would be breaking one of Devlin's many rules if she wore one. If she had learned anything over the weekend it was that his orders were always precise and literal. He had said he wanted her to wear nothing underneath except what he had bought for her. Did she want to start her year of slavery with a breach of her obligations?

When she put the vermillion top on without the bra, her very ample, but not oversized breasts swung loose, swaying every time she moved. It would be obvious to everyone that she didn't wear one. She bit her lip in frustration.

In the end, she decided that she would wear it. Devlin had said that he wanted their relationship, or at least the more harrowing parts of it, kept secret. If she started dressing like a high school kid trying to score, it would be obvious to everyone that something had changed about her. She doubted she would see Devlin today anyway. She left it on and hoped for the best.

She got in the back seat of the limo and Carlos drove her to the bank. He didn't say a word to her, thank god. Her bank was on Bayard Street at the corner of Willow about four blocks from the Center. Devlin had introduced her to the CEO of the bank, Mr. Harrington, on Saturday night out at his club and told her everything had been taken care of. No one would blanch at her depositing more than $200,000 in cash into her account.

She walked in, Carlos trailing behind her holding a slim, black valise. She went directly to the branch manager's office and told him that she had a large amount of cash to deposit. She didn't want to do at a teller window with everybody watching. As promised, she had been expected. Mr. Morris, the manager, was punctilious in his politeness. He closed the door after them when they came in. Carlos placed the valise on his desk and sat down next to Anna on one of his visitor's chairs.

Mr. Morris was about 5'6" tall, thin and mousey. He wore steel rimmed glasses and a polyester blend brown suit with light orange pinstripes. He had lost all but a thin crown of hair and he had brushed a few long strands over the bald spot in a vain attempt at disguising it. His desk was neat and clean with only a desk pad, a round container holding about fifteen pens with the bank's logo on them and a picture of his fat wife and three plump kids.

Mr. Morris opened the valise nervously. He peered into it and took in the sight of the neatly banded bundles of cash. "I-I don't think we need to count it here," he said, a tremble in his voice. "Mr. Harrison has made me fully informed. I've already made out a deposit slip. All you have to do, Ms. Addunizio, is to sign it. My teller will count it later. I'm sure that there won't be any discrepancy."

Anna's insides were boiling. She crossed her legs and then uncrossed them before leaning over the desk to append her signature to the instrument of her doom. Her hands were sweaty and her heart was pounding in her chest. Her mouth was dry. She hesitated for a moment and considered what would happen if she just got up now and walked out of the bank. The Center would have to close in less than a week. Scandal would break out over the lost money. Mr. Devlin would make sure that the hounds of legal hell pursued her. She would be disgraced, maybe jailed, for Devlin had her handwritten confession. She was sure he would use it even though he almost certainly knew she hadn't taken the money. Her eyes moistened in self pity and she had to blink twice so that she could see where to sign the deposit slip clearly. She took a deep breath and signed the warrant of her embondment.

Mr. Morris took it from her quickly and placed the valise on the floor behind him. "If you'll wait right here, I'll have the deposit slip stamped in," he said before rushing away.

Anna sat back in her chair. Carlos was a lurking, evil presence beside her. He was broad shouldered, with a large mouth that always seemed to be set in an ironic smile. His cheek carried a small, narrow scar suggestive of a knife point flicking across his skin. He had large, strong hands that Anna remembered taking purchase on her body, molesting her breasts, covering her sex, twisting and turning her love lips until she squealed with pain. She tried not to think of his thick, long cock as it had choked her the other day and that she would certainly experience again. She lowered her gaze and kept it on her folded hands in her lap. There was an aura of electricity in the air, like just before a thunderstorm. She could hear Carlos breathing.

The bank manager came back quickly. "Here's your receipt," he started to say as he proffered the damning document to Anna. Carlos reached out and snapped it out of his hand.

"I'll take that," he said in his raspy voice. Anna looked at him. He was smiling that evil smile that he had. She looked quickly away.

"Is there anything else I can do for you, Ms. Addunizio?" Morris asked her standing next to his desk.

"N-no," Anna replied. "Thank you."

She and Carlos got up and left.

It was a short drive to the bank where the Center's accounts were kept. Her checkbook was in her plain, black, snap topped pocketbook and she took it out and wrote a check for $227,475.28, the amount of the County grant Carol had absconded with. She made it payable to the Lincoln County Center for Young Women. She followed Carlos into the bank. Devlin had specified that he wanted a copy of the check so she went to an assistant manager and asked for her to make one for her. The young woman, dressed in a matronly business outfit much too mature for her, smiled and took the check. She came back a moment later with the check and the copy.

Anna handed the copy over to Carlos and then went to the service counter for a deposit slip. She had the account number written down in her small diary she kept in her pocketbook and copied it out. There was no choice now but to go through with it to the end. Devlin's money was already in her account and the die was cast. She looked at the large number on the deposit slip after she wrote it. "It's okay," she told herself. "I'll get through it somehow and the Center will be saved. It'll be worth it. I just know it will."

She stepped over to a teller. There was a large woman, past middle age, in front of her wearing a long puce colored wool coat that went down past her knees. Anna tapped her foot as she waited for her to complete her transaction. Carlos was hovering menacingly by her shoulder. Even though it was too late to turn back now, a thousand butterflies were doing the jitterbug in her belly. When the older woman stepped away, Anna stepped up and handed the teller the check and the deposit slip. The teller, a young Asian man, hardly looked at her. He ran the check and the deposit slip through a machine, tore off the back sheet of the deposit slip and handed it back to her. He looked up and gave her a manufactured smile. Anna took the receipt and stepped away. Carlos had his hand out and she handed it to him.

Everything was done. She was almost relieved. All the angst she had suffered about whether to go ahead with her deal with the devil had gone. The deal was sealed. The only options she had now were to be Miles Devlin's slave or take off and keep running for the rest of her life. She knew that he would keep his promise to make sure that she suffered grievously if she double crossed him. His gangland connections would chase her down eventually. So there was really no choice at all. A year wasn't an eternity. She would get through it somehow.

There was one more stop to make. Carlos halted the limo at a hardware store and placed his hand out. Anna put the key to her apartment into it. Devlin wanted no barriers to his use of her. She dreaded the idea of having to worry about whether he would show up at her place, or coming home and finding him already there, going through her most intimate things. Or maybe waking up in the middle of the night as he let himself in. It was the worst part of the whole thing. She would have no sanctuary, no place where she would be safe from him.

When Carlos came back, he gave her back her key and drove her to the Center. He had hardly said a dozen words to her. She half expected him to demand a blow job before he let her go. She wondered what she would do if he did. Mr. Devlin hadn't said anything about performing for him. Maybe she should just refuse. But sooner or later, he would have her alone in the fourth floor room that had been her cell at the mansion. If she refused him now, what would he do to her then?

To her great relief, he didn't ask. She shut the door to the limo after she got out and watched him drive away, the evidence of her guilt, the evidence with which Devlin would damn her if she crossed him, in his pocket.

It was a quarter after 9 when she walked into the old house that served as the Center's home. It had been conveyed to her in the will of the old woman who had saved her life, lifting her out of degradation. Anna had gifted it over to the Center a little over a year ago. It was the only way she could get the mortgage for the expansion that included more dormitory space, a bright new refectory and a nice lounge for the girls who lived there. Anna didn't mind. She wasn't in it for the money.

She turned and looked at the buildings that housed the Center. The older part, the former residence, was a three story Victorian dwelling. It was built in the 1920's by a rich businessman with a large family. The front of the house had a porch that went around the front and about half way around the sides, six steps up from street level. On the ground floor it originally had a large sitting room, facing east and referred to as the morning room, a formal salon off to the left of the entrance hallway, a spacious dining room, a family room and a large kitchen. On the second floor was another large sitting room with a balcony that overlooked the street. There were two large adjoining bedrooms separated by a common bathroom, which were designed for the husband and wife. Both had spacious dressing areas. On the third floor were four bedrooms for the children and above that an attic.

Anna's office was on the ground floor in what had once been the morning room. It had a beautiful view of a park across the street. The windows were large and the woodwork was exquisitely carved. Anna had mounted pretty, chintz curtains that recreated, in her mind, the Victorian atmosphere of the place. She had a large, spacious desk positioned so that she could see out of the window and a sitting area where she sometimes had one on one meetings with her staff and met with girls who lived there to discuss one troubling issue or another.

The large formal salon on the other side of the entrance hall had been converted into two rooms. In the front was the conference room. It was here that staff and Board meetings were held. Toward the back of the building, the other half of the salon was converted into offices. This is where Carol's office was and the office of the head of development, the Center's principal fundraiser. The rest of the ground floor was devoted to the kitchen and a cramped cafeteria.

On the second floor were offices for the other staff, mainly counselors and caseworkers, a lounge for the girls, a meeting room and a staff lounge. There were also two training rooms where the girls were taught word processing and other secretarial skills in one, and basic skills like reading and writing and basic job hunting skills in the other. There was a small library and reading room too.

The girls' bedrooms were on the third floor, enough room for twelve girls, three to a bedroom, and a bedroom/apartment for the staff resident, the woman who minded the girls after all the other staff went home for the night and on weekends. For the first years of the Center, that seemed to be enough. After a while, though, it was clear that dozens of eligible girls were being turned away because of space considerations. Even after they had started putting four girls to a room, there hadn't been enough space.

That was when Anna started to campaign for enough money to build the annex. Fundraising went into high gear. Anna was busy, it seemed, every night, at this social event or another, networking and seeking out rich donors. It was how she had first met Miles Devlin. It had been at a Community

Chest event, the countywide charitable fundraising organization. It was an awards banquet and Anna had received an award for the Center's work. In her acceptance speech she outlined the Center's need for more space, pleaded for an understanding of the importance of her agency's work in the lives of the young women it served and pointed out the huge population of girls in their city separated from their homes for one reason or another and who were daily sinking into lives of sexual exploitation, drugs and even death.

Devlin approached her after the banquet and offered his services. Anna had heard of Miles Devlin. No one who lived in their city had not. He was well known for his 'associations' with underworld figures and existing at the borders of many significant scandals. He had even been indicted once on a bank fraud charge, but the State's two principal witnesses mysteriously disappeared never to be seen again. The indictment was dismissed.

Devlin offered a donation of $50,000 towards the building fund. When Anna brought his donation back to the Board of Trustees, they immediately voted him a place on the Board. Two years later, he was the Board President. It was he who had arranged the financing for the annex once the original building had been signed over by Anna. It was at the grand opening for the new wing that he had first asked her out. Anna had politely refused. She had always since seemed to have been able to find a reason to dodge his luncheon invitations and invitations to his many parties.

The two story annex allowed them to almost triple the beds for the girls. The local community college held a business class there. There was a workout room. A larger kitchen had been installed and a comfortable, bright, airy cafeteria. The second floor was devoted to a dormitory. There was enough room for thirty four girls. There was a large playroom on the first floor with a ping pong table, a large screen TV and some computer games.

The older girls were now housed two to a room in the original building. The oldest was 23. The girls in the annex were generally between the ages of 18 and 21. Girls who were younger than 18 were usually sent to foster homes until they reached the age of majority.

Anna took a deep breath. The Center would continue. There were still many problems. The primary one now was a replacement for Carol. She had been Anna's first assistant. She had done much of the scheduling and had managed the agency accounts. That was how she had gotten into the position to walk off with over $200,000, their quarterly County grant. Anna had trusted Carol implicitly, to her dismay. Now that she had to be replaced, she was looking for someone who could take some of the staff supervision duties off of her as well. That meant a trained social worker, which Carol had not been. She also wanted the new person to be able to help with career placement for the girls, something that was kind of haphazard now. The whole point was to secure for the girls good futures.

Devlin had told Anna that he was sending by today a woman he was recommending for the job. Under present circumstances, Anna knew that his suggestion was tantamount to an order to hire her. Anna had determined that she would give the woman a chance to convince her that she was qualified for the job but if she clearly wasn't, if she was just one of Devlin's bimbos he was looking to palm off on her, she would tell her no and take her chances with Devlin. After all, she was sacrificing enough to save the Center. She wasn't about to let it go to pot because someone unqualified was working there.

Anna walked up the steps and entered the building. She was a little later than she usually got there and the place was already bustling. There were several phone messages. Anna's secretary, Phyllis, sat right outside her door in the foyer, and also served as the greeter for visitors. She handed Anna her messages. Phyllis was a tall, thin, attractive redhead. She was in her forties and sometimes tried to mother Anna a little bit. When Anna went to take the messages from Phyllis's hand, Phyllis held on to them.

"Nice earrings," she crooned. "Has Anna found a sugar daddy?"

Anna smiled. It was hard to get angry at Phyllis, even when she was nosey. Her disposition was always pleasant.

"Oh, these," Anna replied. She had prepared her story in advance.

"They were a gift from my aunt several years ago. They've been just sitting in my drawer ever since. I decided that I shouldn't waste them any more. Aren't they pretty?"

"They sure are," Phyllis agreed. Maureen, one of the counselors, was coming down the stairs. "Look at Anna's earrings," Phyllis said. Maureen came over and looked.

"Wow," she commented. "Diamonds are a girl's best friend. They look fabulous. Where'd you get them?"

"They were a gift from her aunt," Phyllis interjected. "Or so she says." A smirk crossed her face.

"Everybody has their secrets," Anna retorted before she knew what she was saying. She realized as the words left her mouth that truer words were never spoken. If these women, or any of the women who worked for her had known what she had done, would they understand or would they hold her in contempt?

"I came down to talk about my schedule," Maureen said. "I'd like to shift some things around."

"And you told me to remind you that the money needs to be in to the payroll account by Tuesday," Phyllis said. "And a couple of the vendors are clamoring for payment."

These were things that Carol had handled.

"Yes," Anna replied. "Can I talk to you about it this afternoon?" Anna asked Maureen.

"Well, okay, but I need to know as soon as possible so that the girls can rearrange their schedules," Maureen said. "And there's some other matters I need to talk to you about. And Katie and Marsha have some scheduling issues too. They asked me to tell you."

Anna sighed. She still hadn't gone through last week's case notes on the girls, something she usually did on Saturdays. And then there were next week's schedules to work on and several applications for new girls that Carol usually screened and wrote up for her. The Community Chest representative was coming at 1 to discus their grant application and she needed to set aside some time to talk to the new caseworker, Linda, about her case notes. They really needed to be more thorough. The woman Devlin had sent was coming at 10. There were three more interviews in the afternoon. It was going to be a hectic day.

"Okay, I can see you at 11," she told Maureen. To Phyllis she said, "I'll work on the payroll this afternoon too, as well as the bills. Is there coffee?"

"I just made a pot and one of the girls brought in bagels. Do you want me to get you something?" Phyllis asked.

"That would be wonderful," Anna replied. "I didn't have time for breakfast this morning." The truth was she had had a bowl of cereal but had thrown it up. "I wouldn't normally ask, but I'm just so harried today."

"I know, sweetie," Phyllis replied. "It's no problem. Sesame seed with butter and milk no sugar, right?"

Anna smiled nervously. Phyllis knew almost everything about her. How was she going to hide the thing with Devlin? "That'd be fine," she said.

She walked into her office. The in basket was filled with some purchase requests from staff, a couple of trip requests for the girls, letters from other agencies regarding coordination of services and some invitations for social events she usually attended for PR reasons. There were inquiry letters to write to potential employers for the girls and other correspondence to get out too. Then there were the phone calls to return.

Anna put her overcoat on the rack and then plopped herself into her chair. Was she the same person who had left this desk on Friday night, she wondered. The short answer was no. She felt like the weekend with Devlin had been a shift in the paradigm of her life. Nothing would ever be the same.

She picked up her phone to return the first of the calls. She was still on the phone when Phyllis came in with her coffee and bagel. She gave the woman a nod of thanks and continued with her call. She wolfed down her coffee and bagel in between returning calls and fielding new ones. It was ten o'clock before she knew it. She hadn't even looked at the case notes when Phyllis buzzed her to tell her that a woman was here for her interview. Anna had forgotten to tell Phyllis about it and she sounded a little miffed. Well, she would have to live with it.

"Send her in," Anna told her.

The woman who entered looked to be in her mid-thirties. She had dirty blond hair cut in a flippant style. She was tall and slender and pretty. Anna noticed that she had full makeup on and painted nails. Her blue and white dress was just above her knees and she wore tall high heels. The dress was cut a little low in the front. To Anna, she had bimbo written all over her. Her stomach clenched at the thought of confronting Devlin about her. But she had to draw the line somewhere.

Just as the woman sat down in one of her visitor's chairs in front of her desk, Phyllis buzzed her again.

"It's Mr. Devlin," Phyllis said. "And he sounds pissed. I told him you were in a conference, but he was insistent."

Anna's blood ran cold. She knew she had to take the call. "Okay, I'll take it," she replied.

She picked up the phone, one resentful eye on the woman sitting before her.

"Yes, Mr. Devlin," she spoke into the phone.

"I don't ever want to hear from that bitch that you're in conference when I call ever again. Do you understand me?" Devlin spat out.

"Y-yes, Mr. Devlin," Anna replied nervously.

"Is Ms. Johanson there?"

"She just walked in, Mr. Devlin," Anna told him.

"Good. I want her to start work tomorrow. Understand?"

"Y-yes, Mr. Devlin."

"And Anna, Carlos told me that you are wearing a bra today. Get rid of it."

Anna wanted to protest. How could she go around all day without a bra? Eyes would turn.

"I mean now, Anna. Do it now. I'll hold."

"Y-yes, Mr. Devlin," Anna replied. She looked up at Ms. Johanson. Devlin would probably ask her later whether Anna had obeyed. So she couldn't fake it. She put down the phone. She couldn't possibly take off the bra right here in front of this woman. She would have to go to the bathroom. But what would she do with the bra when she took it off? She couldn't come waltzing out with it in her hand. She would have to throw it in the trash.

"Excuse me a moment, please," Anna told the woman. "Would you like some coffee?"

"No thanks," Ms. Johanson responded. "But thank you anyway."

Anna nodded. She got up from her desk and walked out into the foyer. The bathroom was down the hall. Phyllis looked at her inquisitively as she passed. Anna said nothing. When she got to the bathroom, she locked the door. She didn't want to pull her vermillion top up over her head, it would mess up her hair. Reaching her arms under, she unsnapped the bra strap behind her back. She would have to take it off like they did in high school. She pulled her arms up out of her top and then slid the bra straps off of them, the top around her neck. She watched her breasts bounce free. She then reinserted her arms and pulled the top down over them. It was just like this morning. You could tell right away. The bra kept her ample orbs set up high. Without it, they hung low, not sagging, but giving in to their natural weight.

She recalled when Devlin had first demanded that he see them, after dinner that first night. Her embarrassment at the time seemed now almost quaint. He had seen all of her after that. She had spent practically the whole weekend naked. And he had fucked her several times. And then there had been Vincent and Carlos too. They had both seen her naked. And they would again, this weekend, if not before. Anna watched as tears came into her eyes. Devlin had reached into her sanctuary and despoiled it. Was this what it would be like? And he had demonstrated to Ms. Johanson his power over her. But she would know that already, or at least part of it. He had probably told her that the interview was just a formality.

Anna went to toss her bra into the garbage bin. It was empty. Anyone who came into the bathroom after her would be able to see it. She grabbed several towels from the dispenser and wrapped the bra in them and then dumped it into the wastebasket. When you looked down you could still see it. She quickly pulled out some more towels and placed them over it. It was not much of a covering, but it would have to do. After Ms. Johanson' interview, she would come in with her pocketbook and put the bra in it.

She rushed back to her office, not giving Phyllis a glance. Ms. Johanson was waiting patiently. Anna picked up the phone as she sat back down at her desk.

"Hello," she said.

"I don't want to have to ever tell you this again, Anna," Devlin said, his voice ominous. "You belong to me now, body and soul."

"Y-yes, Mr. Devlin," Anna answered, her voice shaky.

"Are you wearing panties?"

"No, Mr. Devlin."

"Do I have to send Carlos over to check?"

"No, Mr. Devlin."

"Don't think I won't."

"No, Mr. Devlin," Anna replied. Devlin's voice was loud. She wondered unhappily if the woman could hear him. She hoped not.

"That's all for now," Devlin said. He hung up.

Anna placed the phone in its receiver. She looked up at Ms. Johanson. She expected to see a smirk on her face, but there was none, only the somewhat anxious face of a job applicant. Maybe she was wrong about her after all, Anna thought.

"I'm sorry for the interruption," Anna said. "I under-stand that you know Mr. Devlin?"

"Yes," the woman replied.

"And how do you know him?" Anna asked, surprised at her own audaciousness. After all, everything she did or said with this woman would probably go right back to him.

"He's the friend of a friend," was all that Ms. Johanson answered.

"May I see your resume?" Anna asked.

Ms. Johanson handed Anna two sheets of ivory bond. As Anna leaned forward, she felt her breasts shift under her top. She noticed Ms. Johanson' eyes flit to her chest and then look up right away. It was going to be like this all day.

The resume was neat and orderly. Anna leaned back in her chair and read it. Her full name was Esther Johanson. She had graduated from Michigan State 15 years ago, which made her probably 36 or 37. Anna was surprised to see that she had a masters in social work from the local City University. She had worked in a state program for disabled children for her first seven years. She had had her own counseling business for five. After that, she worked for a private counseling service out of state for three years. Miles Devlin was her only reference.

"How do you feel about working with teenage girls?" Anna asked.

"I worked with a lot of teenage girls when I had my own business," Esther said. "It's challenging, but rewarding. There are so many issues for them to deal with, so much more than boys."

"Do you have any experience with substance abuse issues?"

"You can't counsel teenage girls without it," Esther answered. "I'm a few credits short of obtaining a substance abuse counselor's certificate," she added. "I'd like to finish that up this spring part time. If my working schedule permits it, of course."

The interview went on for another half hour. Anna could see nothing wrong with her, except for those three missing years out of state. She would have to check up on that. She was surprised that Devlin had actually sent her a candidate that was qualified. More than qualified. She had Carol beat all over. It might be nice to have someone experienced with case work to talk things over with. She seemed alert, responsive, able to communicate well. She had a certain lack of self assurance, but Anna put that down to her natural nervousness about the job interview. It was possible, after all, that she didn't know that Devlin had put his thumb on the scale for her.

It was just that there was something about her that didn't seem right. She tried to pry a little bit about her personal life, but Anna knew she could only go so far with that or be in violation of equal opportunity laws. She wore no wedding ring on her finger. When Anna told her that she would have to spend some nights at the Center to monitor the girls, she didn't seem to have a problem with that, so she probably didn't have any children. Her attire was a little bold for a social worker, but that could easily be taken care of. Wouldn't it be nice if her search for Carol's replacement was really over?

Well, the decision had already been made for her anyway. With this resume, she had no grounds to oppose Devlin's demand.

"Okay, you have the job," Anna told her. A broad, gratified smile broke out over the woman's face.

"Oh, thank you, Ms. Addunizio," she said.

"Can you start tomorrow?"

"Oh, yes, Ms. Addunizio," Esther replied.

"Okay. Please be here by 8 A.M. Your normal hours will be from 9 to whenever your work is done, but tomorrow I want to give you an orientation and show you the facility. "

"Certainly, Ms. Addunizio," Esther agreed.

"And please call me Anna. We're all informal here."

"Yes, of course, Anna,"

"See you tomorrow then."

"Yes, bright and early."

Anna watched her leave the room. She still had an undifferentiated feeling that there was something wrong about the woman. But it was too late to do anything about it now. Except to check that out of state reference. She made a note to herself.

The rest of the day went by rather normally. She did the other three interviews anyway, cutting them short. She told Phyllis to cancel all the rest, that the job had been filled. Phyllis was surprised, but said nothing. No one said anything about her lack of a bra either, although Anna was conscious of it all day. There had been several somewhat startled looks though. She had surreptitiously retrieved her garment from the bathroom after Esther left.

That night, Anna got home after 8 p.m. She took a cab since she didn't have her car. She was tired. There was something about her apartment that was not right. She detected it immediately as she came in. There was not much to it. There was a small kitchenette and a dining area. She had a small sitting room where she sometimes watched TV and read. Then there was the bedroom. She had a queen sized bed and it filled up most of the room. There was a second hand dresser for her foldable clothes, a chair in the corner and a closet that was a little large considering the size of her living space.

When she went in the bedroom, she noticed that the closet door was slightly ajar. She hadn't left it that way, she was sure of that. She immediately went over to it and opened the door the rest of the way. She was shocked to see a number of the dresses she had bought with Devlin's money on Saturday. On the floor were several of the shoes she had purchased. She went over to her dresser and opened the underwear drawer. All of her panties and bras were gone. In their place were the scanty things she had bought with Elaine. Someone had been in her apartment! It had to be Carlos. She cringed at the thought of the man pawing through her things. She sat on her bed for a while, tears in her eyes. Then she shook herself out of it. What could she do about it anyway? This was the deal she had made. She would have to live with it.

She ate a small dinner and went to bed early. Her hand went to her pussy, remembering Devlin's instructions. But she was tired. It had been a long, stressful day. He would never know. She rolled over and went to sleep.

CHAPTER TWO

Tuesday, wearing her new, immodest underthings, she gave Esther her tour and introduced her to everyone. Esther was dressed a little more demurely. Anna had one of the other staff members cover the phones while Phyllis broke her in to the accounts payable and purchasing procedures. Anna had her sit in on a staff meeting. She seemed to be getting off to a good start.

About 1:30 Devlin called. Anna had instructed Phyllis to put him through immediately regardless of what she was doing. Phyllis gave her another one of her looks but said nothing.

First, Devlin asked her what she was wearing. She told him and dutifully indicated the new delicates she had under her clothes.

"That's good, Anna. Don't think I've forgotten about yesterday. You will have to be punished for that."

"Yes, Mr. Devlin," Anna answered, her blood running cold.

"I've purchased a membership at the Downtown Club for you. I want you to spend an hour there every day working out. Do you understand?"

"Yes, Mr. Devlin."

"Starting this afternoon. There's already a locker picked out for you and it's filled with all you'll need. Workout clothes, shampoo, soap, makeup, a hairbrush, everything, so there's no excuse for not going is there?"

"No, Mr. Devlin," Anna conceded.

"You have an appointment with your trainer at 4. Be there. That's all," he said and hung up.

At 4, she showed up at the Downtown Club. It was a ritzy gym, full of stockbrokers, upper level corporate management and a few up and comers. It was very exclusive and very expensive. Anna knew that Devlin must have had to pull a few strings to get her a membership.

She went to the main desk. A beautiful, shapely, young blond girl in tight fitting workout clothes was behind it. Anna explained who she was and that a membership had been taken out in her name.

"Oh, yes," the woman said sweetly. "Mr. Devlin arranged everything. You have locker number 47. Here's the key. Would you like me to give you the tour?"

"No, thanks," Anna replied. From the look that the girl gave her, she realized that she thought that Anna was one of Devlin's bimbos. Well, she was, wasn't she?

The girl pointed out the way to the locker. "Your trainer's name is Cathy," the girl told her. "She has brown hair in a long ponytail. You'll find her in the trainer's room," she said helpfully.

The locker room was plush and well appointed. The floor was carpeted and there were polished wooden benches in front of them. The fronts of the lockers were made of polished wood too. Beautiful, refined women, ranging from about 27 or 28 to well over 50, self confident, well maintained, were all around in various states of undress. Anna remembered how it had been in high school. Girls would be trying to hide their nudity from each other as they rushed to dress and undress for gym class. Things had changed. These women had no compunction about letting it all hang out. They had no reason to. They all seemed to be perfectly formed, trim, vibrant. None of them were sex slaves, Anna was sure of that. Their banter was confident, jestful, challenging.

Anna went to her designated locker. She opened it with the key. It was full of workout clothes and toiletries. Anna looked at some of the labels. The clothes were top of the line. The toiletries too. There was a pair of Reebok trainers, white with pink laces, just in her size. Anna realized that Devlin, or whoever bought these things since she doubted it was him personally, had gotten her sneaker size from Carlos when he ransacked her closet.

She dressed silently and quickly in a pair of blue gym shorts and a matching sports bra. She knew that the black and blue from her beating had not yet faded and she was embarrassed that any of the other women might see it. She was ashamed of her denuded pussy too, although she saw one or two of the other women the same way. That didn't help much. She still thought of it as being lewd and obscene. She tied up her sneakers and went out to the gym.

The trainers' office was right off of it. She saw a handsome, fit man, obviously one of the trainers. He directed her to Cathy. She was compact, about 5'4", and had a fit body. She looked to Anna to be about 22. She shook Anna's hand friendlily and led her out to the workout room. She gave her a quick tour of the machines, one for each type of exercise and laid out a routine for her.

She pinched Anna's soft, not quite flabby arms. "We'll get these trimmed up nicely in no time," she said confidently. "Your legs and ass too. You might lose an inch or so off your boobs, but the rest of you will be trim enough so no one will notice. And believe me, when I'm done with you, no one will ever throw you out of bed."

Anna recoiled at the girl's statement. Devlin had done just that the first time he fucked her. He had literally thrown her on the floor and then whipped her with his belt for being an unresponsive fuck. Did the girl know? Had Devlin told her all about her?

Under the watchful eye of her trainer, Anna performed the various exercises demanded by the machines. It wasn't long before she was sweaty and tired. But Cathy kept her going on and on. "Come on," she called out to her, "you can do better than that! Don't be a pussy!"

By the time they were finished, Anna was drained. Her muscles screamed with ache. Cathy made an appointment for her the same time the next day. When Anna was leaving to go back into the locker room, Cathy said. "See you tomorrow! And say hello to Mr. Devlin for me."

Anna showered and dressed quickly.

She went back to the Center for a couple of hours. She wanted to stay later, but she was worn out from her workout. When she got home, a little after 7:30, she ate a can of soup and went to bed. She slept all the way through.

Devlin called her a little after 2 o'clock the next afternoon, Wednesday, with her instructions for that evening. He told her about the change of plans about her dress and to be ready and waiting by 7. Anna went to her workout, as required, and drove straight home afterwards, exhausted, like the day before.

Now, at exactly 6:55, she was all dressed and made up for her master's pleasure. She had suffered Devlin's scorn when she had been 5 minutes late last Friday. She didn't want to risk it again.

When the doorbell rang, Anna jumped. She grabbed the small silver purse that had been purchased as an accessory for the dress and went to the door. Devlin had said nothing about an overcoat and so she didn't put hers on. Besides, she had nothing that would match the mod stylishness of her dress. It would have looked stupid.

Carlos was there. On the street, behind him, was the long black limousine. Anna stepped out of her apartment and walked the 100 feet down the cement path to the car door. Her high heels clicked as she walked, reminding her of when she walked across the slate floor of the foyer to Devlin's mansion. Like then, she felt like she was walking to her doom.

Carlos opened the door for her. She tried to get in without having her dress pull up, but she was unsuccessful and it came up almost to her waist revealing her hairless mons.

She blushed as she felt Carlos' eyes on it. She tried to keep her thighs pressed tightly together.

Devlin was sitting on the other side of the backseat. He was dressed in a finely tailored, dark blue suit. His short, black hair, as always, was perfectly trimmed and combed. He had a strong, very masculine face. He was broad shouldered. Anna wasn't sure of his age, but she guessed it to be somewhere between 38 to 42. On his left hand was a solid gold ring with an insignia on it. It reminded Anna of the insignia of the club they had gone to. It was on the door of the nightclub that was called The Blue Cantina.

When she had slid into her seat, Anna first tugged at her skirt, pulling it back down her thighs as far as it would go and then put her hands behind her back. This was per Devlin's standing instructions. She didn't say anything, but waited for Devlin to speak. That was also one of his rules.

"Good evening, Anna," Devlin said, his voice deep and creamy, as the limo took off from the curb. "You look marvelous. Let me see your pussy."

Anna was startled by the request, not because of its nature, but because it had come so quickly after her arrival. Dutifully, her heart beating wildly, her stomach a flutter, she turned on the seat and drew the hem of her dress back up to her waist. Devlin was to her left and she lifted her left leg up on the seat so that she could spread her legs. She had to shift her bare bottom over on the leather seat and lean back so that he could get a good view of her mons.

Devlin reached out his hand and took possession of it. "Very pretty, Anna," he said. "I've been thinking about your pussy ever since Sunday. I see you shaved it very recently. That's a good little girl." She had, in fact, shaved it each morning after her shower, a procedure that was both strange and titillating, and, just to be safe, an hour before Devlin's arrival.

His thumb was working up and down the divide between her exposed love lips. Anna felt her heat rising right away. "Oh, god, he's going to fuck me," she thought desperately.

"It's a little rough. Did you shave recently?"

"Y-yes, Mr. Devlin," Anna replied.

"Did you use a lotion afterwards?"

"N-no, Mr. Devlin."

"You need to use a lotion to keep your pussy nice and soft. I'll have something delivered. Make sure you use it."

Anna didn't answer. She had learned the hard way that Devlin's comments didn't require a response. Only his questions.

Anna kept her elbows down on the seat of the car for balance as they sped along. Devlin continued to work her puss until it had moistened and he could sink his thumb into it easily. Anna sighed and closed her eyes.

"You really are a whore, Anna," Devlin said finally, removing his hand. "Maybe I should put you out on the street so you could earn for me, maybe get some of my money back. Would you like that, Anna?"

"N-no, Mr. Devlin," Anna replied. Her eyes were glassy with tears. Why did he have to insult her so? Hadn't she done everything he asked? And then she thought. No, she hadn't. She hadn't jilled off last night or the night before. She didn't know if she could lie to him, but she had to or else he would punish her.

It was the very next thing out of his mouth. Anna had remained in position, her thighs widespread, her pussy proffered for his visual, and if so desired, tactile enjoyment.

"So have you been a good girl, Anna? Have you made yourself come every night like I told you?"

Anna's stomach flipped. She felt herself sweating. Her mouth was dry and her throat felt thick. "Y-yes, Mr. Devlin," she muttered. She knew right away that he didn't believe her.

"You're lying, Anna," Devlin said, harshness in his voice. "Do you know what happens to people who lie to me?"

"Y-yes, Mr. Devlin," Anna replied, sickened with fear.

"What happens to them, Anna?"

"Th-they get punished."

"That's right, Anna. They get punished. And do you deserve to get punished? Were you lying to me?"

Anna panicked. If she confessed, she doomed herself to suffering. If she lied again and he didn't believe her, she would make it even worse. The fact that she knew she could not make herself sound convincing dictated only one possible response.

"Y-yes, Mr. Devlin," she murmured. She was trembling. How could she have been so stupid! She wanted to beg him not to punish her, to grant her forgiveness. But she knew better than to talk.

There was a long silence. Devlin had his hot hand on her naked thigh. She could feel her lips trembling. In a moment, she was going to burst into tears. She would ruin her makeup. Then what would he do?

"We'll deal with that later," he said finally. Dread covered Anna's heart.

"Come here," he told her.

Anna brought herself to her knees on the seat and approached him cautiously. He took hold of her arm and dragged her closer so that their bodies touched. He took a handkerchief out of his right pocket and began to dab her eyes with it. "There, there, Anna," he said. "No crying now. We're going to have a good time tonight. And there's a little surprise for you too. You'll like it."

There had been a moment, this past weekend, when she was walking down the stairs of his mansion with him, when he held her hand in his, that Anna had felt an unnatural warmth passing through her. Here was the man who had tormented her and caused her to suffer excruciating pain, but yet she felt closer to him than anyone in her past. That feeling passed through her again now. It was such a rare feeling, one she had searched for for so many years, that her eyes began to brim with tears again. In a moment, she would be bawling.

"Come on, now, Anna," Devlin said, his voice soft and warm. "Chin up. I know you want to be a good girl. It's going to take a lot of practice. And I have to punish you when you've been bad. You know that don't you?"

"Y-yes, Mr. Devlin," she moaned. Somehow what he said was comforting. She was a good girl. That's what was important.

"I want you to suck my cock now, Anna. That'll take your mind off things."

Anna gave him a little nod.

"Open my fly and take out my cock. And remember, hands behind your back."

Anna nodded again. His words were a statement, not a question.

She fumbled a moment with his fly and then zipped it down. He wore silk boxers and she was able to reach in and extract his cock through the slit in the front. It was already at half mast. She propped herself up as best she could, one knee on the seat, her right leg on the floor, placed her hands behind her back and took his instrument in her mouth.

The salty maleness was familiar to her. She slid her lips down his hardening pole as far as she could and then drew them back again. He had been right. This took her mind off her prospective punishment, but it brought it right back to his reference to her as a whore. Carlos was in the front seat listening to the whole thing. Her dress was still up around her waist, revealing her round rear cheeks. And the sensation of having his prick between her lips, feeling it hardening by the second and finally having it's full, steel hard length within her, made her pussy burn.

She sucked him slowly, leisurely, as he liked it. It was difficult to keep her balance and a few times she had to rest her breasts on his thigh so that she wouldn't fall over. His hand wandered to her naked rear haunches and stroked them softly. "Mmmmmmmmmmmmm," he moaned lowly. "That's good, Anna. That's good," he said.

Anna had no idea where they were going or how long it would take them to get there. It was dark outside and she hadn't had the chance to see even which direction they were headed in before Devlin had secured her undivided attention. She just knew that she had a task to fulfill and that she better not make him come before he was ready. She was alert to his slightest moan or movement. His hand drifted up her back and began stroking her head gently, soothingly.

Fifteen minutes later she felt the limousine slowing to a stop. Bright lights shined in the windows. They were tinted, but she could hear people talking outside the car. The idea of her sucking Devlin's cock in the midst of a crowd of people, even though they might not be able to see her, made her whine with unhappiness. She did not flag at her duty though. She kept slowly raising and lowering her head, washing the iron pole with her tongue, pushing its tip deep into her throat, as she had been taught, on each downward stroke.

She heard the front window of the limo opening and Carlos talking to someone about a pass. Her insides ran cold and she tried to lift her head up off of Devlin's cock in panic. He grabbed her hair behind her head and kept her in place. "Don't even think about it," he growled. "You're not done yet."

Anna whined again. She began to quicken her strokes to try and get her ruler to want to come, but he held her head steady and forced her to slow down.

"I can see that Carlos is going to have to give you another lesson in cocksucking, Anna," he told her sternly. "Maybe I'll have him take you to a public park at noontime, the one across from your office, and make you blow him there where everybody can see it. Maybe then you'll get over your stupid ideas of modesty. Modesty is inappropriate in a whore, Anna. You're going to have to get used to that idea. Now take your time. I'll tell you when I want to come."

Anna cringed at Devlin's words. She believed his threat. And she knew he was serious about further lessons from the coarse Hispanic. She pleaded in her mind for Carlos to shut the window. Anyone passing might look in and see her. She did not know where Devlin had taken her, but it might be someone that she knew. The way that Devlin had gripped her hair, her face could be plainly seen.

She was relieved to hear the window roll back up and the limo begin to move again. Her jaw was beginning to ache. Devlin's cock was a rude presence in her mouth. The vehicle began a series of starts and stops as if it was in a line of traffic. She realized that wherever they were, there was probably valet parking. Any moment the door to the limo would be opened by one of the valets. He would see her with Devlin's cock in her mouth. "Please! Please! Please come! Please!" she thought frantically.

Suddenly, Devlin's hand began to force her movements to become faster and faster. She heard him groan. "Okay, Anna," he said, his voice strained. "Make me come! Now!"

Anna sucked at Devlin's cock for all she was worth. Her tongue began an energized series of washings along its stem. She had lost control of her movements. Devlin's hand was dictating her hectic pace. The head of his cock delved deeper and deeper into her throat making her choke. It was getting hard to breathe. Devlin's thighs quaked and she felt his cock begin to pulse in her mouth. He pushed her face down hard, until her nose pressed against his stomach, and jetted himself directly into her belly. She had to grip her hands behind her to prevent herself from fighting him, from trying to lift her head from his loins. She knew she couldn't last much longer. The need for air was becoming acute.

Just as suddenly as his convulsions had begun, he gave a great sigh and relaxed. He eased her head up slowly. "Keep your lips tight, Anna. Don't get any cum on my pants," he told her.

She did as ordered. Her mouth was blocked, but she took in a deep breath through her nose. It felt wonderful to have the air flowing. Devlin released her head.

"You can get up now, Anna," Devlin told her. She rose, letting his cock slip from her lips. The residue from his orgasm slipped off the end of his dick and onto her tongue. She dutifully swallowed it.

Just as she rose, the rear driver's side door was pulled open and a young, male voice said, "Welcome to Eastside Bank and Tru...."

Anna looked up. It was a young man, probably not over twenty. He was wearing what looked like a college varsity jacket zipped up to his neck against the cold. It said "STATE" across the front. His eyes bulged a little when he saw her. It was obvious to anyone what she had been doing. Her legs were still spread and her dress was hiked high. Devlin's fly was still open and his softened cock was hanging loose.

"Put me away, Anna," Devlin ordered her.

Shame rushing through her, Anna tucked Devlin's cock into the slit in his boxers and, not without some difficulty, pulled up his fly. Her eyes were pointed down, but she could feel the eyes of the young boy washing over her.

When she was done, Devlin moved to get out of the car. Anna followed him, pausing only to grab her little silver pocketbook from behind her. Her skirt remained hiked until she was able to stand up. She quickly pulled it down, but not before the people getting out of the car behind them gave her a startled look.

Devlin was several steps ahead of her. She had to hustle to catch up with him. As she was trotting shakily on her high heels across the tarmac, she realized that they were at her bank. This was its corporate headquarters. The building right in front of her went up at least thirty floors. It was a traditional corporate monolith of steel and glass. The area was brightly lit. Fifteen feet of macadam separated the limo from the steps leading up to the entrance. There were twelve long, white, granite steps stretching across the front of the building. A large fountain was spouting water high into the air illuminated by blue, yellow and green spotlights. A steady stream of people were advancing up the steps ahead of and behind her. She wasn't worried about the ones ahead of her, but her skirt was so short that she was afraid the people behind and below her would see her bare ass.

Devlin paused for a moment, letting her catch up and then took her by the hand. His hand was large and strong and it made her feel like a little girl all over again. They ascended the stairs and reached a wide landing that led to the entrance. The first floor of the building was surrounded by glass that went all the way from the ceiling to the floor. She could see inside a number of finely dressed, elegant couples who had already gathered there.

Then she remembered. She had seen it in the paper. Tonight was the night that the bank was dedicating the Nathan Rosenfeld mural. Rosenfeld was known worldwide for his expressionistic murals. The bank had paid $750,000 for it. It was going to be the centerpiece of its cavernous foyer, a testament to the bank's commitment to art and its wealth. If you could spend $750,000 on a mural, you were doing pretty good.

Devlin pulled her into the building. It was cold outside and Anna knew that her teats were like darts. It was just what she had been afraid of. They approached a greeting desk and Devlin showed his invitation. The woman behind the desk was just beyond middle age and was dressed in a crisp, well tailored business suit. Her finely crafted hair was frosted grey. "May I have the name of your guest, Mr. Devlin?" the woman asked.

Devlin told her. "She's from the Lincoln County Center for Young Women," he added.

The lady, who was wearing a name tag with the bank's corporate logo and the name Martha Schopenhauer, Director, Community Relations on it, wrote out Anna's name and affiliation on another one. She handed it to Anna and smiled. "Nice to meet you, Ms. Addunizio," she sad. "I've heard such good things about your organization. Give me a call sometime and we can discuss some internships we can set up for your girls."

Anna was pleased, despite her earlier humiliation and treatment. She could still taste Devlin's cum in her mouth. And she was very conscious of her bare pussy and hardened teats. "Thank you, I will," she replied.

"Here's my card," Martha proffered.

Anna took it and placed it in her pocketbook. She took the label, pealed off the back and placed it on her dress. It just fit on the strap that held up her bodice. Otherwise, she would have had to place it on her tit.

Devlin led her into the milling crowd. Waiters were circulating with trays of *hors d'oeuvres* and plastic glasses of champagne. Devlin grabbed two glasses. He handed one to Anna. "Drink it," he told her.

Remembering Devlin's literalness, Anna poured the dry, sweet liquid down her throat. She received immediately a slight buzz. It felt good. Devlin took that glass from her and handed her the other. "Drink it," he ordered again.

Anna took that glass and downed it as well. She let go a little burp when she was done. Another waiter was passing by and Devlin stopped him. He put the empty glasses on the tray and took two more. He made Anna drink them too. When she was done, she had to pause for a moment to let the wave of dizziness pass.

"Okay, now," Devlin said. "Mingle. Make some contacts. If you see Ted Harrington, be nice to him. Got that?"

"Yes, Mr. Devlin," Anna replied.

"When they unveil the mural, I want you to be standing over there by the elevators. I'll meet you there."

Anna was tempted to answer with an affirmation, but caught herself. It was an order, not a question. She had to keep on reminding herself.

Anna was somewhat appalled to be out in a crowd like this dressed like a Miami Beach disco queen. She knew that inevitably she would meet people she knew. As she watched Devlin walk away, her prediction proved true immediately.

"Anna!" she heard from behind her. It was Doug Malsby from the County Child Welfare Agency. He sent the Center lots of referrals. Once in a while, she was able to wheedle some grant money from him.

They talked for about fifteen minutes. He saw someone else he knew and he begged off. Anna had felt his gaze flitting from her tits to her face, down at her legs, to her tits again and than around the horn. Word would be out tomorrow around the small community of social agencies around the county about how she was dressed and who she was with.

An hour later, she was still drifting amongst the crowd. There was a jazz quintet playing. People were laughing, chattering. Anna had had two more glasses of champagne. Devlin had not said that she could, but he hadn't said that she couldn't. She couldn't very well mingle without a glass in her hand, could she? Besides, she wanted to deaden herself as much as possible for what was going to come later.

Suddenly, she felt a tap on her shoulder. It was Mr. Harrington. He was tall and thin, handsome, with grey flecked hair. He was formally attired in a dignified yet contemporary black tuxedo, a ruffled, white shirt and a large, black bow tie. At the club, where she had first met him, he had seemed a little out of place, tentative. Here he seemed to be in his element. Before he could say anything, two different people accosted him, shaking his hand in congratulations and patting him on the back. Anna wanted desperately to flee. He had some nefarious relationship with Devlin and his club. He had taken Elaine away to fuck her that night. He had ogled Anna lugubriously. But Devlin had said to be nice to him. What did he mean by that? Certainly it didn't mean running away the moment he saw her.

"Good evening, Anna," Harrington said. "You look alluring tonight."

"Thank you, Mr. Harrington," she replied. She noticed that he didn't tell her to call him Ted.

"Did Mr. Devlin tell you to be nice to me?"

"Y-yes, Mr. Harrington," Anna replied, taken aback by his bluntness.

"Good. Then I want you to come with me."

He took her hand and pulled her towards the elevator. He pressed the button and the door shushed open. He pulled her in and the door shushed closed. He took out a key and turned it in a button marked 'Executive Offices'. The elevator began a powerful ascent.

Less than fifteen seconds later, the door shushed open once again. Harrington had spent the entire trip staring at her with a satisfied smile on his face. Before they got off, he turned the key, locking the elevator. They stepped off. It closed and hurtled back down to the ground floor.

The hallway was as quiet as a church compared to the lobby. Anna had a terrible feeling in her belly. The floors and walls were black marble. A thick, navy blue rug ran down the middle of the corridor. A large reception desk sat just opposite the elevator. Behind it, on the wall, was the bank's logo.

"This way," Harrington told her.

She followed him down the plush hall. Beautiful paintings, all looking like originals, lined the walls. At the end of the hallway, there was a pair of double doors with a large plaque on it stating that it was the office of "Theodore H. Harrington, Chief Operating Officer and President." Harrington pulled another key out of his pocket and opened the door. He stepped back to let Anna pass.

The office was spacious and splendiferous. His desk, naturally, was as large as a city block. It was mahogany and looked like the trimming on it had been hand carved. Two elegant, padded chairs with arm rests stood before it. Along the wall, on the right side, were two brown leather couches fixed at right angles to each other and a long, glass coffee table in front. The floors were polished oak and large, hand woven area rugs sat underneath the desk and visitor's chairs and the couches and coffee table. The wall behind the couches was paneled in oak to match the floors

On the opposite wall was what looked to Anna like a well stocked bar. It was mirrored and reflected herself back to her. She cringed at the sight.

There were more paintings on the walls, but these seemed more exquisite and more valuable than the ones in the hall. One of them, Anna was sure, was an original Renoir.

Harrington had turned on the light when they entered. It was on a dimmer, and he kept them down low. He was standing there, watching Anna absorb the impressiveness of his private domain. She walked around slowly, taking in the exquisite pictures until she reached the desk. The wall behind the desk was all glass. From it, you could see for many miles. The city lay below them, lit up brightly. A stream of little white and red dots showed where the freeway was. Several of the neighboring buildings, almost as tall as the bank building, but not quite, had floors that were lit, but most were dark. When Anna got near the window and looked down, she could see the plume of the fountain near the entrance. She seemed to be miles above it.

Harrington had moved to the bar. She heard him fumbling around with ice and glasses. "Rob Roy, straight up, isn't it?" he asked her. He had to make his voice loud to stretch over the vast area of the office.

It didn't matter to Anna what she drank. It was what she had had ordered for her by Devlin the night she met Harrington at the club. It would do. Anything would do right now.

"That would be nice," Anna replied. There was that word again, nice. What did it mean? There was nice, polite and then there was nice, nice and all that it implied. Anna was thinking that Mr. Devlin had meant the latter and her stomach was taut with apprehension. Is this why he had been brought here tonight? To be nice, nice to Ted Harrington? Was that the big surprise that Devlin had promised her?

She heard Harrington approaching behind her. He was carrying two wide, crystal cocktail glasses. One contained a murky, dark red liquid and the other was clear as water. It had three onions in it. Her Rob Roy had a cherry.

He handed her glass to her. He didn't bother to toast. His eyes flitted up and down her figure. He took a sip of his Gibson. Anna took a sip of her drink. A large sip. It was cold and bit sharply despite the sweet vermouth.

"You are beautiful, Anna," Harrington told her. "You are quite a catch."

A catch? Yes, that's what she was. Devlin had caught her in his nefarious net, just like that unknown woman who had been at the mansion on the fourth floor when she had. She had heard her walking down the hall after she had been returned to her locked room. And then there was Esther Johanson. Was she a catch too? And Elaine? How many women did Devlin have in his clutches? Did he pass them all around like he was apparently passing her?

Anna wanted to get it over with. Harrington, it appeared, was of the same mind.

"Finish up your drink," he said coldly. "I haven't got all night."

Dutifully grateful for the numbness it would bring, Anna tossed back the rest of her Rob Roy. She shivered when it entered her. Harrington took the glass from her and then tossed back his martini.

"Take off your dress," he ordered.

A stab of helplessness and shame pierced her. She glanced out the window and wondered if people could see up into the office. She wanted to ask if they could do it over by the couch, but she was afraid to question him, just like she was afraid to question Devlin.

There were two little buttons at the top of her dress behind her neck and she reached back and loosened them. Her motion caused her breasts to lift. When the buttons were loose, she lowered the zipper and then shimmied the dress down her torso, over her hips and down her legs. As she stepped out of it carefully, making sure she didn't catch either of her high heels in it, she could feel her breasts sway and jerk. When she stood up again, she saw that Harrington was looking at them. She tossed her dress aside.

"Hands behind your back," he ordered her sharply. Anna complied. He placed the two empty cocktail glasses down on his desk and stepped forward. He placed his hands on her breasts, squeezing them, weighing them. He flicked her stiffened nipples with his thumbs. "Very nice, Anna. Very nice," he said. He leaned over and took one of her nipples in his mouth. He sucked on it gently, running his tongue over it and then shifted to the other and did the same. Anna, despite her revulsion at being treated this way, felt her lusts begin to rise.

Having satisfied himself at her breasts, he took hold of the hair behind her head and pulled her against him. He took her lips in his and insinuated his tongue into her mouth. His tongue was insistent. He had her breast in his other hand and while he explored her mouth, seeking out her tongue and dancing with it, he massaged and caressed her breast. Anna let out an involuntary moan.

Harrington pulled back. "Get on your knees," he instructed her. Suppressing a sob, Anna sunk to her knees. Harrington had his stiff cock out in a minute. It was long, but thin. The head was bulbous, a little out of scale with his shaft, as if it had been cemented on from another model. It was angry red.

Anna didn't wait for instructions. She leaned forward and took it in her mouth.

Harrington moaned and groaned as she suckled him. She scoured the length of his rod with her lips, using her tongue to enflame it. She suckled at the end, running her tongue over the tiny slit. She couldn't help think of the incongruity of her nakedness with his well tailored, formal attire. Would this become one of her tasks now? To come by Harrington's office whenever he desired her to suck him off, nude but for her stockings and high heels, in his elegant, finely appointed office? She was conscious of the window at her back. Could people in neighboring offices see her? One of the nearby office buildings was fairly close and there had been lights on in a few windows on the upper floors.

"That's good, Anna. That's good," Harrington kept repeating. She could sense his trembling every time she descended her lips to the bottom of his shaft, lodging his cock's helmet in her throat. He let her go on for about ten minutes.

He slipped his cock from between her lips. "Get up," he spat out at her. When she obeyed, he dragged her over to his desk by her arm and told her to lean over it. Her breasts were crushed against its cool surface. She spread her legs without being told. She felt him approach behind her and then the tip of his cock begging entrance to her womb. It slid up and down her moistened cleft and then plunged inside.

Anna sighed with unwanted pleasure as she was pierced. Her hands were still behind her. Her head was laying on the desk, turned to her left so that it was resting on her cheek. Her view was of the glass wall and the bright array of lights beyond it.

Harrington was pumping quickly, urgently. She felt her passion rising. His hands were on her hips and holding them tight. He groaned loudly. Anna knew that in a moment he would fill her with his spunk. She whined in misery even as her pussy burned with pleasure. When he came, he shouted loudly, "Oh, yeah! Oh yeah! Oh! Oh! Oh!"

His exclamations were contagious and Anna felt her pussy explode. His spurts and throbs within her were met with fierce, body wracking contractions. "Oh! Oh! Oh! Oh!" she called out. "Ohhhhhhhhhh!"

As his ardor melted away, Anna's body shivered and quaked. Her pussy was still giving her echoes of her orgasm when he withdrew from her.

"I have to get back downstairs," he said, his breath still short. "There's a bathroom behind that door. Wash your-self off and come down right away. The unveiling is in ten minutes."

Anna was still prone across his desk when she heard the door open and close. She was trying not to sob. Mr. Devlin was right. She was a whore. It didn't matter whose cock it was. Now she was Harrington's whore too! Where would it end?

Suddenly, she tore herself from her unhappy reverie. Mr. Devlin had told her to be by the elevators when the unveiling ceremony began. She had to hurry. She slipped her dress on without buttoning it. She ran into the bathroom and got some tissues to wipe off her pussy. Harrington's spume was leaking from her. She didn't have time to get it all. She ran from the office as fast as she could in her high heels and went to the elevator. She pressed the button, shifting nervously from foot to foot as she watched the numbers above the door reveal its location. When it opened, she dashed inside. Then she remembered her buttons. She put her hands behind her and tried to button them. Her hands were sweaty and her fingers trembling. What if she didn't get there in time? She had already earned a savage punishment by lying. She didn't want to increase it.

When the elevator doors opened, she had only got one of the two buttons closed. Her hands were behind her neck, her pocketbook under her arm. A man and a woman, older, dignified, glanced into the elevator as she stood there. It was obvious she was putting her dress back on. "Oh god!" Anna thought. "What will they think?" They will think the truth, that's what.

She stepped from the elevator. Devlin was already there. Someone at a microphone was calling everyone to attention. Devlin looked surprised. "What are you doing there?" he asked. "Where have you been?"

"I was with Mr. Harrington," Anna replied meekly. "You said I should be nice to him."

Harrington broke out into a loud guffaw. "You mean you fucked him?" he asked in a loud voice, incredulous.

"Y-yes, Mr. Devlin," Anna replied, confused, embarrassed at Devlin's outburst. Thank god no one was nearby.

Devlin laughed. "I didn't tell you to fuck him. I said to be nice to him. Are you stupid or something?"

Anna felt like breaking out into sobs. "N-no, Mr. Devlin," she replied.

He laughed again. "We'll talk about it later, Anna. You've earned another punishment. I told you not to fuck anyone unless I consented to it. You are one stupid whore!"

Anna wanted to protest, but she knew she daren't. Just then the speaker introduced Mr. Theodore Harrington, CEO and President of Eastside Bank and Trust.

While Harrington spoke, applause interrupting his confident, self satisfied speech from time to time, Anna trembled and fought off tears. She knew that as soon as she left this place tonight, she would begin to bawl uncontrollably. She listened to Harrington drone on. She had a good view of him. He probably didn't know that he had a little wet spot near his zipper.

Harrington introduced the artist and there was more applause, this time louder. The artist mumbled a few things into the microphone. It was mostly unintelligible. When he finished, the jazz band played a fanfare and the curtain that had obscured the tall mural was pulled off, flowing gracefully to the floor.

It was impressive. It was at least 30' tall and about 50' long. Bright reds, blues, oranges yellows and greens all swirled together like a giant cyclone. Shards of colors were being tossed off of it, speeding to the edges of the mural. They almost looked like different countries' currency being whirled around. Here and there Anna thought that she could make out the dim portrait of a dignified man or woman like you could see on bills. The meaning of the mural was clear. The bank was a giant cyclone drawing money into it all around and then spitting it out for its stockholders.

After the applause died down, Harrington got up to speak again. He was extolling the bank's commitment to the community. All of a sudden, she heard her name. It startled her. She looked at Devlin. He was smirking. "Go on up," he told her.

Anna, clutching her little pocketbook in front of her as if it contained some talismanic quality that could ward off evil, stepped unsteadily to the speaker's platform. Harrington welcomed her with applause and the crowd followed suit.

"I can't think of anyone I know who is more dedicated to her role in life than Ms. Addunizio," he told the crowd. "Her work with the Center for Young Women has produced remarkable results and saved dozens and dozens of young women from exploitation. In honor of Ms. Addunizio's work, it is my pleasure to present her with this check from the Eastside Bank and Trust Corporation in the amount of $50,000 made out to her agency."

The room erupted into applause. Anna stood here, speechless. So this was Devlin's surprise, not the other. How could she have been so foolish? Devlin would never give her an order to fuck someone in such a vague manner. He was right! She was stupid! And Harrington had gotten a free blow job and fuck out of it.

Harrington handed her the check and invited her up to the microphone. As she stood behind it, it seemed as if a thousand flashbulbs were going off, recording for all posterity her whorish getup. What was worse, she could feel Harrington's semen trickling down her thigh. She had to get out of there as quickly as possible. "Thank you," she murmured into the mike. And then she ran off.

That was the end of the party. Anna had to issue a thousand thank you's as she followed Devlin to the door. She placed the check in her little pocketbook. It would come in handy. She had wanted to hire another staff member and this would do it.

The crowd moved slowly to the doors. The limos kept coming and going swiftly. Anna stood freezing in the cold night air as they waited for Carlos to pull up. The wind had picked up and it swirled around the hem of her dress lifting it slightly, causing her no end of apprehension that it would be blown up to reveal her hairless coosh. She kept her free hand down on her thigh to try and prevent it. Her other hand was held firmly in Devlin's

Finally, the limo pulled up. One of the valets, thankfully not the kid who had opened the door for her when they arrived, swung the door open from the driver's side. Devlin made her get in first. She did it as modestly as she could under the circumstances, but she knew that the kid got a good glimpse of her ass. She slid over the seat to make room for Devlin. "Thank god!" she thought. "Safe at last!" The warm air of the limo's interior comforted her. She breathed a sigh of relief.

The limo zoomed away. Devlin turned to her. "Take off your dress," he said.

CHAPTER THREE

Anna burst into tears. All of the night's pressures, all of its indignities, exploded within her at once. It had been a horrible experience. Harrington had raped her, she had been paraded around like a bar girl on the make. Her picture, with perhaps a sparkle of wetness on her thigh, would be in all the papers tomorrow for everyone to see. And now, just when she thought that the worst was over, she had to face Devlin and her upcoming punishment. It was too much to bear.

She knew better, though, to disobey him. She immediately unbuttoned the one button she had managed to get fixed and lowered the zipper. She slid the dress off of her, under her rear and over her feet. She looked up and saw Carlos peering at her nude body in the mirror. Tears were streaming down her face. She was trying to get a hold of herself, but she couldn't. Devlin had not said what to do with the dress when she got it off so she held it in her hands, looking at him, misery written across her face.

Devlin snatched it from her. He zipped his window open and let it fly out into the night. His abrupt disposition of her dress was so bizarre that she had a hard time believing that it had happened. She realized immediately that she was now a prisoner. She couldn't go home without a dress. She would have to walk naked to her apartment from the car. Was this what he was going to make her do? No, it wasn't.

"Go directly home, Carlos," Devlin told the driver.

"Yes, Mr. Devlin," Carlos replied. Anna felt a sinking feeling in her gut. Vincent was there. Vincent would whip her. He would take her to that room full of mirrors on the fourth floor and he would whip her.

Anna was sniveling. Her body was wracked with sobs. Devlin stared at her, a look of disdain on his face. He reached into his pocket and pulled out his handkerchief. "Here," he said, "wipe your nose. You're disgusting."

She took it from him. Her hands were trembling. It was like she was another species of being than the others in the car. They were dressed and she was not. They were men and she was not. They had rights and she did not. When she had wiped her nose, she handed it back to him, but she could not stop crying. That too went flying out the window. "Turn around," he ordered her.

Anna turned her back to him, dutifully placing her arms behind her. There was a pause and she felt him binding her wrists together with a thin leather cord. A feeling of helplessness and doom swept over her. When he was done, he ordered her to turn around again. She saw that there was a compartment built into the back of the seat between them. Devlin retrieved a long, thick gag from it. "Open up," he said. It was clear that he was holding his anger in, a whirlwind that she would soon reap.

"P-please, Mr. Devlin…" she started to utter. She wanted to plea and beg for mercy. It was too late to escape. She was naked and bound and the car was traveling at over 50 miles per hour. She knew she shouldn't speak without permission, but she was so afraid she couldn't help it.

"Shut the fuck up and open your mouth!" Devlin snarled.

With a sob of misery, she spread her lips. Devlin rudely shoved the gag in. He made her turn around and buckled it behind her head. The thick intruder was foul and oppressive. She bit down on it fiercely. Before she knew it, Devlin had draped a black sack over her head and pulled it taught around her neck.

"Pull over, Carlos," Devlin said, "and put this whore in the trunk. I can't stand her caterwauling any more."

Anna felt the car swerve to the side of the road. "Not the trunk! Oh, please! Not the trunk!" she thought madly.

She turned to Devlin and began to whine. The car pulled to a stop and she heard the front door open and close.

"...eeeeeeeeeease1 ...eeeeeeeeeeeeeease!" she screamed from behind her gag. She pulled at her bound arms and shook her head wildly. She was deathly afraid of confined spaces, an inheritance from her days with her father. She heard the car door open next to her. "...eeeeeeeeease!" she screamed desperately.

Carlos dragged her out by her arm. She writhed and struggled as he led her to the back of the car. Other cars were whizzing by. "Some one will see me! Someone will help me!" Anna thought frantically. She heard the trunk pop open.

"...ooooooooo! ...eeeeeeeeeeease!" she screamed again.

Carlos lifted her and tossed her in. She felt him fiddling with her legs and soon he had her ankles tied together. He connected them to her wrists, hogtying her.

"....ooooooooo!...eeeeeeeease!" she shouted. The trunk lid slammed closed. Within a few seconds, the car was on its way again.

Anna screeched and yelled and struggled with her bonds, terror, as stark as any she had ever felt, running through her. It took her several minutes to calm herself to anything remotely resembling a normal state. She could hear nothing from outside her little prison, not even the sound of other cars. She concluded that the trunk was soundproofed. She moaned in misery. It felt like she was suffocating, even though she could feel the breeze from a fan circulating the air around her. She could hear its little motor faintly whirring.

"Oh, god! Oh, god! Oh, god!" she thought. "Please help me! Please! Please!"

She knew that it was a long way to Devlin's mansion. At least 45 minutes. It was way on the other side of the city, out in the suburbs. She didn't know if she could stand it. Darkness, cruel, frightening darkness was all around her, eating into her brain, opening up terrible memories, giving life to the horrible monsters of her id.

She knew she had to calm herself. There was no choice. Those memories were long ago. She had overcome them once, she could do it now. Soon, not long, 45 minutes wasn't that long, she would be out. She would face Devlin's punishments. She would obey him in all things. She would be a good girl. She promised! She promised! "I'll be good! I'll be good!" she screamed in her mind. And then she began to cry again.

* * * * * * * * * * * * *

Almost 45 minutes later, Devlin's sleek limousine pulled up his long curvaceous driveway. Carlos carefully executed a 'k' turn when they pulled up to the mansion and then backed it into its spot. He hopped out of the car and opened Mr. Devlin's door.

"Leave her in there," he told his driver. "I'll send Vincent out for her later."

"Yes, Mr. Devlin," Carlos replied.

"I'll have Vincent send one of the maids down to you. You've earned it."

Carlos grinned. "Thank you, Mr. Devlin," he said. "Rosalita?"

"If that's your wish," Devlin replied. "She won't be here much longer so have as much fun with her as you want. Don't mark her up though. A buyer is coming on Saturday to take a look at her."

Carlos' grin got wider. "Yes, Mr. Devlin," he said. "Thank you, Mr. Devlin."

Devlin crossed the stone filled driveway towards the front door. His footsteps made crunching sounds as he walked. When he reached the door, it opened for him virtually automatically.

"Good evening sir," a deep, sharp voice spoke out.

"Good evening, Vincent," Devlin returned.

"How was your evening out, sir?"

"Very good. I spoke to Mr. Velasquez, the immigration attorney. He has three new prospects for us. He'll send them all over next week. I want you to pick out the best one and keep her here. She'll replace Rosalita who I expect will be gone on Saturday. The other two you can place on rotation for now."

"Yes, Mr. Devlin," Vincent replied.

"Who do we have upstairs?"

"Marina, sir. She's on your bed all ready for you. I had to give her five strokes because she was late."

"Ahhh, Marina," Devlin thought. The big titted Russian girl. She was just 25 and had pale white skin. It bruised so marvelously. She was truly desperate not to be deported back to Russia where she was wanted for bank fraud. The fact that she was just a fall girl for the bigger guys who had gotten off scott free didn't matter much. She had been convicted in absentia and given 25 years. She had a pretty face and a voracious cunt. But this lateness was beginning to worry him. It was the third time this month.

"I think we've played our string out with Marina," Devlin said. "When I'm done with her tonight, lock her up on the fourth floor. I'll send a couple of the boys from the Blue Cantina over tomorrow. After she's trained, she can spend some time there and then I'll try and get a buyer for her. The Mexicans go crazy for blondes. Send Diego Garcia her picture and vitals. Tell him he can take a look at her in two weeks or so."

"Yes, Mr. Devlin," Vincent replied.

"And send Rosalita to Carlos' quarters."

"Yes, Mr. Devlin."

Devlin started to head to the stairs. He stopped and turned around. "I almost forgot. Ms. Addunizio is in the trunk of the limousine. Let her stew there for an hour and then bring her up to the punishment room. I'll be along later. I want to punish her personally."

"Yes, Mr. Devlin," Vincent answered.

* * * * * * * * * * * * * *

Anna knew that the limo had come to a halt. She felt the car rock slightly as the doors were slammed closed, indicating that Devlin and Carlos had gotten out. She expected her prison to be opened at any second. She had held on longer than she expected. She had been taking deep breaths, counting up and down to a hundred, trying to remember things from her past. The few good things, not the bad. There were scheduling issues she needed to work over with Esther, calls she had to make. She went over her grocery list, thought of songs from her childhood, tried to remember the capitals of all the states. She had them all except Nevada. Was it Jefferson or Carson City? No, Jefferson was the capital of Missouri. She tried to think of anything but where she was and what faced her tonight.

Despite her heroic efforts to pretend she was not gagged and bound inside a tiny, little space, it kept creeping into her consciousness. Her body would shudder and she would burst out into frantic, soul wrenching sobs. She would yell and scream for someone to save her, her voice muffled by the thick leather plug between her lips. She would try and pull her hands and ankles apart. She would roll this way and that, or at least as much as the trunk space permitted. There were tools and various other boxes and things and she kept rolling over them. They poked painfully into her and she would roll back unhappily. She would count to ten. Then to a hundred. Then to five hundred.

But then, when the trunk lid didn't open, she began to cry all over again. They were going to leave her out here all night!

She just knew it! There was no way she could last all night! She'd go crazy! "Oh, please, God! Please!" she prayed.

But last she did. It was lonely, dark and had started to get cold almost as soon as the car engine had stopped. She had begun to shiver. She hadn't had anything to eat at the party, except for Devlin's sperm before it, and her belly was growling. She twisted and pulled at her bound limbs. She bit down on her gag. She tried shouting and screaming for help again. She cried a lot. Why she had ever agreed to Devlin's harsh terms, she did not know. What could be worse than what she was going through now?

When she heard the trunk lid pop open, a long, long time later, she was overwhelmed with joy. Hands, familiar hands, untied her ankles and helped her from the car. Her hood was left on. It was cold outside, even colder than inside the trunk, making her bear skin erupt in goose bumps. A hand took hold of her arm and escorted her over the stone driveway. She could hardly walk. It was a man. A tall man, she could tell that. It was Vincent. It had to be Vincent. She wanted to thank him, cover him with kisses, do anything for him. But then she thought of the punishment she was due and that he was the one who was probably going to mete it out. She began to cry and tremble once again.

Vincent took her directly to the fourth floor. Once there, he brought her to the punishment room. Anna knew where she was right away because she heard the echo from her high heels off the wooden floor. She gave a moan of unhappiness.

The tall, callous butler left Anna standing, hooded and bound, in the middle of the room while he stepped over to a closet built into the mirrored wall. He opened it and rolled out a small steel cage, about 3' by 3'. Anna heard the rumbling of its rubber wheels on the floor and wondered unhappily what it was.

When Vincent had it in position, he locked the wheels and then withdrew the black cloth from Anna's head. She looked around the room frantically. She had hoped she was wrong about where she was, but now knew, to her dismay, that she had been right. She began to whine again, her eyes darting about desperately, seeking solace and mercy somewhere. She was greeted by the myriad reflections in the mirrored walls, her naked, bound body, the grotesque leather shield from the gag across her face, the cruel, dour butler dressed in his grey, featureless suit. But nowhere did she see either mercy or solace.

Vincent had opened the door to the cage. "Get in," he told her.

Anna keened. It was so small! She would be crushed into immobility! How long would they leave her there? She hesitated, proffering her jailer a piteous look. Vincent's hand leapt out and he took hold of the nipple of her right breast. He twisted it harshly. Anna screamed and bent over, trying to dislodge his grip. It only became tighter. She moaned and fell to her knees. Vincent released her teat.

"Get in!" he repeated harshly.

Sniffling, crying, well over the brink of despair, Anna crept into the small enclosure. Since her hands were still tied behind her back, she had to shuffle forward on her knees, her neck bent, her breasts crushed against her thighs. She continued until her nose touched the bars in the front. She could go no farther.

Vincent went back to the closet and brought out a narrow, deep pan. He bent down behind the cage and placed it between Anna's thighs, pressing it up against her vulva. "Piss," he spat out.

Anna cringed at performing this function for him, but knew that if she pissed while in the cage, she would earn additional punishment. She closed her eyes to drive out the mirrored image of her shame and let herself go. She filled the dish right to the brim. Vincent stood and brought it to the water closet where he dumped it out. He returned to the cage with a cloth and wiped Anna's hairless slit dry. He closed the back of the cage and locked it.

He came around to the front. Anna looked up at him piteously. "Mr. Devlin will be up in a while," he said sternly. "He intends to whip you himself. When he is done, I will whip you for being slow to obey me."

Anna closed her eyes and cringed. She had earned yet another punishment! How was she ever going to stand it?

Before he left, Vincent took the cane from the closet and hung it in front of Anna's cage from a hook in the ceiling. He didn't have to say anything about it. Anna knew what it was for and why he had left it there. A moment later, he stepped from the room.

Anna began a long, seemingly interminable wait. She tried to keep her eyes closed to block out the many mirrored images of herself reflected around the room, but she could not keep them closed. The mirrors were slightly angled so that when she looked in the mirror in front of her, she could see the reflection of her hindquarters jammed up against the steel bars behind her. She could just turn her head, and when she did she saw the reflected vision of her sides framed by the silvery bars of her tiny prison. All around the room she could see the reflected image of the dangling cane.

She had been in this room once before and had never wanted to return. She had promised herself then, after her cruel beating at Vincent's hands, twelve vicious strokes, that she would obey Devlin's every rule to the letter. That she would be compliant in all things. And yet here she was. Her road to doom had begun on Monday when she wore a bra to work. Her rebellion had deepened Monday night when she had neglected to bring herself to pleasure. She had compounded her errors since then. She was going to be punished for fucking Mr. Harrington.

How unfair was that? It was a stupid mistake, yes, but one made with the spirit of being obedient.

And she had lied to Mr., Devlin! That was, she was sure, the worst of her transgressions. How had she ever imagined that she would get away with it? Devlin seemed to have pierced her very soul. He had the key to her psyche. She could never lie to him. She should have known that. So she would be punished for not bringing herself off and for lying about it.

Her terror went up and down. She tried to convince herself that she could tolerate her upcoming whipping. She had been through it once. How much worse could it be? She had lived. She would live again. She was strong, resolute. She would endure, no, triumph.

But then she remembered the experience of being whipped with the cane. She had begged and pleaded for mercy at the top of her lungs. She had screamed and moaned. It had been a horrible, scarring experience. And she was to suffer it all over again! The last time, her transgressions had been minor, mistakes of protocol essentially. These sins went much deeper. So deep that Devlin was going to whip her himself. It was then that her despair grew deepest, then when she would begin to cry again, then that she wished that she could levitate her body a hundred miles from there.

Being caged like this was a horrible, new experience. All around her was space, made to seem even larger by the mirrors around the room. And yet she was confined to less than a cubic foot of it. It was incongruous. It seemed that it couldn't possibly be real. She couldn't really be a naked, bound prisoner here! She wasn't really gagged and caged! She was dreaming it! She had to be! All of this, Devlin, Carol, the Blue Cantina, whatever that was, all a terrible dream. She would wake up any second! She had to! She just had to!"

How had she ever fallen into the hands of such cruel people? She had met some pretty bad ones when she was on the run from her abusive home. She had even been raped once, by a bouncer from a bar she had been dancing at. She had to face him the next night, but he had never repeated it. Once was enough for him. But it was not going to be near enough for Miles Devlin. She had thought that she was trading her body for the money to save the Center, but she had been really selling her soul.

After a long while, she heard some trudging up the steps. Along with it came the sound of a woman on high heels. Was it the same woman who had been here last time? The one who seemed to be a mysterious tag team with her for Devlin's pleasure? The footsteps went past the door to the punishment room. She thought she heard the woman crying. Another door opened and slammed shut. She imagined Vincent, it was his footsteps she had heard, she was sure of that, tying the woman up as he had tied her last weekend, gagging her and putting a black bag over her head. She wished the woman no harm, but she could spare no sympathy for her. She wasn't going to suffer a beating. She wasn't bound up in a little cage. She wasn't going to have her picture in the paper tomorrow looking like a cheap whore.

A short while later, she heard the door opening and closing again. Vincent walked up the hall and waited outside the door. Anna cringed and whined with the thought of him hovering there. It meant that Devlin was not far behind.

Sure enough, a few moments later, she heard another heavy set of footsteps coming up the stairs. These were unmistakably Devlin's. His footsteps had a firm determination that Vincent's lacked. Vincent's were more plodding, inevitable, doomsaying.

She listened as the steps came up to the door. There was a moment's hesitation, and the door swung open.

Devlin strode in. He was wearing a red and black robe over his fit frame that belted around his middle. On his feet were leather sandals. Anna's body shivered and a feeling of dread permeated her. Her tears began anew.

Vincent walked in after him. His face, as always, betrayed nothing of the thoughts behind it.

"Hello, Anna," Devlin said. He took hold of the cane that had been dangling over her like the sword of Damocles and swished it through the air. A chill ran through her. She wanted to beg and plea for mercy so badly, and yet, she knew it would do no good.

He lowered the cane and then tapped it a few times against the sides of her cage. Anna could feel its reverberation. It was heavy and hard. But she knew that already.

"I've been going through our evening in my mind," he said, his voice even and rational sounding. "And I've been trying to discover where I went wrong with you. You see, even though it was you who sinned, I feel somewhat to blame. I let you leave here somehow last Sunday night without a true understanding of your obligations to me." He was tapping the cane at his side now, staring down at her. She was staring up at him, her neck strained, seeking, perhaps, one iota of mercy. But what she heard was just the opposite.

"I was too lenient with you. I like you, Anna. I really do. I was hoping to spare you the worst of my nature. But you see what happens when you get soft. I'm sure you've experienced it at the Center, some caseworker who you let slide for this or that. In a short while, you have a real problem on your hands. Like the one we have tonight."

Anna squirmed in her cage. What Devlin was telling her did not sound good. Panic raced through her. If she had been spared the worst last time, what would she suffer now? A great sob escaped her.

"I sense that you see what I'm getting at, Anna," Devlin said. "And I need some help from you. I can't decide which offense is worse, lying to me or letting someone use your pussy without my permission. What do you think?"

Anna knew that this was a game for Devlin, that he enjoyed tormenting her. He intended to extend her suffering as much as he could. If he had calculated that it would increase her terror, he had been right. His coldness bespoke a measured, calculated evil. She was no more a person to him than was a cow or a dog or a cat. She doubted he saw anyone other than himself as a full person. He was a psychopath, incapable of empathy or remorse. Yet, she knew she had to try and answer him. Silence would just mean more pain. But which was worse, lying or fucking someone without permission? She would have to guess lying. It was more personal, more direct. It was committed right in front of him.

Her voice was choked off by the gag, but she could still make some sound emerge. Her throat was dry and it was difficult to form any words with the obstruction between her teeth. She tried nonetheless.

"....eyiiiiiiii," was all she could get out. It didn't sound much like a word.

Devlin leaned over. "What did you say, Anna"" he asked.

Anna's whole body was shaking. "....eyiiiiiiii!" she tried to shout.

"Did you say 'lying,' Anna?"

"...es, i-er e-in," Anna said miserably.

Devlin drew back up. "That's what I thought initially too," he said. "But then I thought that a lie could always be taken back, like you did yours, to your credit I might add. Fucking someone can never be taken back. Once it's done, it's done. And I'm always looking out for lying. I expect it. But using your pussy without permission, that's very bad. It's like an act of rebellion. And rebellion must be squashed harshly and immediately, don't you think?"

Devlin had driven Anna past the point of distraction. "...eeeeeeeeee, i-er e-in! ...eeeeeeee ...own! eeeeeeeeeeee! I ...orrrrrry!" she screamed from behind her gag, "...eeeeeeeee!"

Devlin smiled. "It's good for you that we always allow begging and pleading in the punishment room, or you'd be in for more unhappiness. Let's get started, shall we?"

He nodded to Vincent. The taciturn butler went to the back of Anna's cage and released the door. Ann started to bawl. She considered refusing to come out of the cage, but she didn't have to courage to rebel. Miserable, she backed herself out. Her tears were flowing down her face. When she was free of the cage, Vincent took her by the arm and set her on her feet. Devlin was inches away from her. He reached out and took gentle hold of a nipple and shook her breast playfully, smiling.

Vincent got the chain ready for her mounting. It ran from the wall to the ceiling and then through some pulleys to the center of the room. When it was dangling from the ceiling above her, he stepped to her back and released her hands. He brought them forth and inserted them into the leather handcuffs connected to the end of the chain.

Anna didn't resist but didn't cooperate either. Her knees were weak and she felt like she was going to collapse. When her second hand was locked in the cuff, she pulled on her bindings for stability. Vincent went to the wall and pulled on the chain. Anna's hands were lifted high above her. Devlin was tapping the cane in his hand while Vincent connected Anna's ankles to a ring in the floor so she would be unable to dodge the blows. After he rolled the lacy tops of her sheer, black stockings below her knees, he rose to his feet and removed her gag.

Anna sputtered and coughed. Her lips were turned down in a piteous frown. Her face was a mask of misery. Her mascara had run down her cheeks and she looked much like a sad circus clown.

"Since we agree that fucking Mr. Harrison was your worst transgression, tonight's punishment will be all about that," Devlin told her. "I will leave the rest of your punishments for the weekend. It's better that you suffer for each of your sins separately so that they can be burned into your mind. Is that all right with you, Anna, or do you want it all at one time?"

Anna moaned with misery. It was a terrible decision to have to make. But to endure it all at once might drive her mad. She shook her head, afraid that if she spoke she would disgrace herself. She knew that she would be issuing wild supplications for mercy in a short while, but she wanted to hold on as long as possible.

"I'm going to take that as your decision to split it up. Is that right, Anna?"

Anna nodded silently. Her arms and shoulders were strained with the bulk of her weight. She could only just touch her toes to the floor. She was still wearing her silvery high heels and her stockings. Tears continued to stream down her face.

"Now is there anything that you want to say before I begin, Anna. Go ahead, say what you want. I won't punish you."

Anna's lips were trembling. It was hard to catch her breath in her distended position. "I'm sorry, Mr. Devlin," she was able to mutter softly, a pitiful obsequiousness to her voice. "Please don't hurt me. I won't lie to you ever again. I promise." Her lips were trembling so hard that it nearly made her lowly spoken words unintelligible.

"I'm sure you won't, Anna, but tonight's punishment is not about lying, it's about fucking Mr. Harrington."

"I-I was confused," she protested, her voice soft and murky. "I thought you meant me to. It was a mistake. Please, Mr. Devlin, it's not fair," she whined unhappily. She was surprised at her audacity, but Devlin had never lied to her, so she spoke freely.

"I grant you that it was a mistake, Anna, but it was a mistake you made because you didn't listen. Why would I use a euphemism like 'nice' when I meant you to fuck him? I would have just told you to fuck him. Don't you agree?"

Anna saw the truth in what he said. She had been stupid. But it was like he had laid a trap for her and she had fallen

into it. But what he was saying was right.   "Y-yes,   Mr.
Devlin," she whispered unhappily.

"Okay, then," Devlin said stepping away from her. "I'm
going to give you five strokes of the cane," he told her as he
drew off his robe. He was naked underneath and his cock was
steely rigid in anticipation of his task. "That's the first part of
your punishment. Then I'm going to take the flogger and
whip the insides of your thighs and your pussy. I don't know
how many strokes, but until they're nice and red. That will
take care of the whipping. The rest you'll find out when we're
done."

"Ohhhhhhhhh!" Anna cried. She watched Devlin rear
back with the cane.

"Pleeeeeeeeeeease!" she screamed. "Noooooooooo!"

Devlin let loose. The cane struck her across her thighs. It
made a 'whoomp!' sound as it landed. Anna screamed in pain,
"Ohhhhhhhhhhhhhhh! Ohhhhhhhhhhhhhhh!"

The second blow landed across her breasts. It made her
body rock. It took her breath away and it was a few moments
before   she   began   to   groan,   "Uuuuuuuugh-hhhhhhh!
Orrrrrrrrrrrrrrgh! Orrrrrrrrrrrrrgh!"

Her thighs and breasts were pulsing with pain. Tears were
streaming down her face. Her body swayed from the blow.
"Plllllllleease,   Mr.   Devlin!   Pleeeeeeeease!   No   more!
Pllleeeeeease! I'll be good! I will! I'll never do it again!
Pleeeeeeeease! Pleeeeeeeease!" she shouted. She hardly knew
what she was saying. She would have said anything that came
into her mind that might help her.

Devlin went behind her. Before she knew what was
happening, he swung the cane forward and struck her
buttocks. Since there was so much padding, he had put his all
into this one. It was like some huge beast had sunk its fangs
into   her.   "Ohhhhhhhhhhh!   Owwwwwwwwwwww-www!
Ahhhhhhhhhhhhhh!" she screamed. "Oh, god, please help
me!" she let out at the top of her lungs.

The next blow crossed her back, just above her kidneys. A tidal wave of hurt flowed through her. She had lost all ability to stand and was just hanging by her wrists. She moaned loudly. It was all she had the energy for.

When the final blow landed, across the back of her thighs, she groaned and her body shuddered. Through her befogged state, she was aware that that was number five. This part of her punishment, at least was over.

She was sobbing heavily. She sensed Vincent releasing her feet. A strap was wrapped around her left ankle. She looked and saw that he was standing again on the stool running the other end through a ring in the ceiling to the left and in front of her. He stepped down and began to pull. Her left foot went into the air. "Ohhhhhhhhh!" she moaned. He tied off the end, leaving her leg hanging wide and open.

She stared at him intently as he went to her right ankle, tied off a long strap to that one as well. In a minute, he had that leg in the air. Her legs were spread wide and she was completely off the ground. Through her spread legs she saw Devlin taking a flogger out of the closet. She whined in misery. He went to work on her right away.

Anna screeched and yelled and pleaded for mercy. The seven tasseled whip kept raining down on her most sensitive places. Its ends were stiff and knotted. The insides of her thighs were soon streaked with red. But it was when he struck her pussy that it hurt the most. When the cruel flails collided with her tender love lips, she arched her back and howled. "Ohhhhhhhh!   Pleeeeeeeease   stop!   Pleeeee-eeeease! Ahhhhhhhhhhhhh! Ahhhhhhhhhhh!"

Although her limbs were bound, that did not prevent her body from swaying and jerking as the punishment was laid down. Her anguished voice echoed off of the mirrored walls. She could see the image of her tortured body and Devlin's fiendish one reflected all around her as if a hundred Anna's were being assaulted by a like number of Devlins. Each time he struck the inside of her tender thighs, she screeched terribly. But when he brought it down over her defenseless, widespread pudenda she howled.

At last, he finished. Sweat covered his body, running down in rivulets. Vincent handed him a towel and he wiped his face and then his body. That he had put his all into was reflected by the bright red skin that ran from knee to knee on his victim.

Anna moaned and moaned. Her thighs burned like they were on fire. Her pussy stung. Her body still swayed slightly. The places where the cane had struck, her breasts, her thighs, and others, all throbbed with a heavy, dull ache.

Devlin gave the towel back to Vincent and approached Anna between her outstretched thighs. "I must say you did very well, Anna," he told her. "Now I'm going to fuck you." He put his hand on her burning quim. It was at just the right level for his penetration. He slipped his thumb up and down her divide until it began to moisten in self defense. When he was satisfied, he took his cock in his right hand, poked its helmeted head at her angry red gate, and slid himself in.

Anna moaned with dismay. He was adding insult to injury. She could think of nothing more odious than having his prick inside her now. But she had no choice. She had no power to drive it away.

He began a slow, steady motion. His eyes were rolled back and his back arched. Every time he pressed his meat home, his hips collided with her tortured thighs and she moaned in pain. His arms circled them, pulling her suspended body back and forth to meet his thrusts.

He looked at her. "This feels so good, Anna, especially after a workout like that. Do you know what I'm doing now, Anna? Can you tell me that?"

Anna knew better than to disregard a question no matter how foolish or taunting. "Y-yes," she replied unhappily.

"What am I doing, Anna?" he asked her, his cock still sliding back and forth.

Despite her pain and the horror that she suffered, despite her revulsion at having him inside her, his motions were beginning to spark her passions. She was trying desperately to fight them, but the questioning was distracting her efforts.

"Y-your fucking me." she replied. "Y-your fucking my cunt."

"No, no, Anna. You still don't get it. I'm fucking my cunt. It isn't yours any more. It's mine. You just carry it around and care for it."

Anna whined at the unhappy truth. It was his cunt. He could do anything he wanted with it or to it. And he certainly had the right to determine who used it.

"And while my property is in your custody, Anna, you have the duty to protect it, to nurture it. You can't be giving it away like you did tonight. Do you understand that?"

"Y-yes, Mr. Devlin," she moaned back. Her pussy, or rather, his pussy, was getting hot. His long, slow and steady motions were exciting it. He was making it perform. She had no power over it. She bit her lip and moaned, "Ohhhhhhhhhhh!"

"That's it, Anna. I want my pussy to come. I want to feel it contracting around my spurting cock. Get it ready for me. Urge it on. Make it work."

"Ohhhhhhhh!" Anna moaned again. For some reason, his ownership of her sex felt right. For years she had virtually ignored it. He had brought it back to life. It yearned for him to possess it, as if it had a mind of its own. It recognized his mastery of it, not hers. It was a sensation and realization that drove her blood hot. It released her from all responsibility for it. She didn't have to concern herself as to whether she was a slut or a whore. It was her pussy's fault. Her pussy had revolted against her and joined the enemy.

And yet, she could enjoy the rewards that her pussy sent her. She could revel in the feel of a hot cock plowing it. Devlin had punished her savagely and the last thing she wanted was to reward him with pleasure from her body. But her pussy did not care. It had no memory. It had only desire, desire for its master and owner. No matter what he did to her, no matter how she suffered at his hands, her pussy would emerge hungry for his stiff manhood.

Devlin's lecture had ended. His thrusts were getting faster and harder. Despite her pain, Anna's need was growing larger and larger. She wanted to thrust back at him, but he controlled her motions. All she could do was receive his benedictions. She moaned again. Devlin placed his thumb atop her burning clit and began to rub it energetically. She gasped as the pleasure shot through her. She felt her lusts rising. Her pussy wanted to come! It wanted to come! It wanted to come! It was coming!

Anna gave out a loud groan and her body started to shake. Devlin was smashing his hips against her ravaged thighs again and again. He too groaned and his cock began to throb and spurt within her. Anna looked into the mirror in front of her and saw a long line of Devlins fucking Annas, his buttocks thrusting madly. "Ohhhhhhhhhh, god! Ohhhhhhhhh, god!" she called out to the same god who a short while ago she had asked for deliverance from her torment. But now she wanted the excruciating pleasure to last forever. It bordered on blasphemy, but she didn't care. "Ohhhhhhhh, yes! Yes! Yes!" she screamed, "Oh, god, yes!"

CHAPTER FOUR

Devlin slipped his detumescing cock from Anna's still throbbing vagina. It had been a good night's work. The psychological profile he had developed on Anna based on what her best friend, Carol, had told him was spot on! She was responding just as Dr. Evans had said she would. He would have to thank her. She was one of the few female members of the club and had designed the protocol for training the girls for The Blue Cantina. She did a thorough workup on all of them and was always consulted when problems cropped up down the road, as they inevitably did. For this, her membership fees were waived and she received a healthy monthly retainer, plus, of course, access to the girls

He donned his robe. Vincent was busy reaffixing Anna's gag around her head. Her night wasn't over by a long shot. By the morning, she would be really ripe.

Devlin left without saying a further word to Anna. He was done with her for the evening and it was Vincent's turn to deal with her. As he stepped out of the punishment room, he had to laugh. Of course his telling her to be nice to Harrington had been a trap. She had fallen right into it and had given him the excuse for inflicting a severe punishment. Dr. Evans had predicted that she would falter on his instructions to make herself come every night. Right again! And she had been right when she said that she would lie about it. We all think of ourselves as individuals, but we all have basically the same psychological makeup. Our triggers may differ based on our experiences, but generally speaking, everything we do is more or less predictable within a slim margin of error.

Take Martina, for example. She had cried and sobbed when he told her that she was spending the night. She was no fool. She had guessed that there was more to his domination of her than trading her sexual services for his influence on her immigration problem. But by then it was too late. It would have taken a heroic effort to overcome her fear of him. She might have been thinking about rebellion, about running away, but the consequences of him catching her afterwards was so severe in her mind that she kept putting it off. He wasn't all that powerful as he made it seem, but it was easy to make the girls think he was. Not that he didn't have assets in that department. He had plenty, but he didn't have the omniscient global reach that the girls often attributed to him.

He had sensed that very soon Martina would muster the courage to take a powder. Dr. Evans had outlined the signs, and lateness for appointments was one of them. It was a like a little practice rebellion on the way to working up to the big one.

When he told her that she was staying the night, she realized right away that she had made a mistake, that her chances of rebellion were at an end. She begged and pleaded to be allowed to go home, making all kinds of excuses. By then, her hands were bound behind her and Vincent had placed a chain around her ankles. Carlos would go by her place tomorrow and wipe out all traces of her. On Devlin's orders, she had, over the last two months, cut off all ties with the few people she knew. They wouldn't even miss her. By tomorrow afternoon, she would be at Dr. Evans' facility getting trained for her new life.

He walked down the hall to her room. He opened the door. She was laying on her back, her wrists tied to her ankles and then tied off to the sides of the bed. Her legs were spread wide and her sweet, hairless mons beckoned as did the little star between her rear cheeks. Her pretty, red high heels were still on her feet. She was gagged and hooded, but she knew that it was him. She whined and sobbed as he closed the door. He went to the closet and took out the dog whip. It was one of his favorites, with a leather handle and a split thong at the end. He would whip her and then fuck her again. Up the ass this time.

* * * * * * * * * * * * * *

Vincent had released Anna from her bonds. She was kneeling on the floor, her head bowed down and her arms stretched out before her, as instructed. He went back to the closet where the implements of pain were kept. He chose the long, thin, leather encased, steel crop.

Anna was exhausted and dazed. She had been tired when she began the evening after her very thorough workout with Cathy. Since then, there was the stress of getting ready on time and fulfilling all of Devlin's orders regarding her appearance, the stress of being caught in her lie, the stress from the party and Harrington fucking her, and all the stress, torment and pain she had suffered since then. Her body was aching from her caning and her pussy and thighs still burned. Devlin had said that she would learn more about her punishment after he was done beating her and she feared what would come next. She knew too that she needed to obey Vincent to the letter or face additional torment at his hands. She already had one punishment coming and she knew that the meticulous butler was not about to forget that.

Vincent approached her and tapped her bottom with the crop. She jumped when she felt it. Her payment owed to Vincent had become due.

"This is your punishment for not obeying me. I will give you three strokes. The next time it will be more."

"Three strokes!" Anna thought. Her stomach quailed. She looked up in the mirror and saw Vincent's arm rearing back. Her body tensed in anticipation. She closed her eyes and put her head down. The crop zipped through the air. A line of excruciating fire broke out across her buttocks. She screamed fiercely, but held her place. She was trying not to cry. She had done so much of it tonight. She could feel her eyes brimming.

Anna didn't want to look up again to watch Vincent as he prepared himself for another blow, but she couldn't help herself. She could see that he was waiting for the sensations of the first blow to subside. He was a patient, methodical man. He reared his arm back again. Anna put her head down and cringed. A second line of fire erupted across her rear cheeks, a little bit down from the first. She clenched her teeth and held her breath trying not to react. But the pain was so excruciating that she could not suppress her anguished wail. "Ahhhhhhhooooooowwwwwwww!" she howled. Her gag muffled most of her exclamation, but it resounded through the room nonetheless. She began to sob. "One more! One more! That's all! One more!" she ranted in her mind. A shrill coldness reverberated through her body as she fearfully awaited the next and last blow. This time, she held her head down and did not look. Looking only made it worse.

She heard the subtle sound of him shifting his weight on his feet to deliver it. She heard the 'whrrrrrrrr!' of the crop slicing the air. She bit down hard on the gag in her mouth. When the crop struck, the pain seared through her.

"Ohhhhhhhhhhhwwwwwwwwww!" she moaned. "Ohhhhhhhhhhwwwwwwwww!"

But it was over. He had said three and she had been given three. She allowed her body to relax even though the wounds on her rear still burned mightily. She heard Vincent walk to the closet and put the crop away. He paused and then came back. He had something in his hand. She didn't want to know what it was.

"Kneel up and put your hands behind your back," he ordered her curtly.

When she had obeyed, she felt him tying her wrists back together. "Spread your legs," he spat out.

Anna dutifully brought her knees wide apart. Her stockings were still rolled down below her knees and she was still wearing her high heeled shoes. Lifting her knees one by one, Vincent pulled her stockings up so that they were back in place. He then reached around her front, applying a wide belt. He pulled it tight. It felt like there was some kind of box on the back. There were straps hanging down the front and some sort of object dangling from it. Anna did not look down to see what it was for fear of punishment. She had committed herself to doing exactly what he said and nothing else.

Vincent came around her front and crouched down in front of her. He took the object that was dangling between her legs and fitted it on her pussy. It had a long, thick prong that slipped inside her and a piece that went over her clitoris. Her pussy was still pliant and wet from her fucking. He adjusted the straps to fix it in place. Holding it with one hand, he took the single strap that hung from its bottom and brought it up between her legs. It nestled into the crack of her ass and then went into the box located in the small of her back. He pulled it tight so that the device on her pussy sunk deeper within her and was pressed tighter against her clit.

Anna was frantic. "What is he doing? What is this for?" she wondered unhappily. She was sure that it had something to do with the additional punishment she had been promised. All she could think of was that it was some kind of torture device. Her blood ran cold.

Vincent spent some time fiddling with the box on the back of the belt. Anna felt a pad being wrapped around her left wrist. It seemed to have some kind of sensor attached to it that went directly over her pulse. She could feel a little wire emanating from it that she assumed went to the box on her back. When Vincent finished attaching the wristband, he stood up.

"Get back in the cage," he ordered.

Anna gave out a whine. It had been horrible to be imprisoned there. But she did not hesitate in obeying. Crying again, her body wracked with fear, she crawled over to the steel confinement and maneuvered herself in. The bottom was padded so that she did not hurt her knees, but the rest of it consisted of just cold steel. She was squeezed into a kneeling position. Vincent stepped away and returned with the pan that she had peed in earlier. He made her do it again. She was grateful for the opportunity to relieve herself, but realized, unhappily, that it meant that she was going to be kept confined for a long time.

Vincent came back after emptying the pan. He swung the door to the cage shut and locked it.

"You will spend the night here. The device will give your pussy both pleasure and pain. If you still have any doubts about who controls your slutty cunt, this should dispel them." He had a transmitter in his hand and he pointed it at Anna. She saw him press down on a button and the box behind her back clicked in obedience. Anna shivered with fear. She whined and unhappily pulled at her bound hands.

She was disconsolate both at the prospect of remaining so cruelly confined throughout the night and at the news about the purpose of the device. She knew that begging would do no good, even if she could. She just closed her eyes and tried to suppress the sensation of anguish that passed through her. She heard Vincent walk away. The door to the room opened. Anna panicked. She looked up. "No! Don't leave! Please don't leave me like this! Please!" she screamed inside her. "Arrrrrrrrrrrrrrgh!" she shouted. "Arrrrrrrrrrrrrgh!"

The door slammed shut. A moment later, the light went out.

It took a moment for it to register. And then Anna released a long, anguished wail.

When she paused to catch her breath, she realized that the prong in her pussy had begun to buzz. Panic shot through her. What was it going to do? Was it pleasure or pain? And then, suddenly, a fierce shock erupted from deep inside her. "Ohhhhhhhhhh!" she moaned. "Ohhhhhhhhhh!" It pulsed through her whole body. It forced her teeth to bite down harshly on her gag. Her belly constricted into a painful cramp. It had only lasted a few seconds, but it was excruciatingly painful.

When it subsided, she noticed fretfully that the prong was continuing to vibrate within her. She braced herself for another shock. It did not come. The part of the device over her clit began to buzz as well. The vibrations became stronger and stronger. Her pussy began to send messages of pleasure to her. She tried to ignore them, wish them away, but the buzzing was insistent. She squirmed her hips. She squeezed her knees together. She bit down on her gag. The buzzing went on and on and her lusts kept rising and rising.

"No! I don't want this! I don't want this!" she thought to herself unhappily. Her heart started to beat heavily. She could feel her breasts hardening. "Arrrrrrrrrrrrrrrrrgh!" she growled in frustration. "Stop! Stop! Stop!" she yelled in her mind. "I don't want this! Stop!" But it kept on going.

Her breathing began to become ragged. Like a primer to a pump that when the water reaches a certain level turns it on, her attempts at denial of the passions induced within her ceased and her desires reversed course. "Ohhhh-hhhhhh!" she moaned. "Ohhhhhhhhhhh!" Now she tried to clamp her pussy muscles around the electrified prong. Her hips began to shift back and forth in an imitation of coitus. Her hands clamped into fists, her pussy seemed ready to explode. And then it did.

Her body convulsed and shuddered. Her eyes rolled back. Her insides quaked. The throbbing of her pussy sent powerful waves of pleasure through her. Her heart pounded in her chest. The buzzing went on and on pushing her orgasm to its limits. Then, as soon as her pussy's convulsions slowed and her heartbeat began to return to normal, the buzzing stopped.

It took her a while to catch her breath. It was difficult with her chest pressed against her thighs and breathing through her nose. She realized that the control box on her back was reading her pulse. When her pulse rate peaked and began to edge its way down, the device turned off.

For a while, she reveled in the warm glow that he pussy was sending her. Slowly, though, she returned to the realization of where she was. With the device inert, the darkness seemed to surround her again. She recalled that she was to spend hours and hours confined this way. The steel bars of the cage touched her all over, defining her space, so tiny, so inconsequential. The pitch black room around her seemed to stretch out into infinity. Devlin and Vincent had probably already gone to bed, sleeping the sleep of the sociopathic. There was no one to help her. No one who cared.

In her dismay, she tried to estimate what time it was. The party had been over about 9. It had taken almost an hour to get to the mansion. She had lain in the trunk for a long, long time, at least an hour. That brought it to 11 o'clock. Her whippings had taken perhaps another hour. That meant it was about midnight. Last time, Vincent had come to check on her about 6 a.m. That meant at least six hours of dismal confinement. Six hours in the horrid darkness.

Did it mean six hours of torment from the device? Would it go all night? Was it on a regular schedule? The idea of it terrorized her. She had experienced both excruciating pain and intense, mind blowing pleasure. But she had the ability to control neither. Vincent had been right. It was a powerful demonstration of Devlin's control of her. But she had learned that lesson! She didn't need to experience it again and again. She would bow down to him, surrender completely. Do anything he asked strictly to the letter. Anything!

She felt the little vibration that had preceded the first shock. She knew it was coming again. It was like a little warning. The shock would come a split second later. "Nooo....!" she tried to yell through her gag.

The shock made her body jump. She groaned loudly. Her stomach felt like it had been tied into a knot. Her pussy throbbed, her teeth ached. Her mind seemed jumbled, with all thoughts burned right out of it. She sobbed and sobbed. And then the buzzing began again. The piece over her clit commenced its vibrations too. A short while later, she was squirming and shaking in her little cage, urging her pussy on to its impending explosion of pleasure.

The box was not set on any regular schedule. It was programmed to be random, with the longest gap between fierce, electrical shocks to be about 20 minutes and the shortest about 5. Each terrible shock was followed by the intense stimulation of her sex until her descending pulse rate told the machine she had climaxed. Between the longest gaps, she managed, despite her anxiety, to fall asleep. The Tell tale vibration in the device sunk within her would awaken her. She would just have time to realize what was happening when the shock would go off. And then, following, a rigidly enforced path to pleasure.

Sometimes, she just knelt there, sobbing. Sometimes, she growled animisticly in protest against her abuse. She knew she could not prevent the shocks. She tried and tried again to prevent her orgasms, but the machine was implacable. Her pussy became sore and tired and it took longer and longer to get her to climax, but each time, she eventually did. When it was done, she would cry and sob some more. She didn't know whether the surge of intense apprehension she felt each time the device signaled that it was about to come alive again was because of the shock or because of the terrible powerlessness she felt as the machine dominated her body, forcing it to perform again and again.

Anna didn't realize it, but the shocks stopped coming about 4 a.m. She had gone through 4 hours of horrid torment. She passed into a fitful slumber.

She didn't awake when the lights were turned on. It was when the back of her cage was opened that she realized someone was there. Hands reached in and loosened the belt from around her waist. The fiendish prong was slipped out of her and the device removed. She began to cry from joy. She looked up to see Vincent walking to the water closet. He returned with the pan and placed it between her thighs. He ordered her to pee. She strained and strained to make it come. Her stomach muscles were so tired that it was hard to put pressure on her bladder. Vincent was patient. He held the pan there until, finally, at first weakly, a stream of water was released. He wiped her and disposed of her urine in the closet.

When he returned, Anna expected him to free her from her terrible confinement. To her bitter disappointment he did not, but instead closed the back again and locked it. He stood next to the cage and pushed his foot against the lever that locked the rubber wheels. He attached a leash to the front of the cage and began to wheel her out of the room.

They went down the dimly lit hallway to a dumbwaiter near the stairs. The cage was shoved in backwards and the door closed. At first, Anna thought she had been locked inside a small cabinet, a new angle on her torment, but when she felt the dumbwaiter begin to descend, she knew what it was.

The cage reached the second floor a little bit before Vincent did and she had to wait to be removed from the small confine. She was happy when the door was opened and she saw the butler's face. He pulled her free and began to wheel her down the hall. She could see ahead and she knew where they were going. They were going to the sun room where Devlin ate his breakfast. When the door was opened, there was a burst of sunlight that at first blinded her. Then she saw

Devlin, sitting in his chair, wearing a brightly colored morning bathrobe, drinking a cup of coffee.

Vincent wheeled her to a spot about ten feet away from him. Anna was shaking and crying. This was the man who determined her torments. This was the man who ruled her, owned her. He seemed as powerful as a god.

Devlin gave her a momentary look and went back to his paper. Vincent retreated from the room. There was total silence except for the rustling of Devlin's paper and the clicking of the cup against the saucer whenever he put it back down after taking a sip.

Anna felt like she was going to explode. This was the man with the power to free her. She yearned to beg and plead for release but was afraid of making a single sound. She felt a whine begin to build in her throat and she desperately fought to contain it. She bit down on her gag and held her breath. To her horror, it escaped. Not a large one, but a small one. One that might not, on a normal day, be even noticed. But Devlin noticed it. He looked at her. He frowned.

"Now, now, Anna," he said disapprovingly. "You know better than that. Don't interrupt me again."

His voice was stern, but avuncular. Like he was the parent and she was the child. Naughty children don't interrupt Daddy when he's reading the paper. You could get a spanking.

Anna, distressed by his insouciant callousness, tried to calm herself. Eventually, he would let her out. He had to. It was the morning. She had to go to work. He couldn't keep her here like this. Could he?

Her muscles were strained by her long confinement. Her body ached where she had been struck by the cane. Her pussy was sore and tired. There was a clock on the wall that said 7:24. Seven and a half hours she had spent in the cage! It seemed like an eternity.

Devlin tossed the first section of the paper aside and picked up the local section. There were several colorful pictures spread across it. He peered at them intently.

He held the paper out for her to see. "Look, Anna! It's a picture of you when you received the check from Harrington. Gee, that skirt looks even shorter in the picture than it did in person. It's a good thing they didn't shoot it from a low angle!" He laughed.

Anna looked at the picture through the bars of her cage. It was just as she had feared. The picture took up a quarter of the page! Everyone would see what a bimbo she was. All the other social workers around the county would see it. Her staff would see it, as would the girls at the Center. And the Board of Trustees would see it and the people down at the Community Chest, and the county Commissioners who voted on her agency's grant every year.

She moaned from unhappiness. Devlin looked at her. "Don't be upset, Anna. You look really hot. Harrington's eyes are looking straight at your tits." He laughed again. "I'll bet he gets a lot of ribbing for that, especially from anyone who saw him bring you upstairs."

Anna moaned again. Devlin pulled the picture away from her. "I don't know what you're complaining about," he said petulantly. "It's great publicity for the agency."

With that he sat back and continued to read. Anna kept her lips tightly gripped around her gag. "Please let me out! Please! Please!" she kept thinking desperately. It was like something surreal: her squashed cruelly and medieval-like in a little cage, naked, gagged and bound, him leisurely sitting in a lounge chair in the middle of his luxurious morning room, dressed in his fine looking robe, reading the paper and drinking coffee. All the normal relations of the world were out of kilter. It required a wholly new definition of reality. At no time ever in her life had she ever thought that she would be in a situation like this. How could she have ever? No one could. She began to cry again, silent, bitter tears.

The door to the room opened again about ten minutes later. It was Vincent and he was carrying a tray of food. He set it down on the coffee table next to Devlin. Devlin put down his paper and smiled.

"Here's what we've been waiting for, Anna. It's your breakfast. I'll bet you're good and hungry. "

He picked up a round, silver lid off of one of the plates. "It's oatmeal," he announced merrily. "And Vincent makes it very good. It's got raisins and little slivers of almonds in it. And he's brought some maple syrup. I love it with maple syrup. I'll pour some on for you. You'll love it too."

He took a small carafe and poured some of the thick, honey gold liquid into the bowl. There was another carafe with milk and he spilled some in, stirring it all up.

Vincent had left as soon as he dropped off the tray. It was just Devlin and Anna again. He put the bowl down, got up and pulled Anna's cage closer to him. There was a hatch on the front. He released it and it fell open.

"Come on now, Anna," he said. "Stick your head out so I can feed you. Be a good girl."

Sobbing, disconsolate, Anna obeyed. She strained forward until her head emerged from the cage. Her face was stained by her dissolved mascara. Hours of stress, pain and terror had ravaged her face. Her chin was trembling. Wasn't he ever going to let her out? Why was he doing this to her?

Devlin took a look at Anna's distorted features. He was sitting on the edge of his chair. He ran his hand through her dirty, unruly hair. "Poor Anna," he said. "Did you have a rough night?"

Anna burst into sobs. It had been the worst night of her life. Devlin continued to stroke her head. "Poor Anna," he said again. "Go ahead and cry. You've earned it. Go right ahead."

Anna's crying continued. She couldn't stop. It was like something had broken inside her. Devlin reached behind her head and removed her gag. He leaned over and kissed her on her forehead.

"I'm so sorry, Anna," he said. "It's all my fault. Just like I said. If I had been harsher when you were here last weekend, none of this would ever have happened. Well, I'm going to make sure it doesn't ever happen again. I promise you that I'll punish you very severely any time you do something wrong. This way you won't ever think of being disobedient. And things won't all pile up on you like they did last night. Is that okay with you Anna? That's right, isn't it?"

Anna didn't know what to say. Did he want her actually to agree to be punished severely? Was he asking for her consent? And then, like a light going of in her head, she knew that he was right. She needed the threat of his cruel punishments to motivate her to comply with all of his outlandish, degrading commands. If she thought for one moment that she could evade them without consequence, she would do it. If, however, she had the deadly fear of him that she possessed this very moment, she wouldn't even think about it. Absolute and complete obedience was what he demanded. She could only obey if the idea of disobedience filled her with a dread so fierce it made her quake. She was a bad girl, full of disobedience. She needed an iron fisted regulator. Someone who would give her no quarter. Someone like Mr. Devlin. Why hadn't she realized it sooner?

He was expecting a reply. She tried to stop crying long enough to answer him. "Y-yes, Mr. Devlin," she finally uttered.

"That's a good girl, Anna," Devlin replied, obviously pleased. "I knew you'd see it my way. And I'm sure that from now on you will do you very, very best to be good, won't you?"

"Y-yes, Mr. Devlin," Anna squeaked out. She was still crying now, but it was tears of relief. Mr. Devlin had called her a good girl. She wanted to be a good girl. She wanted to obey him.

He kissed her forehead again and rubbed his hand through her hair. Then he kissed her on the lips. He held her head still with one hand and slipped his tongue into her mouth. She kissed him back fervently, joyous at the opportunity to please him. She would do whatever he asked, no matter what. She was his whore. She carried his cunt around with her, his tits, his ass, his mouth. He could enter them at any time, do with them whatever he wanted. She would fuck a hundred Mr., Harrington's for him, or not, as he desired. It had been a long, hard night, but now she saw why she had needed it. She had needed to break through that barrier of self. She didn't matter. She was just a lowly creature, deserving of the worst of punishments. All good things came from her master, her owner, Miles Devlin.

It was just the reaction Dr. Evans had predicted. It had all been carefully choreographed. Fear, pain, hunger, exhaustion, loneliness, abandonment, powerlessness. They had eaten away at her until she broke. And when she broke, Dr. Evans had predicted, she would have the zeal of a religious convert. And so she had.

It would not last unless reinforced. But that part was easy. Bits of her self esteem would rear their ugly head from time to time. There were things she would want to rebel against. But her rebellions would be easily crushed, her self esteem easily quashed. It was all in her history. Dr. Evans had read her like an open book. And Devlin had played her like a maestro.

Devlin released her mouth. "That's a good girl, Anna," he said. She beamed at him. Her pussy, even in its battered state, yearned for him. He was life itself.

He picked up the bowl and spooned up a little oatmeal. He brought it to Anna's lips. It was still nice and warm and a little steam rose up from the spoon.

"Open up like a good girl, Anna," he told her.

Anna opened her lips and accepted what her god gave her. It was like ambrosia. It tasted so good it almost made her come. From now on, anything and everything Devlin did to her would take on the attributes of sexuality. It was so bound up with her conception of him, the god who brought pleasure and pain, that it was inescapable for her.

As he continued to deliver spoonful after spoonful of oatmeal to her mouth, her pussy grew warmer and warmer. Her hips squirmed and her breasts were tight. Her bound hands writhed behind her back and her body wriggled, pressing up against the remorseless bars of her little cage. Squashed into a crouch, naked, helpless, her discolored face and dirty, unruly hair jutting out of her confinement like a sideways jill-in-the-box, she looked at him with awe. His fine body, his handsome face. And underneath his colorful robe, in the dark space between his crossed legs, was his cock, the cock she hungered for. But only he would decide when she would get it. He was the master and she was the slave.

As she ate, she thought of last night as being a hundred years ago. It had been a different Anna who had stepped out of her apartment and walked to his limousine, a different Anna who had worried that the valet boy would see her sucking his cock. Now she didn't care if all the world knew.

When the bowl of oatmeal was gone, Devlin helped her drink a large glass of orange juice. There were electrolytes to be replenished. He needed her healthy, after all. For a while anyway.

He put the empty juice glass back down on the tray and shifted position so that he was sitting straight ahead. He took her little cage and rolled it into place in front of him. Anna looked up at him with foreboding. He was about to announce her fate. She was more than willing to serve him. That didn't mean that she craved punishments.

"I want to make something perfectly clear," Devlin told her while stroking her head. "No one has the right to fuck you unless I say so, got that?"

"Yes, Mr. Devlin," Anna said eagerly. She had learned that lesson well.

"And that includes blow jobs, hand jobs, tit fucking, ass reaming, using the folds of your armpits, anything, understand?"

"Y-yes, Mr. Devlin," Anna replied.

"There's one exception to that rule. Do you see this ring?"

"Y-yes, Mr. Devlin." It was the triskelion image on the door to The Blue Cantina.

"Any one who has possession of one of these rings has the right to do anything they want to you. Do you understand?"

"Y-yes, Mr. Devlin," Anna said fearfully. This hadn't been part of the bargain. Or had it? So much had happened within a short week that she hardly remembered what was said the night she surrendered herself to him.

"And you have no right to refuse them at any time or at any place. Understand?"

"Y-yes, Mr. Devlin," Anna answered. Her eyes were brimming with tears. The possibilities for indignity were boundless. How many men wore that style of ring? Had she met any before? Would they come to her office and fuck her right there? Would they invade her home? She wanted to obey Mr. Devlin with all her heart and soul, but this was going to be hard.

"Now what do you do when a man or a woman shows you this ring?"

"Obey them."

"As you would me."

Anna almost said, "Yes, Mr. Devlin." She caught herself just in time. That last was not a question. It was a statement. She was learning. She just nodded.

He patted her on the head. "Good girl," he told her. A little thrill ran through her at his words.

"It's too bad you didn't wait until next week to fuck Harrington, he's to be inducted into the club this weekend," Devlin told her, chuckling. "Then he'll have his ring and you can fuck him as much as you want. Okay?"

Anna quailed at the thought of fucking the man again. She responded, "Yes, Mr. Devlin," just the same.

"I'm going to go get ready for the office. Vincent's going to take you upstairs to your room. I've got some nice clothes picked out for you to wear to work. I want you to shower and make yourself up nice. I'll drop you by the Center with my limo."

Anna nodded her head in understanding. She saw him pick up her gag. She frowned at the thought of it back in her mouth, but she comforted herself that it was only for a while. He was about to put in between her lips when he stopped.

"Oh, and anytime anyone in this house wants to fuck you, that's okay too. And that specifically includes Vincent and Carlos."

Anna nodded sadly.

He slid the gag between her lips and belted it closed behind her head. He gave her head a gentle push until it was back inside the cage and he closed the little hatch. He took a last gulp of his coffee, got up and left.

CHAPTER FIVE

Anna tried to take stock of herself in the interregnum between Devlin's leaving and Vincent's arrival. She realized that she had committed herself to Devlin and his wants utterly and without reservation. She also was smart enough to know that this was the result of the process of pain and degradation he had imposed on her. But, in the end, it didn't matter how she got to where she was. She was here and that's all there was to it. There was such a thrilling feeling of correctness in the idea of her submission to him. When she visualized his presence before her, her body trilled with excitement. Her consciousness knew that it was wrong to feel that way about a man as cruel and callous as Miles Devlin, but some primitive part of her didn't care.

It was like a feeling she had known about herself since her first conscious moment. She was meant to serve. Her body was for others to enjoy and use. Her father had taught her that and her psyche knew how right he was. Her adult mind, the one which caused her so much conflict about this inner, more basic knowledge about herself, was a mere construct superimposed upon the real, more authentic one. It was dictated by the mores and ethics of an artificial culture of civility, rights and taboos. Her whole being re-volted against them. This Anna, the one who was so obsequiously pleased to eat from her master's hand, the one satisfied to await disposition bound and gagged inside of a small, steel cage, that was the real Anna. Devlin had helped her find her again, after being lost so many years.

The door opened. Anna looked up. It was not Vincent as she had expected. It was a pretty, dark skinned girl, young, maybe 22 or so, with long, black hair in a ponytail behind her head. She was wearing a black dress that looked like a maid's outfit. The bodice was wide and low, revealing an ample portion of her generous bosoms. It was tightly constricted around the breasts and waist, pushing her breasts together and demarking her taut belly and her wide hips. There were large, white buttons down the front designed, perhaps, to make her breasts easily available on demand. The skirt of the dress was loose and flouncy with large pleats and came down to only mid-thigh. Its looseness, in comparison to the tight bodice which squeezed her breasts, seemed to be intended to advertise the free accessibility of what was beneath it. She was wearing a golden hued name tag with the name 'Rosalita' etched in florid, black script.

The girl looked at Anna briefly, exhibiting a slight hint of disdain. Without any further acknowledgement of her, she pushed the cage aside so that she could gain access to the tray on which Anna's breakfast had come. She hefted the tray to her shoulder and then turned and left the room.

She was the first of Devlin's servants, besides Vincent, Anna had seen. Last weekend she had been surprised not to see any. It was a large mansion and she would have assumed that it had a large staff. Devlin must have kept them out of view to increase her sense of isolation. Anna had been worried about one of them seeing her marching through the house naked and bound. But now that one of them had seen her, and in much more humiliating circumstances than that, Anna was surprised at her lack of shame.

Vincent entered a few moments later. He came to her cage, reattached the leash to it, and dragged her out the door. He put her back on the dumbwaiter and sent her to the fourth floor. She waited for him in the tiny confine until he opened the door and pulled her out. He took her down the hall, past the punishment room and to the door to what had been her room the prior weekend. He fished a key from his pants, opened the door and pulled her in behind him.

Anna had been forced into the same restrictive position for many hours, and it was not a simple matter to extract her from the cage. Vincent opened the back and helped her to ease out. Just stretching her legs caused her muscles to ache, not to mention the bruises from her caning last night. He helped her to slowly stand and then guided her to the large bed where she laid down on her belly. Her arms were still bound behind her and he released them. Then he used his strong, boney hands to massage her muscles, stimulating the flow of blood. Anna sighed and moaned with pleasure as her circulation was restored. It was so nice to be out of her little prison. And it was heaven to feel the butler's hot, powerful hands on her flesh. Knowing that he could fuck her any time he wanted made her blood run hot. Was he going to do it now?

No, he wasn't. He rose from the bed and ordered her to stand. She rose and stood before him, her hands behind her back as she had been taught.

"You are to shower and make yourself up. I will bring you your clothes when I return. Be finished in fifteen minutes."

Anna nodded. "Fifteen minutes!" she thought. It wasn't much time. She wanted to linger in the shower and enjoy its soothing warmth, but that was not to be. She would have to wash herself quickly if she were to be finished on time.

"And don't forget to shave your pussy," he added.

"Yes, sir," Anna replied in the form that was expected. Vincent tuned and left. She heard the door being locked behind him.

She quickly shucked off the silvery high heels she had been wearing since the day before and drew off her torn and ruined stockings. Then she took off for the bathroom in a flash. She turned on the shower and as soon as the temperature was right, she jumped in. She gasped. The water made her wounds sting. Her thighs and pussy were still angrily red and there were the three lacerations to her rear that Vincent had appended there. It took a few moments, and then the stinging sensations abated. The shower came stocked with a plastic bottle of expensive body wash and a large loofah sponge. She used them to wash herself, treading carefully over her wounds. She shampooed her hair. It was easier now that it was short cut. All in all, she was no more than four or five minutes in the shower.

She used the large, soft towel to dry herself off, patting dry carefully her wounded thighs and pudendum. There was a hair blower for her hair and she quickly had it dry. When she looked in the mirror to brush her hair in place, she was taken aback by the black and blue bruises to her breasts. She looked down at the front of her thighs, which she had not carefully examined in the shower, and saw the same thing: a dark line of black and blue straight across them. She realized that when she went to her exercise later today, her bruises and the irritation of her inner thighs would be clearly seen. They would be difficult to explain. She couldn't see the back of her thighs, but she assumed that the same thing was there. She would have to wear sweatpants instead of her exercise shorts.

She tried to remember if there were a pair in the locker full of stuff Devlin had provided for her. Otherwise, she would have another dilemma. Was she permitted to wear workout clothes other than that provided by Devlin? She stared at her image in the mirror. She felt queasy in her stomach. Then, she recalled her strict schedule to get ready for Vincent and she put that upcoming crisis out of her mind.

She made up her face and brushed her teeth. The diamonds in her ears sparkled in the mirror. Applying her face was one thing she couldn't rush. She carefully lined her eyes and mouth as she had been taught at the salon last weekend and applied a dark lipstick to her lips. She shaded her eyelids with light blue and applied light mascara to her eyebrows. She turned her head right and left to make sure everything looked good.

There was no clock so she didn't know how much more time she had left. She quickly filled a bowl with hot, soapy water and brought it and a razor out to the bedroom. She sat on the bed, her knees raised and her legs spread wide. She dipped the razor in the water and quickly scraped away the 14 hours or so of growth. It was easy and she was finished quickly.

Just then she heard Vincent's footsteps coming up the stairs. She rushed into the bathroom, dumped the water in the toilet, flushing it, and tossed the razor on the edge of the sink. She was running to her position just as Vincent put his key in the lock. When he opened it, she was standing where designated, her hands behind her back, her chest heaving and her heart beating heavily.

The butler gave her a careful, examining look. He had a wooden hanger holding a dark blue garment bag in his left hand. He hung the bag on a hook behind the door and then turned back to her. He stepped close to her and, placing his hand on her chin, tilted it up so that he could examine her makeup. He seemed satisfied.

"Spread your legs," he told her curtly.

Anna dutifully obeyed. He drifted his hand over her pudendum, feeling its smoothness. Anna had yet to get used to the free and easy way he handled her body. Perhaps she never would. His hand was hot and strong and she felt a rise of passion as he stroked her. His fingers seemed to linger at a particular spot, just adjacent to the joinder of her right thigh with her loins. Anna felt a surge of fear pass though her. She had done the job quickly, perhaps a little too quickly.

"You missed a spot," he told her in his deep, cold voice. Anna trembled at the news.

"Get up on the bed," he told her sternly. "Hands behind your back, forehead to the mattress.

With a deep foreboding, Anna crawled up onto the bed. She knelt in presentation position. Vincent went to the closet where the whips are kept and returned with a thin riding crop like the one he had used on her last night. He took a position behind her and without ceremony, reared back his arm and let the whip fly. Anna released a loud screech of pain. It felt like a ragged glass had been drawn across her rear cheeks.

"Go get the razor," he told her coldly.

Tears in her eyes, Anna crawled from the bed and dashed into the bathroom. She returned with the razor and handed it to him.

"Get up on the bed, lift your knees and spread your legs," he ordered.

Anna complied. He pushed her right leg open further and then, with his left hand, pushed on her pudenda so that the skin at its side was taut. "Raise your ass," he told her.

Anna lifted her rear cheeks of the bed. She felt Vincent scrape the razor along her skin lightly. He did it three times, coming close to her thigh and near to her perineum. "Okay, let it down," he told her when he was done.

Without a word, he went into the bathroom. Anna heard him washing off the razor. In her rush, she had left the towel and her makeup out. She knew she should have hung up the towel and put the makeup away, but she hadn't had time. Fear of another punishment ran through her. She heard a closet door opening and closing. He returned with a jar of ointment and a tube of antiseptic cream in his hand.

"If I see the bathroom in that condition again," he told her, "I will whip you. Do you understand?"

"Y-yes sir," Anna answered, her voice tremulous.

He came to the end of the bed and opened up the jar. "Scoot down to the end here," he ordered. Anna maneuvered herself closer to the end of the bed. He took a generous dab of the cream from the jar, leaned over and began to apply it to her wounded inner thighs and pudenda. It felt so good going on. He worked it in carefully, his touch light as a feather. Anna could almost feel the ointment's healing propensities right away. When he rubbed it over her mound, the heat of his firm hand made her catch her breath. She could feel her pussy begin to tingle. He looked her in the eye and ran his thumb up her labial divide, stopping at her as yet dormant clit. He rubbed it lightly in a circular motion and Anna felt a message of nascent pleasure pass through her. The room was deathly silent and Anna knew that he was debating whether to make use of her. Their eyes were locked together. She gasped as his thick thumb penetrated her, moving back and forth slowly, pressing aside the walls of her crevasse. Then, apparently thinking better of it, he drew some more lotion from the jar and finished the job of covering her wounds. Anna's pussy burned in its abandonment.

When he was done with her front, he made her turn over and raise her rear end. He dabbed the antiseptic ointment over the angry red lines that had been produced from her whipping last night and the new wound he had just inflicted. Anna felt oddly comforted by his concern even though she knew that it was in service of his master's interests to keep her body smooth and inviting.

When finished, he brought the ointments back into the bathroom and put them away. Anna heard him cleaning up her makeup and wiping the sink clean. He came out and went to the dresser where the garment bag was hanging.

"Get up," he said.

While Anna rose to her feet, he opened the bag. He produced a black, shirtwaist dress with thin, vertical gold stripes about four inches apart. "Put it on," he told her.

Anna took the dress from him and stepped into it.

She drew it up over her hips and onto her shoulders. There would be no bra today. Nor any underwear. She quickly buttoned it up the front, leaving the top two buttons free. Vincent leaned over and opened the third button as well, making her cleavage visible.

It was not one of the dresses she had picked out last weekend. Devlin must have taken her sizes and ordered more clothes for her. The dress was tight in front and on her hips. Its skirt came down just above her knees. It was another young girl's outfit as far as Anna was concerned, but she knew that if Devlin wanted her to wear it she had no choice. He handed her the belt to the outfit, a wide, gold band with a large, ornate, golden buckle.

Vincent produced a pair of dark, sheer, self supporting stockings, much like the pair she had worn last night. She sat on the bed and pulled them onto her legs, lifting the hem of the dress so that she could draw them up her thighs. It was a particularly intimate gesture and Anna felt a tug of shame at doing it in front of him.

When the stockings were on, he drew a pair of black high heels from the bottom of the bag. Anna usually wore plain black shoes with low heels to work. These were nothing like that. They had a stylish cut and had three inch heels. They had been polished until they gleamed. Anna put them on dutifully.

Vincent had her stand there while he went into the bathroom. He returned with the expensive perfume that Elaine had had her buy last Saturday. He opened it and put a dab on his pointer finger. Reaching out, he placed it behind Anna's right ear. He put another dab behind her left and between her breasts. When he put his finger to the tiny, sculpted bottle again, he told her to lift her dress. Anna picked up the hem and, with some difficulty, shimmied the skirt up to her hips. He placed the final dab on her belly just above her hairless slit.

At his signal, Anna dropped her skirt while Vincent returned the bottle to the bathroom. When he came back, he said, "Carlos will bring another bottle over to your apartment this afternoon. Use it. Do you understand?"

"Yes, sir," Anna said timidly. For a moment, she had been afraid she had earned another punishment.

"He will also drop off a blush that you are to apply to your nipples and some lip gloss. The lip gloss is for your pussy lips. If I see you again not properly perfumed or made up, you will be very, very sorry."

A sourness arose in Anna's belly. "Y-yes, sir," she replied.

"Tomorrow, at 1 p.m., you have an appointment to have your nails done. I will send you the details. Do not miss it."

"Y-yes, sir," Anna acknowledged.

"You will keep this appointment every Friday until further notice unless Mr. Devlin has given you another obligation for that day. They will make sure that your hair is maintained as well. Tonight, when you get back to your apartment, you are to take all of your clothes, other than the ones that Mr. Devlin has purchased for you, and place them in plastic garbage bags. Carlos will collect them. You will wear the clothes that will be provided for you and no others. Carlos will bring something by for you to wear tomorrow when he drops off the makeup. And he will also drop off a diet plan. You are about 7 pounds overweight. You will eat nothing that is not on your diet. Is that clear?"

Anna nodded. Devlin was taking complete control of her life.

"Follow me," he said.

Anna followed him out the door to her room, down the hall and down the stairs. Her high heels made loud 'clicking' noises and she wondered if the other woman who was imprisoned here could hear them, assuming she was still there. She walked with her hands behind her back.

When they reached the ground floor, they went into Devlin's office. He was on the telephone. He did not react to her presence. As usual, he was berating someone for not doing something he had ordered. His voice was sharp and authoritative and had a tinge of anger to it. When he was done, he slammed the telephone into the receiver and turned to Anna. Vincent was standing behind her.

"Ahhhhhh, Anna," he said, his mood changing instantly. "You look wonderful. Elaine and I picked out that dress and some others yesterday afternoon. You need a decent set of work clothes. Yours are way too schoolmarmish. Did Vincent tell you what to do with your present clothes?"

"Y-yes, Mr. Devlin," she answered.

"Everything, and I do mean everything. Do you understand?"

"Y-yes, Mr. Devlin." Anna thought of all her things, the special blouses she had bought for herself here and there, her blue jeans, her sweatshirts, her favorite t-shirts, lots of old, comfortable stuff she had accumulated over the many years. It didn't seem fair that she should have to give all those things up. But she knew she had no power to oppose him. Nor to question him.

"Come here, Anna," Devlin ordered, his voice friendly and light. Anna felt like a little school girl as she approached him. When she got near, he reached out and stroked her face. "You smell nice," he told her. "Like a French whore."

Anna cringed at the appellation, but said nothing. His hand was stroking her face, almost lovingly.

"I hope we understand each other better now, Anna," Devlin continued. "Do we?"

Tears welled up in Anna's eyes. She knew it was wrong, terribly wrong, but she felt like falling to the floor and kissing his feet. He had done something to her, something that needed to be done. His touch, which could be so cruel, could also be so gentle. "Y-yes, Mr. Devlin," she murmured.

He took hold of her hair at the back of her head and drew her to him. He leaned down and crushed his lips against hers, invading her mouth with his tongue. She felt helpless in his grip. With his free hand he popped open the buttons on her dress, down to her waist and slipped out her breasts, mauling them with his strong, heavy hand. Anna kept her wrists crossed behind her back as it they had been bound there. Her knees felt weak and her pussy tingled. Their kiss went on, a minute or more. Her tongue mingled with his as he explored seemingly every portion of her mouth's interior. Her breasts, no, his breasts, felt hot and she reveled in their rough handling.

When he broke his lips away, she was breathing deeply. She could feel his cock pressed up against her. "Go and lean over the couch, Anna," he said. "I want to fuck you."

Her hands behind her back, her pussy yearning for penetration, she moved obediently and quickly to his long, beautifully apportioned couch and leaned over it, just as she had a few nights ago. She felt his hands drawing her skirt up and over her hips. Her legs were spread. She heard his zipper descend and a moment later his cock pressing against her enflamed love lips. It hesitated there a moment, seeking the proper angle for entry, and then slipped inside.

Anna gasped when he felt his cock push aside her tender inner tissues. He fucked her with deep, rapid, strong strokes. His hands were on her hips, pinning her down. She thought, for a moment, of the fact that Vincent was watching. Last night was the first time he had witnessed Devlin fucking her. She had been too far gone to make note of it. Besides, she was bound and unable to resist. Here she had surrendered herself willingly, more than willingly, her true, sluttish nature on display.

But the thought passed quickly. All of her mind focused on the thick meat that was plowing her. Her master was possessing her. She yearned to receive his spume. Her lusts were suffusing her body, making, it seemed, every cell rejoice. She heard him groan. His grip grew tighter, his thrusts more emphatic and then he groaned again and again, signaling his climax. Her pussy exploded with delight. Its hard contractions made her belly spasm and roil. Her heart was pounding in her chest. She moaned loudly, filling the room with her exclamation of ecstasy.

He gave a great sigh and then he slipped from her. She heard his zipper being pulled up.

"Time to go," he announced. "Victor, get a cloth for Anna to sit on. I don't want her leaking all over my seat."

"Yes, Mr. Devlin," Vincent replied. By the time Anna had raised herself from the back of the couch, he had returned. He handed a white cloth napkin to Devlin. In his other hand, he had a small, black pocketbook with a large, golden clasp. He handed that to Devlin too. "All of your things are in it," he said to Anna.

Devlin hadn't said anything about pulling her dress down or rebuttoning it, and so Anna was standing there with her skirt around her hips and her breasts lying out. Devlin headed for the door and Anna followed him. Vincent opened it and they passed to the outside. The limo was waiting. Carlos was standing there, holding the door open. Devlin handed him the napkin.

"Let Anna in on the other side," he told Carlos. "And put this napkin on the seat. I just got done fucking her and she's very leaky."

Anna blanched as her post coital state was announced in such crude terms to the driver. She sheepishly followed him to the other side of the car. When he had opened the door and laid the napkin on the seat, she maneuvered herself in. As she passed him, Carlos gave her naked buttocks a caress as if to remind her that they would soon be spending some time together again. Devlin had said she needed more cocksucking lessons and he never said anything like that lightly. Anna's stomach grew tight at the thought of it. She sat down on the seat, careful to center her pussy on the napkin and keeping her arms behind her back.

Carlos got in the driver's seat and the limo took off. He turned on the music and a light Vivaldi concerto came on, filling the back of the car with beautiful music. It was enchanting, elevating her mood. Anna closed her eyes and let it pass through her. Her bare breasts jiggled and swayed as the limo maneuvered itself along the curvy roads. Her legs were ajar and she could feel the cold morning air covering her thighs. The heat came on and the hot air emerging from the floor vents felt good too. It was so strange being dressed and not dressed at the same time. The important parts of her were exposed for the world to see. Her dress just served as a frame for them.

Devlin was quiet. Anna could sense his heavy bulk near to her. It was comforting. After about fifteen minutes, he spoke to her, his voice low.

"Come and sit closer to me, Anna, where I can touch you," he said.

Anna's eyes sprung open and her body trilled at the thought of his touch. She raised her hips and slid the napkin over closer to him and sat down on it. She leaned back and closed her eyes again.

She felt his hand slip over her breast, squeezing it gently, playing with her stiffening nipple. It just felt so right to have his hand there, to have her body subject to his whims. He caressed her other breast, squeezing it a little harder.

"Mmmmmmmmmmmmm," he sighed. "You have such great tits, Anna," he said. "I could just play with them for hours."

Anna smiled. That sounded fine with her. His touch was so comforting. She had been all alone in the world, but was so no more. She belonged to Miles Devlin.

His hand slipped down her belly and between her thighs. "Spread your legs," he told her. His hand took possession of her mons. She moaned with pleasure at the contact. His heavy hand laid upon it while his finger slipped along her slippery divide. He stroked her idly, leisurely as they traveled along. His finger seemed magical as it slid inside her and then drifted northwards to circle around her clit. "It's his cunt," she thought. "He's playing with it. It feels so good."

She lost all track of time. The rhythm of the road lulled her into a passiveness that was comforting. She thought of her ride to Devlin's mansion in the trunk just last night. How much different she was now. How much better was it to be obedient then rebellious. Good girls got pleasure, bad girls got pain.

He brought her to the edge once or twice, making her breathe hard, but then his finger retreated until she cooled. She hardly noticed it when the limo came to a stop. His finger was circling and rubbing her love button. It was becoming more and more insistent. She raised her knees, pressing her left one against his thigh. Her passions were beginning to boil. "Don't stop! Don't stop! Please! Please!" she thought desperately. The finger kept going and going. Her pussy grew hotter and hotter. She could feel her orgasm growing from someplace deep inside her. She gave out a great groan and then it came. "Ah! Ah! Ah! Ah!" she called out at each fierce contraction of her crevasse. "Oh, god," she thought madly. "That's so good! That's so good! That's so goooooooooooooood!"

Her pussy was still giving her strong echoes of pleasure when the hand removed itself. "We're here, Anna," Devlin told her. "We're at the Center. It's time for you to get out."

Anna panicked. "At the Center?" Her face felt flushed and she was still breathing heavily. Her dress was still around her waist; her pussy gave off a strong odor of her arousal. Would he let her dress herself properly before she got out? It would be awful if somebody from the Center saw her like this. She could lose herself in her fantasies while in Devlin's presence, but there was a real world out there that she had to live in. It would be mortifying for anyone to see her this way.

"Pull your dress down and button up, Anna. You can't get out of the car like that," he told her.

She gratefully shimmied the skirt down over her hips and then buttoned the top of the dress. She was careful to leave the top three buttons open, as Vincent had instructed her. She looked to Devlin for permission to leave.

"You can go, Anna," he said, amused. He handed her the stylish black pocketbook that went with her outfit. "Now don't forget your workout at 4," he added. "I know you'll be tired, but you'll just have to do the best you can. And remember, you're to follow Cathy's instructions to the letter. Do whatever she tells you. Do you understand?"

"Yes, Mr. Devlin," Anna said meekly.

She opened the door and returned to the world.

* * * * * * * * * * * * * *

It was 20 after 9. She was late again. Twice in one week, something totally out of character. She burst through the door. Phyllis looked up from her desk quizzically. "Where have you been?" she asked. "There was a staff meeting at 9, or did you forget?"

"Oh, shit!" Anna declared to herself. "Yes, I'm sorry. Ask everybody if they can get together in about ten minutes. I had an errand I had to run."

"They're all still in the conference room waiting."

"Okay, okay," Anna replied impatiently. "I'll be there in a minute."

"By the way, nice outfit," Phyllis said. "You're really coming up in the world."

Anna shrugged off the comment and ran into her office. Her head was whirling. She had to make the shift from obsequious slave to decisive, committed head of a social service agency. She sat down in her chair behind her desk. The newspaper was on it opened to the page with her picture. "Oh, shit!" she thought. She had forgotten about that. It also brought to mind that the last time she had seen it she was locked, bound and gagged, naked in a cage. If somehow that ever got out, how Devlin treated her, she didn't know what she would do.

She took a deep breath. She found the agenda for the staff meeting and her notes. She got up, strode confidently through the door to her office and across the hall to the conference room. All of the staff members, 15 of them, were there.

Anna sat down at the head of the table. She cleared her throat. "I apologize for being so late. Something came up this morning that I had to take care of. Now, item one on the agenda is…."

* * * * * * * * * * * * * *

The meeting had gone quickly. There were several matters she had to skip due to time constraints. The staff all dispersed to their daily tasks without ado. Esther came up to her. "I had a call from Martha Schopenhauer from the Eastside Bank and Trust Company. She was looking for you, but you weren't here so Phyllis passed the call to me. She has a job opening that needs to be filled right away. It's for a branch office down state. She wanted to know if we had someone who could interview for it today. I sent Wendy over. I hope that's okay."

Wendy was a diminutive, pale skinned, red headed Irish girl. She had had a job opportunity withdrawn from her at the last minute a week ago. She was ready for placement and had been crushed. Wendy is who Anna would have sent.

"That's fine, Esther. Thanks for your quick thinking. I hope it works out."

"You're welcome," Esther said, beaming. "That's part of my job, isn't it?"

"Yes, it is, although I like to be informed of job placement decisions before they happen. I met Ms. Schopenhauer last night at an affair at the bank. They unveiled the new

Rosenfeld mural. She told me that she wanted to work on some internships with us, but I didn't think she'd call so quickly."

"Yes, I saw your picture in the paper. You looked beautiful, very sharp."

"Thank you," Anna said coldly. It was not something she was anxious to discuss.

Anna went into her office. Esther had reminded her about the check. She pulled it out of the little black purse Vincent had given Devlin. The pocketbook was Italian, from a well known manufacturer. Anna guessed that it cost well over $500.00. People were going to wonder where she had gotten all this money all of a sudden.

She buzzed Phyllis. She came into her office a moment later.

"Here is a check that Mr. Harrington of the Eastside Bank and Trust gave me last night. Give it to Esther for deposit."

"Yes, Anna," Phyllis replied.

"And dust off that job description for the new counselor. I want to send a memo to the members of the Board of Trustees so that they can approve the new position at our meeting next week.

"Yes, Anna," Phyllis acknowledged. She paused before leaving.

"Are you okay, Anna?" she asked. "You seem very distracted lately."

"I'm okay," Anna returned. "But thank you for asking. I guess I've been a little harried with Carol gone and all. Everything should be fine now that I hired Esther. What's the scuttlebutt? Is she working out okay?"

"The staff love her so far. She's picked up on everything very fast. You should have seen Wendy's face when she told her about the job interview."

"I'm sorry I wasn't there."

"And by the way, you look mad hot in that picture in the paper. I'll be you get a lot of calls for dates. It's about time."

Anna had a mental image of her sliding off the silvery dress at Harrington's command last night. Yes, she might get lots of dates, but what kind? She thought of Devlin's instructions about men with the ring. She shuddered.

There were some calls to return, some staff reports to read. Wendy came back around 11:30. She was ecstatic. She had gotten the job. They had a place for her to live and everything. She rushed upstairs to get her things and was back in a flash. The bank's limousine was waiting for her. Ms. Schopenhauer had come in with her. She was dressed in a conservative, grey business suit.

"I'm so glad we met last night, Ms. Addunizio," she said. "This job offer came across my desk yesterday. When I came in this morning I thought of you immediately."

"Thank you so much," Anna replied. "It is going to mean a lot to Wendy. She's a great girl."

"I can tell," Ms. Schopenhauer answered. "She's lovely. You've done a great job with her."

"She's worked hard," Anna explained.

Wendy was standing there, out of breath. She had turned 19 a few weeks ago and had been in the Center for almost a year. She had been picked up turning tricks for a drug dealer down on Fourth Street when she was 16. She had done six months at a court ordered drug treatment facility and then assigned to a foster family. At 18, she received the boot. It was either back to the street or the Center. Anna had recruited her personally.

She had a pretty face and a terrific figure, buxom even. And she had the sheen of youth. Anna was very happy for her. She liked to screen employers before the girls were sent away on jobs, but since it was the bank, she had no problem with it. And it would be good for Wendy to be downstate, away from all her old haunts.

"Oh, Anna," Wendy gushed. "I don't know how I can ever thank you. All of this has been wonderful. I promise, when I'm on my feet, I'll send part of my salary here every week!"

"You don't have to do that, Wendy," Anna told her. "Living a good life will be the best reward for us."

Wendy jumped into her arms. She was crying. "I'll miss you so much! It's like a dream come true! I'll write you every day!"

"Once a week will be fine," Anna said laughing. She gave Wendy a big hug and kissed her cheek.

"We've got to get going," Ms. Schopenhauer announced.

Some of the other girls had come downstairs to see Wendy off. She had been very popular. They kissed and hugged and tears were shed all around.

"Goodbye!" Wendy shouted as she walked out the door, her little suitcase in her hand.

Anna went back to work, pleased.

* * * * * * * * * * * * * *

Twenty minutes later, the bank's limousine pulled in behind a small, one story, industrial building in the factory district of the city. Ms. Schopenhauer explained to Wendy that this was an orientation center for new employees. There was a short film for her to see and an interview. Then they would be back on their way.

Wendy followed Ms. Schopenhauer into the building. She didn't notice the dark blue van parked outside. She didn't notice the man holding a white cloth in his hand on her left when she came in. The cloth went over her mouth. She inhaled deeply in surprise. Then everything went black.

About a minute later, two men emerged from the building rolling a large, black case on the ground. One of the men opened the rear door to the van and they hefted the case into it. After securing it properly and attaching the proper hoses, the door was shut and they got into the front seat. A few seconds later, they were on their way. Ms. Schopenhauer watched the van pull out of the parking lot. On its side it said in scriptive letters, "The Blue Cantina."

CHAPTER SIX

It was a long, hard day for Anna. She was tired beyond belief. As she sat at her desk, reading reports, fielding phone calls, her mind kept drifting off. She reexperienced her time in the cage, an association she could not help but connect to both the terrible shocks she received and the subsequent, mind blowing orgasms. She thought of her obsequious submission to Devlin. Now that she was free of his immediate dominion, the paradigm by which she accepted her slavish surrender seemed more remote. And yet the echoes of it remained. Her pussy warmed as she recalled his use of her, both in his office before they left the mansion and later in the limo. His cock and hand had thrilled her, experiences made more acutely passionate by the thought of her obedience to his demands.

She thought of the ring that he had showed her and its meaning. How many men bore it, she wondered. How would they recognize her as being subject to their will? When would she meet one of them and, when she did, would she be able to give herself over to the callous use by a complete stranger as readily and as wholly as Devlin had indicated she should?

The thought of escape ran through her mind. She knew what she had experienced at Devlin's was terribly wrong. She was being drawn into a mode of existence which was contrary to everything she believed in. And yet it had a mesmerizing appeal. She was like a person who had experienced their first shot of heroin. She knew the dark places it would bring her to, descending the dark ladder into nothingness. It could only end in destruction of everything she held sacred. And yet, she knew that she was going there nonetheless. She couldn't go back now, even if she wanted to. The draw of the fierce, thrilling emotions it sparked in her was too much to resist.

At lunchtime, she ran out and bought a pair of sweat pants to bring with her to the gym. Her heart beat wildly in her chest, her hands trembled as she waited by the checkout. She knew that she was committing a terrible sin. But the thought of revealing her wounds to Cathy, her trainer, or to the other men and women at the gym was too much to bear. She could only hope that Cathy would not betray her.

At 3:45, she took off for the gym. There was a new girl to be interviewed at 4:15, but she had to obey Devlin's command. She got Esther to cover it.

When she got to the gym, she rifled through the clothes that had been supplied to her in her locker, hoping that there was a pair of sweatpants there she could wear and not be breaking one of Devlin's rules. There hadn't been. Rather than change in the locker room, she went off to the bathroom and changed in one of the stalls. She put on a sports bra and over that one of the t-shirts that had been in her locker. She emerged into the gym with trepidation. She was so tired, she didn't think she could do the whole workout today. She intended to ask Cathy if they could take it easy for once.

Cathy bounded up to her when she saw her. She was dressed, as usual, in a pair of very brief shorts and a tank top. She was all smiles. "Hello, Anna," she said. "Good to see you." She eyed Anna's long sweat pants. "Those aren't regulation, are they?" she asked.

"N-no," Anna answered, "but, you see…" she started to explain.

"That's okay. It'll be our little secret, won't it?" Cathy interrupted.

Anna was surprised at Cathy's response. How much did she know?

"Mr. Devlin called and said to keep your workout light today anyway. I figured we would do some stretching exercises. Is that okay with you?"

Giving out a sigh of relief, Anna agreed.

Cathy led her to one of the side rooms. The floor was covered by a large, green gym mat. The room had no windows. It was small, about 15' by 15'. The walls con-sisted of whitewashed cinderblock and were padded up to about three feet. The glass on the door had been covered up with brown paper to give the users of the room privacy. Anna had just turned around after walking in when she saw Cathy turn the lock on the door.

"Just so we won't be disturbed," she said. She had a wry grin on her face.

Anna's belly started to flutter. Something was happening. Something she probably wouldn't like.

"Okay, take off your pants and t-shirt, Anna. We're going to get you all stretched out," Cathy announced. She was standing about five feet away from her, her legs spread for balance, her hands on her hips.

But that had been the whole point of wearing the long pants, so that Cathy wouldn't see her bruises. Besides, she wasn't wearing any underwear.

"I-I can't," Anna replied. "I don't have anything on underneath."

"That's okay, Anna. I've seen plenty of twats. "

"But I don't want to. Can't we just do it with my pants on?" Anna knew she was going way out on a limb, but the idea of being naked in front of this woman, having her see her shame, was too much to bear.

"Listen, Anna," Cathy said, her voice firm, "I was willing to overlook you wearing the pants to begin with, but I don't want to hear any shit about taking them off. What did Mr. Devlin tell you?"

Anna hesitated. He words were as clear as a bell. "Do everything you tell me to do," she murmured unhappily.

"That's right. I'm your trainer, not your buddy. Now strip before I get on the phone to Mr. Devlin. As a matter of fact, take off whatever you have under that t-shirt too. You might as well be totally naked."

Tears of shame in her eyes, knowing that she was bound to obey, Anna drew off her t-shirt and then the black, stretch sports bra underneath it. She kept her vision down as her breasts sprang free. Then she hooked her thumbs in the waistband of her sweat pants and pulled them down. She stepped out of them, pulling them over her sneakers.

"The sneaks and socks too," Cathy added.

Dismally, Anna shed her sports shoes. She picked everything up and moved them to the side of the room where they would be out of the way. She returned to her spot in the middle of the room and stood there, her eyes downcast, awaiting instructions.

"Man, Devlin really got you good!" Cathy exclaimed. "You must have been a very naughty girl!"

Anna mumbled a response. Her front had two long purple stripes, one across her breasts and one across her thighs. They had started to dissipate, spreading the discoloration and making the lines of purple somewhat fuzzy. Despite the lotion Vincent had placed on her inner thighs, they were still red and irritated.

"Turn around so I can see your back," Cathy ordered.

She obeyed. Cathy whistled when she saw the long strips of black and blue. "I betcha that hurt," she said. "Well, I'm going to get you feeling real good again. And just to show you that fair is fair, I'm going to get buck naked too."

She drew off her top with a practiced ease and then stepped out of her shorts. She removed her sports shoes. She wasn't wearing any underwear either. She had on a grey sports bra and she slipped that off last. Her breasts were taut and small, like inverted coffee cups. Her bush was trimmed but for a little tuft of brown hair over it and around the sides.

"Okay, lie down on your belly. We'll work out some of the crimps in your back and arms. "

Reluctantly, dismally ashamed at her treatment, Anna obeyed. When she was lying flat, Cathy placed herself atop her, her knees next to her hips, Anna's buttocks between her thighs. Anna could feel her coosh pressing against her bottom. She leaned forward and placed her hands on Anna's shoulders. Her fingers dug deep into the muscles there.

'Arrrrrgh!" Anna called out as the pain shot through her.

'Keep still," Cathy said. "It'll hurt a little at first, but it'll feel better after a while, you'll see."

Her efforts accompanied by an occasional grunt, Cathy worked over Anna's back and shoulders. She was right about the pain. After a while, it went away and was replaced by a type of bliss. She work her way down, kneading the muscles in her lower back, then her buttocks and then her thighs. She even did her ankles and feet.

She ordered Anna to flip over and began to work on her front. Anna kept her hands up over her head and her eyes closed. She flinched when she felt Cathy's strong hands on her breasts.

"Just relax," Cathy said. "Lay back and enjoy it."

Her touch was stimulating to her mammaries, but not in a sexual way. Anna sighed as she massaged them, digging into the tendons and muscles. She did her belly and the insides of her thighs. Anna could not help feel a slight surge of arousal as Cathy's hands neared her pudenda. She was glad that she didn't have a cock because she was sure she would have had an erection.

When she finished massaging Anna's front, she had her turn over again and started working on the stretches. She pushed her legs back until Anna groaned. She flexed her ankles. She had her kneel up and placed her arms around her, twisting her torso to the right and to the left as far as she could. Her body was jammed up against Anna's and she couldn't help feel aroused by the hot, soft, sweaty flesh, the sensation of having Cathy's naked breasts pressed firmly against her back. As she maneuvered Anna around, her hands began to flit across her more sensitive parts. Her hand would rest on a breast, squeezing it gently as she pushed her this way or that. When she had Anna on her back, pushing her legs back until her knees touched her chest, her fingers rested on Anna's mound, causing a stimulation to ripple through her.

Anna's arousal was beginning to rise, when she found herself wrapped up in Cathy's body, her arms trapped behind her, her legs spread by Cathy's feet. She had her left arm around Anna's shoulders, her hand resting on her chin. It was like some strange wrestler's hold. Anna couldn't move a muscle.

She became frightened when Cathy kept holding her there. She felt the woman's free right hand slip over her belly and down over her pussy. The touch was gentle and soft and, Anna knew, not part of any muscle stretching exercise.

"Please...." Anna murmured.

"Shhhhhhhhhhh!" Cathy whispered lowly. "Don't talk. Just relax."

Anna made a desperate effort to get free. Cathy just tightened her hold. Somehow, she was able to twist Anna's arms until she felt exquisite pain in her shoulders. "Ohhhhhhhh!" Anna complained.

"Shhhhhhhhh!" Cathy said again. "You're not going anywhere, Anna, until you get the full treatment. Just let your body relax and enjoy it. It's what I call 'the happy ending'."

When Anna felt Cathy's hand return to her pussy, she tried to jerk herself free. The idea of another woman touching her there was anathema to her. She knew a few gay female couples and all that, but the idea of what they did together was repulsive to her. The idea of it now made her stomach turn.

"Pleeeeeeeease, don't!" she begged earnestly.

Cathy took hold of her love lips between her thumb and forefinger and gave them a twist. Anna cringed with the pain.

"I told you to keep still!" Cathy scolded her. "If you give me any more trouble, I'll really punish you. And believe me, I know how to hurt a body!"

Anna whined her surrender. Cathy's hand returned to her pussy. Her fingers flitted over it as lightly as a butterfly. They passed down her thighs and up over her belly. They flew to her breasts, giving her nipples light tweaks. Her lips came into contact with the base of her neck and her tongue slipped slowly and sensually across her skin.

Despite her revulsion against a woman's touch, Anna was beginning to become aroused. When Cathy's fingers returned to her hairless puss, they found an incipient moisture there. "Mmmmmmmmmmmm," Cathy moaned. "You're all wet, Anna," she said languorously. "What a good girl. I'm going to tell Mr. Devlin what a good girl you are. Would you like that, Anna? Should I tell Mr. Devlin that you're a good girl?"

The juxtaposition of Devlin's name and the phrase good girl set off a thrill inside Anna. She couldn't help it. She wanted to be a good girl in Devlin's eyes. There was nothing she wanted more. "Y-yesssssssssss!" Anna moaned.

Cathy's hand was becoming more insistent. It flowed across the insides of her thighs, over her belly and seized her breasts, one at a time, giving them, firm, exquisite squeezes. "Yes, what, Anna?"

"Y-yes, please," Anna sighed. Cathy's fingers were revolving around her clit and her lusts were rising sharply.

"That's 'Yes, please, Mistress Cathy,' Anna. You're to call me Mistress Cathy from now on. Say it again, right this time."

Cathy had taken hold of her stiffened love button and was pinching it harder and harder. Anna moaned from the pain, pain that made her fires of lust rage.

"Say it, Anna! Say it!" Cathy demanded.

"Yes, please, Mistress Cathy!" Anna shouted. "Please! Ohhhhhhhhhh!"

"Good girl," Cathy announced again. "You're a good girl." Her left arm, the one that was around her shoulders, pushed Anna's head sideways so that it was facing her. Cathy placed her lips on Anna's and pried her mouth open with her tongue. Anna moaned again. Her body wanted to wriggle and squirm with her excitement, but Cathy kept her firmly bound with her own. It was like being caged all over again, but this time someone was in there with her, tormenting her into pleasure. Cathy's hand rubbed over her belly and took hold of her breasts again, squeezing them hard. Then they flowed back down to her puss. Her thumb slipped over her pleasure nubbin and her long fingers entered her.

"Here it comes, Anna," Cathy said as she pulled away from her lips. "I'm going to make you come now."

The thumb began a steady caress of her clit while the fingers drew in and out of her. Cathy took possession of her lips again and her hot tongue slipped and slid over Anna's, driving her passion. She could feel her orgasm coming closer and closer. Like last night, she wanted to deny it, but knew she couldn't fight it. She tried to arch her back, strained at the limbs that were confining her, moaned into Cathy's active mouth. When her climax hit, her body jerked and twisted. Wave after wave of pleasure shot through her. Her assailant's thumb and fingers drove her on and on. Her hot tongue and breath accentuated and deepened her excitement. Her warm, sweaty body, pressed against her accelerated her passion. Anna had never known that fucking a woman could be like this. It was like she knew all of her triggers, just how to delight her. She moaned and groaned as ecstasy flowed through her.

Finally, her excitement waned. Cathy's fingers drew out the last, diminishing shocks from her pussy. Her tongue became less insistent. When she broke their kiss, her hand wandered up over her belly and breasts again. "Now, that's better, isn't it, Anna?" she asked.

"Y-yes, Mistress Cathy," Anna replied, her voice languid and satisfied.

Cathy released her. "Get up on your knees," she told her. "And put your hands behind your back. It's my turn now."

Cathy stood up, towering above her. Anna cringed at the thought of what she was going to make her do. The young, fit, well muscled girl spread her legs and placed her hands on her hips.

"Okay, now, Anna. I want you to lick my pussy until I tell you to stop. Got that?"

"Yes, Mistress Cathy," Anna whined. Devlin had ordered her to obey Cathy in all things. Her instruction to gemauch her pussy was as if it came directly from him. She inched herself forward on her knees on the soft, green mat until she was just in front of Cathy's spread legs. She bent her neck up, gazing at the already engorged organ. She brought her face forward, let her tongue out of her mouth and licked her slit from bottom to top. It was salty and musky. The aroma was familiar, not unlike her own. It surrounded her like a fog. She licked the pussy again and Cathy moaned. Anna felt surprised at the sense of excitement she felt. Cathy took hold of the sides of her head, forcing her head closer to her cunt, and she went to work.

She, of course, knew how to pleasure a pussy. It had been done to her dozens of times. She knew just where to flick her tongue, just when to slip her tongue in deep and wriggle it, just when to take her love button between her lips and suckle it. Cathy moaned and sighed while she did it. She stroked her active head and gave her little sounds of encouragement. It did not take long for her to come. She groaned loudly, thrusting her hips at Anna's mouth, pressing her head down firmly with her hands.

Even when she was sure that Cathy's orgasm had faded, Anna kept to her task. She was waiting for a sign from her mistress to relent. Finally, Cathy pushed her head away. "Okay," she said breathlessly. "That's enough for today."

She took a deep breath and stepped away from Anna. She scooped up her shorts and bra from the floor and put them on. Anna was waiting for a signal that she could get dressed. She watched Cathy go to the corner of the room and retrieve a long, floppy, rubbery stick.

"Get on your hands and toes and raise up your ass, Anna," she told her.

Anna knew she was going to be whipped. But for what?

"I told you that your wearing those sweat pants would be our little secret, but I didn't say I wouldn't punish you for it. And you were a little slow to obey me before. Mr. Devlin told me to punish you ruthlessly after every infraction. So I'm going to do it."

Anna sniffled and whined. She knew better than to disobey. She put the palms of her hands on the mat, stretched out her legs until she was on her toes and then raised her back side so that it was up in the air.

"Put your legs together," Cathy ordered.

When Anna had tearfully complied, Cathy took up a position next to her.

"Now this stick won't mark you up or wound you, but it does carry an angry bite. Next time, do what you're told. Understand?"

"Y-yes, Mistress Cathy," Anna answered. She readied herself for the blows.

"There'll be five for wearing the wrong clothes. You knew that that was very bad and did it anyway. I'm going to only give you three for failing to obey since this was your first time and to reward you for a good pussy licking job. It was pretty good for a first effort. But you'll have to do better. Understand?"

"Y-yes, Mistess Cathy," Anna whined.

She heard Cathy take a deep breath and then the sound of the stick moving through the air. The blow struck Anna across her upraised buttocks. It felt like a dozen bees had stung her. "Ohhhhhhhhhhhhhh!" Anna exclaimed.

The next four came rapidly in succession. She gave out a loud, agonized expression of pain at each blow. She could feel her ass getting heated. There was a pause and then three more came. Anna was screeching in pain by the end. It had grown progressively worse. Tears were flowing from her eyes and dripping on the mat underneath her.

"Okay, you can get dressed now," Cathy said.

She watched as Anna assembled her clothes again and put them on. When she had tied her workout shoes, Anna stood, her feet apart, her hands behind her back, her eyes lowered. The memory of how the young woman had overpowered her and made her come ran through her mind. She could still taste her pussy juice in her mouth and her backside burned like someone had taken sandpaper over it.

"Okay," Cathy said, looking her over approvingly. "We'll see you tomorrow. And I want you to drop off those sweatpants at my office before you leave. Understood?"

"Yes, Mistress Cathy," Anna replied obediently.

She skipped her shower. She would take one at home. When she brought the sweatpants to Cathy's office, she was already working with another client. Anna obediently placed the pants over her chair and left.

* * * * * * * * * * * * * * *

All the way on the taxi ride home, Anna kept going over and over her experience with the domineering trainer. Getting pleasure from a woman had been a totally new experience. It had not been what she had anticipated at all. The flesh was smooth and soft, unlike a man's even despite Cathy's fit frame. Her touch had a gentleness far different than a man's softest caress. And to have had her mouth on her pussy, to experience the strange, smoky taste, had been thrilling. She had expected to be revolted by it, but she had liked it. It tasted like passion.

Licking her to crisis had, in a way, been just like giving a blow job. There was a strange juxtaposition of power and subjugation at the same time. Power, because of the immense pleasure it brought the recipient, compelling their desire. Subjugation because of the submissive posture, the bending to the dominant person's loins, the obedience to their commands and needs.

But was she going to have to go through that every day? Cathy was her trainer. Was she going to be training her so that she could serve women with the same alacrity and skill as she did men? And did she have to add Cathy to the growing list of people who had ready access to her body?

She also thought of the time that being Devlin's sex slave was consuming. She had been late for work twice and had to leave work every day early. She had returned to the office on Monday and Tuesday evenings, but not last night and not tonight. Tonight she was just too damned tired. And when was she going to get done the work she usually did on weekends? It would pile up fast. She could see that she was going to have to rely on Esther more and more. And the other women too.

The taxi left her off just opposite the door to her little apartment. She was glad to be home. It had been almost 24 hours since she had been here. As she walked up to the door, she remembered that her task tonight was to get rid of all her old clothes. It was going to be hard to throw all those things away. But she knew she had no choice. It was either run away or obey.

When she entered her apartment, she looked for signs of Carlos. He was going to drop off the makeup and perfume as well as tomorrow's clothes. The makeup was in a bag on the kitchen counter. Next to it was a box of black plastic garbage bags. The clothes were in a garment bag hanging on the bedroom door. Anna took a look at them. It was a red skirt that looked like it would be very tight around her hips and a gold blouse with brass buttons. There was a new belt, thin with a gold buckle, not much different than the one she wore today, red shoes and a red pocketbook. Anna dreaded going to work looking like that. It was a style totally foreign to her and would make tongues wag.

She put aside her concern for the moment. There was a bottle of scotch in her cabinet that was calling out to her. When she opened the door, she saw that her half consumed bottle of Red label had been joined by a full, unopened bottle of 12 year old Black Label. There was a bottle of premium gin there, a fine imported vodka and a bottle of bourbon. There were also several mixers, tonic, soda water and ginger ale. It looked like Devlin was planning to party at her place, or, in the alternative, make her place suitable for a party for anyone else who happened by. She thought of the men with the ring and shivered.

Taking out the Red Label, she poured herself three inches in a glass. It would have been the height of presumption for her to drink the Black Label. That obviously belonged to Devlin and she would suffer a harsh punishment if she opened the bottle without permission. She took her scotch straight. She felt the fiery liquid warm her insides. Everything seemed a little less intolerable with a little booze in her. She kicked off her shoes and sat down in her chair that she used for reading. She was damn tired, that was for sure.

She closed her eyes for a moment and then opened them right away. She had seen something on her bookshelf that had never been there before. It looked like a computer modem. It had several wires going into it. Anna followed one from the unit to the floor, across the floor to a corner of the room and then up to the ceiling. It ran across the intersection of the wall and the ceiling to a very small camera. It was only about two inches high. It looked like it was all lens. It pointed straight at her.

She followed the other leads. One went into the kitchen area, another, on the neighboring wall, into her little dining nook. Her whole apartment was covered. There wasn't a place where she could hide. Another pair of leads went into her bedroom. The cameras were over her bed, one looking at it from the foot and another from the side. She dashed into the bathroom. The door had been taken off and the camera on the side wall could see straight into it. She slid the shower door open and there was a camera in there too. All of the cameras had little red lights on them indicating that they were on.

Panic and revulsion ran through her. It was Devlin's work, she knew that. She was going to be on view for every moment she was in her apartment. Nothing she did, and she meant nothing, would be private. Who was watching? It was the same question she had had when she saw the cameras in her fourth floor room at his mansion and in the punishment room. For whose enjoyment were these recordings being made? She couldn't live like this! It was out of the question! Devlin had gone too far!

At that moment, the modem beeped. There was a slight crackle and a voice came on. It was Devlin's.

"Good evening, Anna," it said. "I was waiting for you to discover my little addition to your home before I spoke to you. How do you like it?"

Anna didn't know what to say. She hated it! She knew she had to answer him; she knew she had to be honest. "I don't like it, Mr. Devlin," she said finally. She felt like she was speaking to a phantom, a dream person. But she knew it was Devlin. She was looking at the modem. She wanted to attack it. Attack it, run to her car and flee. That's what she would do.

"I didn't think you would like it Anna, but I had my men put it in just the same. Now I can check on you every night to make sure you are obedient and get yourself off. Or I can check every other day or once a week. You'll never know when I'm looking and when I'm not."

She knew that this was true. That was part of the horror of the thing.

"I want you to stand in the middle of the room and look up at the camera opposite your chair, Anna. I want you looking at me when I talk to you. Do you understand?"

"Y-yes, Mr. Devlin," Anna replied dismally. She stepped towards the middle of the room and looked at the camera. She felt like she was looking at a distant god who lived in the stars.

"That's better, Anna," Devlin said. "Now that you are my slave, I want to know what you are doing all the time. You have no right to hide anything from me. This sort of emphasizes that point."

Anna knew better than to respond. Her empty stomach was churning. She was trembling. What had she gotten herself into?

"I want you to get undressed, Anna," Devlin's voice said.

A chill went through her. She hesitated for just a second and then proceeded to obey. She quickly unbuttoned the blouse of her dress and undid the belt. After shimmying it off, she placed it on the chair. She was about to draw down her stockings when Devlin stopped her. "What are you doing, Anna?" Devlin asked.

"I-I'm taking off my stockings, Mr. Devlin," Anna responded.

"I told you to get undressed. That means take off your dress. Can I make myself any clearer?"

"N-no, Mr. Devlin," Anna replied tearfully. She had forgotten his literalness. To un-dress meant to take off your dress.

"You've got to listen, Anna," his voice said. "I'll have to punish you for that."

Anna suppressed a sob. She already had a reserve of sins to expiate when she went to his mansion tomorrow. Now she had added another.

"There's a pair of high heeled sandals in your closet. Go in the bedroom and put them on."

She rushed to obey. When she opened the closet, she saw them. They looked Italian. They were certainly expensive. She sat down on the bed and put them on. She was about to run back into the living room when she remembered that he had not told her to. She stood and looked up at one of the cameras.

"Very good, Anna. I see you listened that time," he said. "Now this is how I want you at all times you are in your apartment. The only times you are to take your sandals off is when you go to bed or take a shower. The only clothes you are to wear are your stockings. You may take them off to go to sleep, but only after you have brought yourself off. When you wake up, even before you go to the bathroom, you shall put your stockings and sandals back on. Do you understand?"

Anna was in tears. He was leaving her nothing. It would be like living under a microscope. Her most private sanctum had been exploded. She knew she had to answer him, but she couldn't catch her voice. Her sobbing was too strong. Finally, she choked out a response. "Y-yes, Mr. Devlin."

"Good. I noticed that your hands are not behind your back, Anna," he continued. "That's a no, no."

Anna quickly moved her hands into place.

"That's better. There will have to be a punishment for that too, I'm afraid. I made you a promise to punish you harshly whenever you disobey and I'm going to keep it. It's for your own good, you know."

She cringed. Her life would be one long torment of pain if this kept up.

"There's a box at the bottom of your closet. Go get it and open it up. Take the object inside it out."

Still sobbing, Anna made her way to the closet. There was a small box there, about 12" by 12". She took it out. It was taped shut and she had to use a pair of scissors she kept in her nightstand drawer to cut it. When she opened the box, she pushed aside the little Styrofoam squares and found a hard, round object. She took it out. It was a gold plated circlet of steel. It had a little box on it for a latch and a prong that descended down a bit from one side.

"Take it out to the living room and stand near the modem," his voice ordered.

She walked out there quickly. A few seconds after she got there, the modem buzzed and the box on the circlet clicked. It sprang open. Anna jumped.

"Now place it around your neck, Anna. The joinder goes to your right and the little prong goes in back."

Hesitatingly, Anna placed the object around her neck. It was cool and frightening. She was shivering.

"Now close it."

With sorrow and fear, Anna closed the circlet. She heard the latch click. As soon as it did, she tried to tug it open again and it didn't move. It was locked on!

"Yes, it's locked now," Devlin told her. "Every time you go into your apartment you are to put this on. You will wear it always. When it is time for you to leave your apartment, it will open automatically."

Unhappily, Anna accepted this news.

"If you try and leave your apartment, and get more than twenty feet away from the modem, it will give you a shock like this."

At once, the collar released a potent electrical charge. It passed through the prong at her back directly to her backbone and all her nerve centers. It was like she had thrust her head into an electrical socket. She screamed and fell to the floor.

Devlin gave her some time to recover. She was sobbing piteously. Her hands were trying to pull the collar apart so she could take it off. After a few moments of this, she gave it up as impossible and looked forlornly up at the camera.

"Stand up, Anna," he ordered.

She struggled to her feet, placing her hands behind her back. Her face was awash with tears.

"Now all you have to do to avoid being shocked is to be obedient, like a good girl should. You want to be a good girl, don't you, Anna?"

"Y-yes, Mr. Devlin," Anna cried. She wanted to beg him not to do it again. She knew better.

"Now, in order to be fair, I'm going to let that shock be your punishment for not listening before, Anna. But I still owe you one for not having your hands behind your back."

Anna cringed and made herself ready for another shock. It didn't come.

"No, I'm not going to shock you, Anna. I have a different punishment in mind. Go to the hall closet and bring out what you find there."

Anna went quickly to the closet and opened the door. At the bottom was a cage. It was an exact replica of the one she had spent her night in. She gasped and stood back from it as if it were going to attack her. Then she remembered her instructions and the collar around her neck and she brought it out to the living area.

"Very good, Anna," Devlin complimented her. "Now point the door of the cage to the modem and get in it. You should back your way in so that you can close the door behind you."

With dread in her heart, Anna did as she was bade. She backed her way into the cage, but didn't close the door because she hadn't been told to do it yet.

"Okay, now close the door," Devlin ordered. With a sob, Anna closed the door. The modem whirred and the lock clicked shut.

"It will open in an hour, Anna. That will be your punishment. When it opens, you are to eat the dinner that has been delivered for you. It's in your refrigerator and will need to be warmed up. You may finish your scotch after you eat. The rule will be that you can have two ounces a night, right after dinner. No more, no less. Every night. Then I want you to round up your clothes. Eating and putting your clothes away should take no more than an hour and a half. I'll allow another fifteen minutes for a shower. I'm going to set your alarm for two and three quarters hours. If you're not in bed by then, you will be punished. There's another modem near your bed and it will know. Once you are in bed, don't get out until the alarm goes off in your bedroom. Do you understand all this?"

Anna looked up from her little cage to the camera. "Yes, Mr. Devlin," she said dispiritedly.

"There are a few more rules and there will be more when you get used to the system. The first that you should know is that when you feel the collar tingling like this...." A vibration went off in the collar. It couldn't be missed. "...you'll have twenty seconds to come out to the living area, get on your knees, put your hands behind your back and look up at the camera. You will stay there until released either by another tingle or by a verbal command. The collar will know if you move away."

Devlin paused to let the rule set in.

"The second rule is that if you hear the modem beep three times, like this,..." The modem issued three loud beeps. "...you have thirty seconds to get yourself into your cage. You will point it like this so that the door is facing the modem and close it. Is all that clear?"

Anna's heart was heavy with dread. How would she be able to live like this? She had told herself earlier today that she wanted an iron like rule over her. Now she had it. What would it be like? "Yes, Mr. Devlin," she replied miserably.

"Good night now, Anna. I'll see you tomorrow evening."

There was a whirr on the modem and the audio went off. Anna whined with unhappiness as she realized she would be a caged prisoner in her own apartment for a full hour. The steel bars of the cage pressed up against her skin. Knowing that she had no alternative, she gritted her teeth and tried to settle down for an hour of dreadful confinement.

Two hours later, Anna was finishing up putting her clothes away. It was chilly being naked and all and she had turned up the heat. She yearned for her clothes as she put them into the black bags. She wondered if she would ever see them again. This t-shirt she had gotten in New York a few years ago when she went on vacation with Carol. It said "New York, New York" on it in multicolored, bold letters. One of the skirts she had had ever since she had been a social worker. She had bought it for the graduation ceremony from college. Some of the clothes the woman who had befriended her had bought. Then there were the comfortable worn and natty blue jeans. It took a good year to really break in a pair of jeans. Now she would have nothing.

Then there were the socks. Socks were one of those things that she often bought when she had just a yen for something new. They were inexpensive and felt good when they were fresh and clean and had never been worn before. She hesitated about the stockings. Most of them were pantyhose and she knew that Devlin wouldn't want them. But there were three pairs of sheer nylons that were still good. They were self supporting like the ones Devlin had bought for her. In the end though, they too had gone into a bag.

Anna was very conscious of the red lights on the cameras above her. It was like being on stage in some boring drama about her own life. Except that her life now was anything but boring. Her hand went to the collar. It was cooler than her skin. It was smooth. It fit her neck exactly and couldn't be turned either right or left, so that the prong in the back would always rest on her spinal cord. She had taken a good look at it in the bathroom. It went well with her olive skin. She shivered with fear when she thought of what it could do to her.

When she had all the bags filled, she looked up at the clock. Had it been 6 or 6:15 when she had gotten in the cage and Devlin had given her two and three quarter hours? She wasn't sure. She couldn't see the clock from her cage. It had been a very long, doleful hour. When the modem buzzed and the lock opened, she had jumped with surprise. It was back in the closet, out of sight but not out of mind.

She really needed a shower. She thought for a moment of skipping it just in case her estimate of her time left was wrong. In the end, the thought of going to bed all sweaty and stinky from working out and making love was too much for her. She would be quick. If it had been six o'clock when she went into the cage, she still had about twenty minutes left.

The shower felt heavenly. She washed her body languidly. All of the stress of the day flowed out of her. Somehow she would make it. She was sacrificing it all for the Center. It was a worthy trade off. And the sex, it was mind blowing. Her relationship with Devlin wouldn't last forever. It was only a year. She could handle that. She knew that he was making things tough for her in the beginning to get her off on the right foot. Things would calm down. They had to.

She stepped out of the shower, dried herself and slipped on her stockings and sandals. She didn't want to forget them. She dried her hair. The heat of the blower felt good. She had to pee before she went to bed and she sat on the toilet trying to ignore the little red light staring at her. She would definitely shit at the office from now on. She didn't want any videos of that going around.

When she stepped into the bedroom, she looked up at the clock. "Oh my god," she thought frantically. It was five minutes to nine, way past her margin of error. Suddenly, she heard the modem under her bed click. "Nooooo!" she shouted as she leapt for the bed. It was too late.

The shock made her squirm and roll back and forth. She fell off of the bed onto the floor. Her whole body felt like it had been wrung out. Tears were flowing down her face. Then she realized that she was out of bed. The modem clicked again. She screamed. The collar sent another mighty charge down through her backbone. Her teeth clenched and her body contracted.

Sobbing dolefully, she crawled quickly to the bed and got on it. She pushed her face down on the comforter and cried and cried and cried. It was too much! She would never be able to stand it! The collar was a remorseless ruler. It had no pity. She never wanted that to happen again!

After a while, she calmed down. She realized that she had a duty to perform. She got up on her knees and moved to her back. She propped herself up against the pillows and spread her legs. When she put her hand to her pussy, it was as dry as the desert. She would have to get herself in the mood, like it or not. She wondered how long she had before she had to finish the job, if there was some time limit. She hoped not.

She closed her eyes and let her hands wander over her belly and breasts. She thought of the day's events. Devlin had fucked her good this morning. And he had made her come in the car. Cathy's fingers had driven her mad with lust. And the experience of sucking her twat, had been thrilling. She realized that she would have had none of these experiences if she had not become Devlin's slave. She would still be keeping her pussy on ice, with an occasional furtive hand job to stave off the blues. Yesterday, in the car, she had sucked Devlin's prick. It had been so hot. His hands wandered her body with a freedom that only ownership can give. And the fuck after she had been whipped last night, that had almost made the beating worth it. Almost, but not quite.

As she dropped her hand to her pussy, finding, to her delight, her crevasse moistening, she thought of what she was doing. Somewhere, someone was watching her. Eyes were drawn to her hairless snatch. They were following her fingers as the delved inside and around it. As she began to frig her stiffened love button, she spread her legs to give her observer a better view. As she got hotter and hotter, she began to think about the severe confines and rules that Devlin had made for her.

She was under his will. He controlled every aspect of her life. There was something thrilling in that, despite her earlier horror at being like a goldfish in a bowl. He could make her do whatever he wanted from wherever he was. He could make her crawl into her cage, kneel abjectly on the floor before him, fuck herself silly, crawl around like a little dog, anything. He had supreme power. All decisions about how to live, what to do, were taken away. It was a wonderful release.

The hotter she got, the more she desired Devlin's iron grip on her life. She thought of his cock and the pleasure it had brought her. It was too bad that he couldn't send that over the modem. But, now that she thought about it, maybe he would figure out a way to do it.

Her breath was coming on harder now. Her pussy was loose and hot. Her clit tingled madly as she caressed it. Her thighs began to quiver and her hips commenced to grind. "Here it comes!" she thought. "Here it comes! Watch me! Watch me! Ohhhhhhhhhh! Ohhhhhhhhhhh! Ohhhhhhhhh!"

* * * * * * * * * * * * * *

Devlin switched off the monitor and laughed. He was in his home office, sitting at his desk. This episode might make the Anna Addunizio Hall of Fame. Dr. Evans had said to keep up the pressure and he had surely done that. What Anna didn't know was that he had cheated a little on the time she had left before the collar zapped her. He had waited until she was out of the shower and was about to get on the bed. She really had five minutes left. He had zapped her anyway using the remote. Her falling off of the bed and receiving another one was a bonus. He hadn't had anything to do with that.

As per Dr. Evans, he would keep changing the rules and increasing her restraints and consequences. She would be constantly off balance.

He thought of the thin blonde woman kneeling naked and bound on his bed upstairs and waiting for him. Esther was a real find. He had come across her as he was planning the con on Carol that resulted in her relapse and defalcation with the Center's money. Esther had been doing two consecutive fifteen year sentences for sexual assault of patients in her counseling business. Both of the girls had been under 16. That made it much, much worse. She had about two years in when he found her. She was ripe for recruitment. Having the chairman of the parole board as a member of the club was a big asset. It was no problem having her paroled to his custody. Of course, he could withdraw it at anytime and the stipulation had been that if she fucked up parole they would add another ten years to her sentence.

Now Esther was putty in his hands. She had spent a few weeks training with Dr. Evans when she was released. Since she played for the other team, she needed to have her heterosexual skills brought up to par and to be conditioned to absolute obedience.

Today was just the beginning of the fruition of his plans. Many of the girls who graduated from the Center were ripe for recruitment for The Blue Cantina and eventual sale, those with no family or other people who would miss them. Esther's job as a placement counselor gave her access to all their files. Once the new girl Anna intended to hire was brought on board, and Devlin had a candidate for that job too, things would be even better. The new job position was for a person to screen candidates for the Center. Some of the girls who might ordinarily be accepted for the program could be rejected on some pretense and redirected to his people. No one would ever miss them. They would just vanish. All he had to do was make sure Anna didn't get wind of his scheme until it was too late. The way things were going, it didn't look like that was going to be a problem.

He was looking forward to Saturday night, Harrington's initiation. He had proved his mettle and value today with the Wendy thing. It was traditional to have a specially invited female 'guest' at the initiations and Wendy, as Esther had described her, was perfect for that role. Afterwards, she would be shipped off to Dr. Evans and returned when she had all rebellion and reticence to engage in varied forms of deviant sex with men, and women, excised permanently.

Devlin had been smoking a cigar. He crushed it out in his ashtray. He had a date with Esther and he didn't want to keep her waiting all night. She had to be at work in the morning.

CHAPTER SEVEN

Amazingly enough, Anna slept that night like a baby. Well, maybe not amazing, she had only a few hours sleep the night before and Cathy had given her quite a workout, even before she forced her attentions on her. And then there was all the stress of the collar and the cameras in her apartment and getting rid of all her old, favorite clothes.

She woke up to the buzzing of an alarm. It was coming from the modem under the bed. She looked at the clock. 6:45, when she usually awoke. Carlos must have gotten the information from her alarm clock, she thought.

She sat up and put her hand to her neck. Yes, it was still there. The collar. She wondered fretfully if it was safe to get out of bed. Devlin had told her that it would be and he hadn't lied to her yet. He had done a lot of other things, but he hadn't lied.

Edging herself off, she attuned herself to the clicking the modem made when it was going to send her a blast. She put one foot down on the floor and then the other. She stood up. Nothing! She breathed a sigh of relief.

She had to pee like a racehorse so she tiptoed quickly to the bathroom. As she sat down on the pot, she realized that she had forgotten to put on her sandals. She cursed her stupidity and then saw that she hadn't taken her stockings off last night when she went to sleep. She groaned in dismay. Two punishments and she hadn't even started her day. If only someone wasn't looking, she thought hopefully. Maybe it was too early. But then she realized all Devlin had to do was to roll back the tape at his leisure and he would know.

She quickly showered, made herself up as she had been told, and was just starting to get dressed for work when she heard the modem in the living room beep three times. For a moment, she couldn't recall whether that meant she should kneel in the living room and look at the camera or get in her cage. It was a matter of no little urgency since if she made a mistake, she would almost certainly get zapped. Then she remembered. It was the cage.

Her heart beating wildly, her throat constricted with fear, her stomach heaving, she ran into the living room to get the cage out of the closet. She was careful to close the closet door once she had it out. She pointed the door to the modem and got on her knees. She was wearing the tight red skirt that Carlos had dropped off for her and the shiny red high heels that went with it. She hadn't yet put on her blouse. Should she take off the skirt or not? She tried to remember exactly what Devlin had told her. She decided that it would be safer if she was nude. She quickly pulled down the zipper on the side and shucked it off. She hung it over a chair and got back on her knees.

Thirty seconds, that was all the time she had. She didn't know how much time had gone by, but it was going to be close! If only she hadn't delayed when she heard the beeps! She edged herself backwards until she was completely in. Then she pulled the door closed. "O, thank god!" she thought to herself. She looked up at the red light expectantly. One minute went by. Then another. Then another. She started to panic. She had expected Devlin's voice to come over the modem right away. The last time she looked at the clock, she had about fifteen minutes before she had to leave for work. If he didn't let her out of the cage soon, she would be late again! She had a meeting with one of the counselors at 9:15! There were calls she had to make!

Anna waited a long, long time. She could tell from the light coming through the windows that it was past 9 o'clock. Her telephone had rung and she had heard Phyllis on her answering machine wondering where she was. Her cell phone went off twice. She realized that she was being punished. But for how long? Was it for not taking off her stockings when she slept or for forgetting to wear her sandals? Or both? Or had she committed some other infraction that she didn't even know about?

It seemed like she had been in the cage for much more than an hour. It had been horrible last night to be a confined prisoner in her own apartment, but at least she knew that she would be released in an hour and that there was nowhere else she had to go. Like last night, the feeling of powerlessness permeated her. Here she was, confined to a tiny little space, the bars of the cage pressed up against her, in the midst of her familiar and formerly safe surroundings. She could hear the faint noise of the morning traffic outside. The refrigerator turned on and off a few times. She apparently hadn't turned the faucet in the bathroom off all the way and she could hear its dripping. She could even hear the whirr of the battery operated clock on the wall behind her. She made a note to change its position so that she could see it from the cage, although knowing Devlin, he would probably nix it. If she moved it without prior permission, he would surely punish her. Her anxiety about failing to show up at work without explanation increased with each passing minute.

The message she was receiving from Devlin was clear. His ownership of her trumped her obligations to the Center. If she couldn't be compliant to his demands, she would be punished even if it meant sacrificing her life's work. She castigated herself for being so foolish as to forget his rules. She vowed again and again to pay more attention to them, to be obedient. It was the only way she was going to be able to survive.

"Oh, please let me out! Please! Please!" she screamed at the camera on her wall. "I'm sorry! I'm sorry!"

When the modem finally buzzed and the door popped open, Anna issued a sob of release. She scrambled out quickly and put the cage away. She picked up her skirt and hurriedly dressed. She knew she should call the office, but she didn't want to speak to Phyllis until she knew she was going to be let out of her apartment. She still had to wait for the modem to unlock her collar.

When she was dressed, she took a seat in the living room and waited. She felt like a criminal waiting for word from the parole board. After a short while, her collar vibrated. Obediently, she knelt in the middle of the floor, put her hands behind her back and looked up at the camera. The modem buzzed and Devlin's voice came on.

"So, Anna," he said. "Have you learned your lesson?"

"Y-yes, Mr. Devlin," she replied meekly.

"That was for forgetting to take off your stockings. This is for forgetting to wear your sandals."

Anna heard a clicking in the modem. Before she had time to take in a panicked breath, her collar came to life. Her body jerked and she fell to the floor writhing in pain. "Ohhhhhhhhhhh! Ohhhhhhhhhhhhhhhh!" she cried out. The blast was only for a few seconds, but it tore through her like a tornado, scrambling and twisting her insides. She lay on the floor sobbing as she tried to recover. Then her collar vibrated. With a sourness in her stomach, she scrambled to her knees and got back into position.

She was panting and crying when she looked up at the camera. Devlin gave her a few moments to regain her composure.

"Are you all right, Anna?" he asked.

"Y-yes, Mr. Devlin," she replied. But she did not feel all right. She felt naughty and bad that she needed so much punishment. She wanted oh so desperately to be good.

Devlin could see her distraught look on her face, but he let the lie pass.

"I've called the Center and explained that I asked you to meet with me this morning, so there will be no problems for you. You can tell Phyllis that we were discussing the new position you are proposing. I have a very good candidate for the job. You can tell her that you interviewed her with me this morning and realized that she is perfect for it. I will email you her resume and her picture in a few moments. Go over it before you leave. I'm going to set the timer for fifteen minutes. Then you will be released. Go directly to the office without making any stops. Call me when you get there. If it takes you longer than twenty five minutes after I release you, I'll know you were disobedient. Do you understand?"

"Yes, Mr. Devlin," Anna replied with trepidation. "Twenty five minutes!" she thought. She would have to fly.

Anna did fly. As soon as she received the signal that Devlin had signed off, she went her computer and checked her email. There was a message from Devlin with an attachment. Anna opened it and downloaded and printed it. It was three pages. Her printer had never seemed so slow. When it was done, she grabbed it and examined it in obedience to Devlin's instructions. Gail Harper. She had social agency experience and seemed, at first blush, qualified for the job. Anna became concerned by the fact that Devlin was loading up the Center with his 'clients'. What could he be up to?

When her collar finally popped open, she made a dash to the car. She ran several yellow lights, something she rarely did. On Carter, the main drag off the freeway to downtown, she seemed to hit every red light. Luckily she had a reserved spot in the parking lot. She rushed in the front door, said a quick "Hello," to Phyllis and went directly into her office. She looked at the clock at the same time that she picked up the phone to call Devlin. She had made it with five minutes to spare. She breathed a sigh of relief. Devlin's secretary put her through to him right away. All he had to say to her was that he was glad she had obeyed and decided to be a good girl. He also reminded her to be at the mansion tonight by 7 o'clock. Anna said nothing. When he rang off, she sat back in her chair and breathed a sigh of relief. She was a good girl once more.

The day went quickly. She apologized to the staff member who she was supposed to meet with and met with her at 11 instead. She skipped lunch so that she could run out and get her nails done as Vincent had instructed. The girl did a wonderful job, doing both her hands and her toes. She got back a little after 2, worked for an hour and a half and then dashed off to the gym. This time, she dressed in the shorts and top that Devlin had provided her with. Cathy said nothing about their tryst the day before although she had a self satisfied smirk on her face. She put Anna through some pretty tough workouts. When she was leaving, she told her that they would do some more 'stretching' exercises on Monday.

Anna showered and changed. She decided that she wouldn't go home before going to Devlin's. She went back to the Center, read through some reports and then left for Devlin's mansion at 6. Traffic was light and she arrived there at 6:45.

It was cold and rainy. Her heart began to beat wildly as she pulled up the long, winding driveway. When she got to the top, she couldn't help think about all she had gone through in the week since she had last pulled up to the large, formidable mansion. Nor could she forget the abuse and she had suffered at Devlin's hands since then. Her throat was dry and her hands trembled. There was a queasy feeling in her stomach. For just a moment, she had the impulse to turn the car around, pull back onto the main road and keep driving until she was a hundred miles away.

As Devlin had instructed her, she pulled around to the back and came in through the servant's entrance. She walked up the five steps to the loading dock and approached a large steel door. It was locked, but there was a bell there and Anna rang it. A few moments later, a tall, heavyset woman, past middle age, with grey hair pulled tightly into a bun behind her head, opened the door. She was dressed in a grey and black shirtwaist dress and a white apron that went up to her waist. She had a scowl on her face.

"Come on! Come on! Don't dawdle there! Come in!" she snapped. Her voice was shrill.

She stepped aside and let Anna pass her. The door led to the kitchen. Another woman, seemingly of the same make and model as the first, was standing in front of a large, black stove minding some pots. She cast Anna a disinterested glance and went back to her work.

The kitchen was large and well equipped with a tall and wide, shiny steel refrigerator, a double oven, a long, steel counter above which hung various pots and pans. The floor was made up of dark brown tile and there were several black mats on the floor. It was large enough to serve a banquet or the type of intimate meal she had shared with Devlin last Friday night.

Anna came into the kitchen and then stood and awaited instructions. The first woman passed her, muttering, "Come with me," and Anna followed her through a swinging door into a long hallway. The woman stopped half way down next to a closet door.

"Take off your things," she said as she opened the closet with a key from a chain that emerged from her waist. Anna blanched at the idea of undressing in front of this woman. She had her purse in her hand and looked around for some place to put it down. The woman turned around and snatched it out of her hands.

"Don't just stand there!" she growled. "Do what you're told! Or haven't you learned that lesson yet? I'll be happy to teach it to you if you'd like!"

"N-no, ma'm," Anna murmured unhappily, and then, panicked, corrected herself, "I-I mean, yes ma'm."

She drew off her brown cloth overcoat and handed it to the woman, who hung it on a hanger in the closet. She was wearing the bright red, tightly fitting skirt that had been mandated as her uniform of the day with the gold blouse and red 3" heels. There had been many comments on the elegance of her attire at the Center that day. Phyllis said something about her 'turning over a new leaf.'

Anna kicked off the shoes and began to unbutton her blouse. Her breasts were naked underneath and she shivered with shame as she handed the woman her top. While the woman placed the blouse on a hanger, Anna lowered the zipper on the side of her skirt and shimmied out of it. She was embarrassed to show her denuded loins to the woman and blushed as she handed her the skirt. The woman ignored her discomfiture and, taking the skirt from her hands, hung that in the closet as well. When Anna went to roll down her sheer, beige stockings, the woman barked, "Leave them on and put on your shoes!"

After stepping back into her shoes, carefully balancing herself, Anna stood there awaiting instructions. Unconsciously, she was shading her intimate parts from the harsh woman's view with her hands. The woman was retrieving something from the closet. It was a small, white opaque, plastic box. Her name was on it, written in bold, black, block letters on a piece of masking tape. Anna could see that there was something in it, but couldn't quite make it out.

The woman turned, holding the box under her left arm. She took a look at Anna. Her right hand flashed out and she struck Anna with its flat side right across the face. The impact made a loud 'crack!' Anna screeched and leaned sideways from the force of the blow. She brought up her hands to protect her face.

"Hands behind your back!" the woman shouted. "Do as I say or I'll make you sorry! Now!"

Anna had hesitated, fearful that the woman was going to give her another blow. Tears running down her face, she quickly brought herself back to a standing position and put her hands behind her. The woman reached out and took hold of her left nipple, squeezing it harshly. Anna moaned in pain.

"You're not on vacation here, dearie!" the woman continued. "Step out of line again and I'll come down on you like a ton of bricks! Do you understand?"

"Y-yes, ma'm," Anna managed to squeak out as the woman's fingers continued to twist her nipple. Anna was bent over and trying desperately to keep her hands behind her. Finally, the woman let go. Anna sighed with relief.

The woman opened the box and, after placing it on the floor, took out a highly polished, dark brown piece of leather. Anna saw what it was right away. It was a collar! It was several inches wide and had shiny brass rings emanating from its front and back. On its front, embossed in gold letters was her name in bold script. The woman put the box down and made Anna turn around. She fastened the collar around her neck and clicked it closed behind her. It was a perfect fit,

While her back was still turned, the woman leaned over again and withdrew something else. Anna felt something go around her right wrist. It felt like a leather bracelet. A moment later, the woman affixed a similar bracelet to her other wrist. She made Anna turn around and she adjusted them so that they were sitting firmly on her wrists. Anna looked down. On the top sides of the bracelets was embossed a scriptive, golden 'D'. There were rings embedded in the leather on the inside part. The left one had an eight inch long chain on it that was doubled up. The woman released one end of the chain and told Anna to turn around again. She grabbed her left wrist and brought it up high behind her back. Anna squealed from the pain. She felt the chain being threaded through the ring in the back of her collar. Then the other wrist was brought high and the chain was attached to it.

Anna's hands were imprisoned high up on her back. It made her shoulders strain and pulled on the collar, nudging it against her windpipe. "Ohhhhhhhh!" Anna complained. The woman spun her around again. Anna looked down in the box and saw that there was another item. It was a gag like the one she had worn on Wednesday night. Except this one had another golden 'D' etched in it and a ring coming out of the shield that went over the lips. Anna gave out a little sob as the woman presented it to her mouth, but she gave her no trouble, accepting it meekly. Once she had buckled it tight behind Anna's head, the woman returned the container to the closet. She took out a six foot leash, closed the door and locked it.

Anna stared at the leash unhappily. She was to be led around like a dog. The woman attached the leash to the ring in her gag and gave it a tug, indicating that Anna should follow her. She led her down the hall and into the large foyer that sat just inside of the front entrance. Her footsteps produced the same loud clacking sound she had experienced last week that echoed throughout the cavernous room. To the right was Devlin's 'library', more of a lounge actually, with a few books thrown about so as not to give lie to the name. To the left was Devlin's office. Both rooms had large, wooden double doors. Devlin had told Anna last week that on her arrival on Friday night, she should stand outside it and wait for instructions from someone. The woman, however, led her past that spot and started to take her up the stairs.

The woman said nothing to Anna as they began their march up the wide, carpeted stairs. Anna had a deep foreboding about their destination. She hoped against hope that they were heading towards Devlin's bedroom. But when they got to the second floor landing, they continued their ascent. They didn't stop at the third floor. Anna had known they wouldn't, but prayed that she was being brought to the little room she had slept in the prior weekend. But when they got to the fourth floor, they walked right past it.

Anna gave out a sob as her worst fear had been realized. The woman took a key from the chain that led to her belt and unlocked the door to the punishment room. Anna's knees grew weak. She knew that she was due for another punishment, but she had hoped that it would not come so soon. Tonight's punishment would be for lying. And there were punishments due after that, for not masturbating in the first place and for wearing a bra on Monday. There were probably others too, but she could not remember them.

The woman, who had not given Anna her name, pulled her into the room. Anna immediately saw a dozen images of herself grotesquely bound and gagged, her legs encased in delicate, sheer nylons, the rest of her starkly nude. The woman brought her to the center of the room, under the chain to which her arms had been attached Wednesday night. Terror ran through Anna like a rabid fever. The woman reached up to pull the end of the chain down. Anna saw that she was about to attach it to the ring on her gag. She collapsed to the floor in fear.

"…ooooooooooo! … eeeeeeeeeee! …ooooooooooooo!" she wailed, her gag malforming her words.

"Get up! Get up!" the woman screamed. She reached down for Anna's hair to pull her up with, but Anna scooted away. The door to the room was closed and she knew that there was no possibility of escape, but the prospect of another session with the whip was too much to bear. Anna scurried to a corner of the room. The woman went to the closet where Vincent kept the whips and emerged with a three foot lash with a wooden handle. Anna watched her approach, crying and sobbing.

"You'll taste my whip sure for this, dearie," the woman snarled. She swung the lash at Anna ferociously. Anna curled up into a little ball.

"…oooooooooo! …eeeeeeeee!" she pleaded frantically. The lash landed across her back. Anna screeched. Three times, the angry woman tore into her, shouting, "Get up you pig! Get up!"

Anna couldn't have gotten up if her life depended on it, which, in a way, it did. The woman struck her three more times, lashing at her back and her thighs. "...ooooooooo! ....oooooooooouuuuu! ...oooooooooooouuuuu!" Anna cried out. Then she felt the woman's hand take hold of her ankle. She had an iron grip. She dragged Anna's body across the smooth, hardwood floor until they were back under the chain. Without hands, Anna had no power to resist her.

"...eeeeeeeeeee! ...ooooooooooo!" Anna pleaded through her gag. The woman took hold of a hank of her hair and lifted her head up. She had brought down the end of the chain that went up to the ceiling with her other hand. She clipped the end of the chain to the ring on Anna's gag and let her go.

As soon as she felt the clasp on the end of the chain snapping closed, Anna knew she was lost. She bent her head to the floor and cried. The woman went to the wall and began to tug on the chain harshly. Anna felt her head jerked rudely upwards. She tried to fight it with the weight of her body, but her opponent was very strong. She soon had Anna up to her knees and then to her feet. She stopped pulling only when Anna's toes barely touched the floor.

Anna's face was pointing straight up. She could only see the woman from the corner of her eye. She watched as she picked up the lash from the floor where she had dropped it. Her face was full of rage. Anna's prior beatings had been administered to her coldly, as lessons to be learned, by men fully in control of their passions. This was different. The woman was hot as a pistol and she angrily battered Anna's body with a succession of fierce lashes. Anna screamed in pain and danced on her toes. Her neck was strained and she felt like her head was going to come off.

Finally, the woman ceased. Anna could hear, amidst her sobs, the woman gasping for breath. She tossed the whip aside again and approached the defenseless woman. She slapped her breasts viciously three times. Anna screeched and wailed. Then she reached out and took hold of her nipples, twisting them brutally. "I'll teach you to disobey me, you filthy cunt!" she roared. "Just wait until tomorrow, when all the men go out! We'll have some fun then, dearie! I promise you that!"

Anna groaned as the pain from her teats coursed through her. "Oh, god! What have I done!" she screamed to herself as the woman's harsh words sunk in. The woman released her nipples, but they continued to throb and pulse as the woman leaned down to roll her stockings below her knees so that Devlin would have ready access to her thighs.

She replaced the whip into the closet and closed the door. She turned to Anna. "Mr. Devlin is out. He'll be back after 10 o'clock. I'm sure he'll tend to you some time after that. In the meantime, just relax and enjoy yourself." The woman emitted a cackling laugh. Then she left.

It was a long time waiting, over 3 hours, before the door to the punishment room opened again. Anna had cried, had raged against her fate, had pleaded with God to help her, had hung there despondently. Her toes soon began to ache terribly and her neck became sore from the strain of looking straight up for so long. While on her previous occasions here she had been able to get a full view of herself while she was awaiting punishment, now she could only catch a glimpse of her reflection from the corners of her eyes.

The time passed so slowly. A few times, she heard what she thought for an instant was the sound of feet on the stairs outside, but she had been wrong. Part of her wanted desperately for Devlin to come, to get it over with. Waiting for someone to appear who was going to cause her agonizing pain was excruciating. Especially with her hands bound so cruelly behind her and her weight on her tippy toes. The other part of her dreaded to hear the sound of Devlin's footsteps, the steady, confident, purposeful sound of his gait.

Now there was a new cause for punishment. Anna worried frantically that she would have to suffer his wrath as well as the woman's for her unforgivable sin of resistance and disobedience.

When she finally heard his footsteps coming up the stairs, Anna's stomach soured and her heart began to beat wildly. The door opened and she turned towards it. If she looked down as far as she could, she could just see his sturdy form in front of her. She issued a long, unhappy whine.

"Yes, Anna," he said as he entered the room. "It's time to pay the piper."

He had doffed his suit coat but was still wearing the finely pressed pants, a fine, pressed, blue oxford shirt and a striped tie. He went directly to the closet and pulled out the flogger he had used on her thighs and pussy on Wednesday night. He swished it several times through the air. As he did, he took note of the long, angry red lash marks on her flesh.

"I see you ran afoul of Mrs. Leopold. That's very bad for you, Anna. I won't inquire. Whatever happened is between you and her. But I should tell you, she is a wasp with a very harsh sting. I'd be more careful to please her in the future."

Anna just moaned. She knew that within a minute she would be suffering the harsh blows of the whip in Devlin's hand. She wanted it to begin. The tension of waiting was killing her.

Devlin approached her and with his free hand began to caress her proffered breasts, ran it across her belly, slipped it over her bare mons. "You notice how I instructed Mrs. Leopold to mount you here tonight, Anna," he told her as he stroked it. "It has direct relevance to your offense. It was your mouth that got you into trouble and so your mouth must bear some of the consequences. As I'm beating you, I want you to remember never, never, ever lie to me again. There are harsher punishments I can inflict than this, Anna. Of that you can be assured. The next time, I'll punish your mouth so harshly you won't be able to talk for a week. Is that clear?"

"Oooouuuuuuuuu!" Anna moaned. Her imagination went wild with the thoughts of what he might do to her. She knew she had to respond to Devlin's question. It was like her voice was frozen, she was so scared. Finally, she was able to force out a response. "...eh, i-er e-in," she moaned miserably.

Her pussy tingled where he had touched it. He ran his hand over her delicate, plump rear cheeks admiringly. He took one of her nipples in his mouth, suckling on it gently. Anna felt the tug in her womb, but it was overshadowed by her dire trepidation.

"Okay, then," Devlin said, pulling away. "Let's get this over with." He reared back his hand and let fly over Anna's defenseless breasts. She screamed.

* * * * * * * * * * * * *

Fifteen minutes, and an untold number of lashes later, Anna's sobbing, pain wracked body hung limply from the over head chain. Her flesh was colored a deep red seemingly all over. She moaned weakly as Devlin put the lash away. When he lowered the chain that led to her mouth, her knees gave out and she collapsed to the floor.

Devlin scooped up the leash from the hook where Mrs. Leopold had left it and connected the end to Anna's gag.

"Come on, get up," Devlin ordered. "We've got some fucking to do."

He took her to his bedroom where he made her service him with her mouth. Then, her arms still bound cruelly behind her, kneeling on the bed with her forehead touching the mattress, he plowed her rear entrance while playing with her pussy with his hand. He made her come three times before spilling himself in her, intoning all the while, "That's good, Anna. That's good. You're a good girl. A good girl."

Anna's mind reeled with the waves of pleasure that passed through her, pleasure paid for in advance by the terrible pain he had inflicted. She reveled too in his approval of her and the rewards it brought. His thick cock abraded her anus's delicate ring. When she came, she screamed into her gag. Being bound and proffering to him the unrestrained use of her body just seemed so right as he was fucking her. It was exactly where she wanted to be. She felt like she had earned it.

She spent the night in her room on the fourth floor. Vincent brought her there. He released her arms from behind her back and fastened them through the ring in the front of her collar and let her use the bathroom. When she had used the toilet under his watchful, intimidating gaze, he wiped her clean and washed off her makeup. He even removed her diamond studs from her ears, cleaned them and her piercings with alcohol and returned them in place, one of Anna's new nightly rituals. Devlin had seen her taking them off before bed on Thursday night and had instructed her that she should only take them out to clean them and the holes in her ears.

It was strange but somehow comforting to be cared for by the tall, dour butler. She was almost used now to being naked and bound in front of him. Her defenselessness and the need to obey him literally and promptly in everything, secured by the ever present threat of violence, was vibrantly thrilling, like a ride through a house of horrors at a carnival, although this one was very real. She could feel the little tremors going through her body as he watched or handled her,

He brought her to the bedroom. After removing her stockings and shoes, he made her lie down on the bed, her legs spread lasciviously as he applied the salve he had used the other day to ease the rawness of her wounded body. His hands were ruthlessly invasive, hard and boney, yet comforting. When he was done, he bent his head to her already moistened crevasse and brought her to a shattering orgasm with his tongue and lips. Using the ring in the back of her collar, he chained her to the headboard and gagged and hooded her, but only after coldly and coolly making use of her mouth.

She lay there for a while, absorbing the night's events and ruing the absolute darkness around her. About an hour after Vincent left, she was awoken from her light, disturbed sleep by the sound of his footsteps on the stairs. He went down the hall past her room. A door opened and closed. About five minutes later, it opened and closed again. Vincent's footsteps returned, accompanied by the sound of a woman's heels on the wooden floor. Anna thought she heard her sobbing. They went down the stairs. She must have been in a deep sleep when the woman was returned because she did not note her passage.

Saturday morning, after Vincent released her, Anna showered, made herself up again and shaved her loins. This time, she had done everything perfectly, from the lip gloss on her pussy lips to her perfume. She had adorned herself with the sheer, self supporting stockings Vincent had laid out for her together with a pair of red, three inch heels. While Vincent examined her pudenda with his hard, boney hand for signs of left behind bristle, she stood there nervously, her legs spread, her hands crossed behind her. He found none.

After binding her arms behind her, Vincent forced her back into the little cage with rolling wheels she had been in on Wednesday and brought her to Devlin's sunroom. Devlin fed her, as he had on Thursday morning, maintaining an amiable conversation incongruous to her imprisoned state, and then discharged himself in her throat. She remained there when Devlin left to begin his day's activities. This time it was a young, blonde girl, dressed in the same lascivious outfit of the girl the prior day, who came to retrieve the tray. Her name tag identified her as Eva. She too ignored Anna as if she was a piece of furniture. Eventually, Vincent came and returned her to her room where she lay on her bed for several hours bound as she was during the night, this time, thankfully without the hood.

Her fear of her looming date with Mrs. Leopold made her stomach queasy. From time to time, her body shivered as she anticipated the torment the woman would inflict. The ever present camera high on the ceiling stared at her, its little red light on. With nothing else to do, her eyes examined very inch of her small room again and again, absorbing every detail. The dresser which contained the instruments of enslavement, the closet that held the instruments of pain, even the white ceiling, with its small cracks and minor defects. Across from her bed was the six foot wide mirror framed in rococo gilt. It was tilted down so that she could see herself on the bed, her long, stocking encased legs, her denuded pussy, her hands bound under her chin, her mouth sealed off by a sheath of leather, her doleful eyes staring back at her.

She didn't know what time it was, but the light from her small window indicated that it was probably past noon when Mrs. Leopold came for her. She made her put on a fresh pair of stockings, sheer black this time, and don a pair of black high heels. Then she released her hands from the front of her collar and forced her arms back up high behind her like she had the previous night. Anna sobbed and quailed as the woman led her by her leash, naked and bound, down the stairs to the kitchen, her high heels click clacketing as she went.

She expected a whipping, but Mrs. Leopold had something else in mind. She brought her to a small room, so small that Anna speculated that it once had been a walk in closet. It was roughly painted in a smeared orange brown and had no window. Mrs. Leopold backed her up to the far wall opposite the heavy wooden door. There was a long, thick, polished board mounted horizontally coming out of the wall and connected to a ratcheting system. She made Anna straddle it. Its top was tapered to a very thin, rounded edge. After affixing Anna's ankles to rings on the floor, she ratcheted up the board until its edge was pushing tightly against her pussy, pushing her love lips aside. Anna could barely keep her toes on the floor. Her pussy was jammed against the edge of the board. As a final touch, the old woman pulled a black, cloth bag over her head and tightened it around her neck. Anna heard the door shut and knew she was alone.

Mrs. Leopold left her there for more than an hour. Darkness surrounded her, making her fraught with fear. The contact point between the board's edge and her pussy began to become painful almost immediately. Within a quarter hour, it began to hurt so much that Anna began to whine and cry. By the time a half hour had expired, she was moaning and sobbing, trying desperately to lift herself off of the board with her toes, but having no luck. Her hands writhed and twisted in their bindings in a desperate, futile effort to free themselves. At three quarters of an hour, Anna was sobbing and screaming wildly for mercy into her gag, begging for someone, anyone to relieve her of her suffering.

When the door opened, Anna screeched her pleas out to the woman. Mrs. Leopold slapped her breasts harshly several times and ordered her to be quiet. Anna could not help emitting frantic whines as she tried to silence herself.

"Have you learned your lesson, dearie?" Mrs. Leopold queried her sarcastically. Anna did her ever best to communicate her affirmation. She cried while the board was lowered. Mrs. Leopold led her by the arm back into the kitchen. Anna stumbled after her, her loins still throbbing with pain. She made her kneel on the cool, hard tiles and removed first her hood and then her gag. The other woman had a bowl of stew prepared and laid it down in front of her.

"Eat it all up, dearie," Mrs. Leopold said. "And lick the bowl clean. Got that?"

Anna nodded her head readily. She spread her knees and leaned over, putting her mouth in the bowl. Despite her pain

and residual terror from her experience, she did as was told.
She was surprised that the stew was flavorful, with large
chunks of soft, tasty beef, carrots and potatoes. It was so good
to be having a positive experience that she ignored for now
her feelings of humiliation at being forced to eat like an
animal and her hatred of the woman who had callously caused
her so much pain. When the bowl was licked clean, Mrs.
Leopold removed it and gave her a bowl of milk to lap up.

When that was finished, she wiped her mouth, reinserted
her gag and returned her to her room. She made Anna kneel
on the bed, her head down, her legs spread. While she played
with her pussy, she laughed and made caustic comments
about her being Devin's little whore and her dirty, slutty pussy.
Anna cringed at the appellations, but she couldn't prevent her
lusts from rising. She groaned as her needs built higher and
higher. The woman's hand was knowledgeable and insistent.
Her touch was surprisingly delicate and she avoided pressing
too hard on the more painful areas of her sex. She alternated
between thrusting her two thick fingers back and forth in
Anna's pulsing canal with rubbing her clit while she caressed
her rear cheeks with her other hand. When Anna came, she
groaned and moaned her pleasure into the small room. After,
Mrs. Leopold bound her up as she had found her, placed the
black bag back over her head again and left.

Anna's pussy trilled with the residuals of pleasure and pain
while she lay there immobile on the bed for several hours in
absolute darkness.

Devlin had her brought down for dinner, which she ate
from an elegant, gold rimmed bowl on the floor in his private
dining room. He examined her wounded pussy, reminding
her of the necessity for full and complete obedience to all of
his servants, and then used her mouth again.

Vincent brought her back to her room and bound her on
the bed. An hour or two later, Carlos came by and gave her
the promised cock sucking lesson. He disregarded her moans

of pain when he fucked her pussy afterwards. She came violently several times nonetheless. He left her hooded and hogtied on the bed.

Late that night, Devlin came by. He was slightly intoxicated and seemed to have had a particularly satisfying evening at Harrington's initiation at the club. He whipped her ass, 'just for fun', he said, and then, to her moans of delight, fucked her there again.

Vincent came by later, allowed her to pee and wash up. He took from her his customary blowjob and then, after making her come with his hand, put her to bed.

On Sunday morning, Anna suffered her last beating of the weekend, this one for not getting herself off at night twice earlier in the week. It was not as severe as the others. Afterwards, she spent a long time cuddled in Devlin's arms as he comforted her and promised her that before she left for home that night, all her punishments would be done for her misbehavior during the week and that they would start Monday with a clean slate.

He made her bring herself off for his visual enjoyment and then fucked her from behind on the floor, in her pussy for the first time this weekend. Vincent later brought her back to her room where she was forced to wear harsh nipple clamps for about an hour for the crime of wearing a bra on Monday. She later spent two hours in her cage in a dark closet as an omnibus punishment for all her lesser offenses.

Carlos came by and fucked her again. Around 4 o'clock, she was brought down to the library where Devlin was watching a late afternoon football game with one of his cronies on a large plasma screen. Vincent had dressed her in a little, flouncy cheerleader's skirt, which hardly covered her sex, with wide, yellow and blue vertical stripes, the colors of Devlin's favorite team, yellow fishnet stockings and blue high heels. The man, dressed in a light blue collared polo shirt and black slacks, looked like he was in his sixties, with grey hair and a mild paunch. He wore one of the triskelion rings. Anna quailed at being half nude in front of him, outfitted so skimpily and adorned with the leather bracelets and collar which so boldly declared her to be Devlin's property and slave. Devlin had told her that he would share her with his friends, but she hadn't expected that line to be crossed so soon.

She served them beers and was sent back and forth to the kitchen for snacks. While she was inactive, Devlin had her kneel on all fours next to his plush, comfortable chair, her legs spread, her ass raised high. He casually played with her pussy from behind as they watched the game, slipping two thick fingers in and out of her welcoming sheath, toying with her little nubbin at the top. Anna fought mightily to prevent it, but a moan of passion escaped her lips. Devlin admonished her to be quiet.

During the second quarter, the man, who Devlin called Ron, asked Anna to get him another beer. She rose from her knees and took a dark green bottle of Heineken from the small refrigerator behind the bar, opened it and brought it to him. His eyes were pinned to her naked, swaying breasts as she approached. He held out his large, rounded glass while she poured it full and placed the bottle down on a coaster on the side table next to him. He called her name, which was boldly proclaimed across her collar, and, after placing his frothy glass down on the side table, had her stand between his knees while running his hands up and down the outside of her thighs, raising her tiny skirt, staring at her hairless, glistening quim and telling her how pretty and enticing it was. Anna's lips trembled as she anticipated his use of her. She was so afraid of inducing Devlin's wrath by failing to cooperate, that her knees felt weak.

The man pulled her towards him and had her lean over so that he could suckle at her breasts. His hot hands held them in place while his lips subsumed her teats, one after the other. When he had satisfied himself, he turned to Devlin and asked,

"Do you mind?" Devlin assented and Anna spent the last portion of the second quarter lying cross his lap, his hand plying her quim, her passions rising. At halftime, he made her stand and brought her to one of the couches. He made her lean back and raise her knees, her bright blue high heels up in the air, her tiny, skirt rising up and exposing her conch. After opening his fly, he fucked her while Devlin watched and gave him verbal encouragement. He captured her lips with his and she roared her pleasure into his mouth when she came. He grunted and moaned as he spilled himself inside her.

When he was done with her, Devlin ordered her to stand in the corner facing the wall, her hands crossed behind her, while they watched the rest of the game. She could feel the man's cum leaking down her thighs

Dinner was at 8. This time, Vincent had Anna dress in one of her nice outfits, a light green dress with a low bodice and a tight skirt. Her eyes were made up in a matching hue and she wore dark green high heels. It was a pleasant dinner, a very robust chicken cacciatore served with al dente rigatoni, a romaine and chicory salad with Caesar dressing and a nice Chianti. Delicious, ripe half cantaloupes were served for dessert along with brandy, of course. Devlin was polite and soft spoken. They talked about some of the ongoing issues at the Center, the new job position, the upcoming Wednesday night Board meeting and some more about Anna's past life. He complemented her on how pretty she was. Afterwards, he took her to his bedroom where he had her undress and then fucked her long and slow, almost lovingly.

Anna cried when they were done, the tenderness after all the brutality she had suffered over the weekend being too much for her. Devlin assured her that as long as she behaved, she would not need to undergo the punishments she had received this weekend again, although he reserved the right to whip her from time to time for his pleasure and that of his guests.

He took her downstairs afterwards, not bothering to have her dress. Mrs. Leopold was waiting. Before he handed Anna over to her, he kissed her long and hard, running his heavy hands over her bare skin, playing with her breasts, and then had her get on her knees on the hard stone floor of the foyer and suck him off. Anna was a little chagrined to do it in front of Mrs. Leopold but, after all, it wasn't like the woman didn't know what she was here for.

She suckled the well used but still sturdy cock lovingly. She reveled in Devlin's groans of pleasure. From time to time, she looked up and gazed into his impassioned face. He was a true, remote, all powerful god. She was privileged to serve him. If only this moment could be frozen in time, she thought idly as her lips ran over the crown of his cock and her tongue flitted across the tiny hole at its top. She pressed her face down as far as it would go, until his cock's head popped into her throat. Devlin's mighty hand held her there for a long time. Carlos had gotten her up to two minutes yesterday and again earlier this afternoon. Devlin must have watched, because he used all two minutes lodged in her throat, stifling the flow of air. Just as she began to feel incipient panic, he pulled her head back and let her take a deep breath. He then pistoned her head on his cock, groaning and moaning. He had hold of her head with both hands and was fucking her face energetically, in total disregard of her needs and wants.

But there was the rub. For it precisely filled her needs and wants, just as Dr. Evans had predicted. Her mind celebrated his callous use of her, his instrument, his property.

When she was done, he patted her on the head approvingly and went into his office. Mrs. Leopold removed her collar and bracelets and gave her back her clothes. Anna meekly dressed in front of her. She led Anna through the kitchen to the back door. Wordlessly, she opened it with a key and allowed Anna to flee.

Anna went directly home. All the way, like last week, her mind was torn between her shattered ideals of feminist independence and the gut wrenching pleasure she experienced when Devlin and the others penetrated her without condescension to her will. She knew that she should have been horrified at her treatment. She should resist her descent into slavishness with all of her rational mind. But it was the irrational mind that was stronger. A vein of pathetic subservience had been uncovered deep within her and Devlin was skillfully mining it. She knew that. He somehow knew something about her, perhaps had intuited it, and he was using that knowledge to reduce her to total abjectness. Although she was unmistakably aware of it, she was on a rapidly descending elevator with no way to stop it and no way to get off. She was in it for the whole ride.

As soon she walked in the door of her apartment, she stripped, except for her stockings, and put on her collar and sandals. She spent some time in her bathroom tearfully examining the wounds on her body from the weekend's activities, remembering the agony she had suffered. Her pussy was still a little sore from its torture at Mrs. Leopold's hands. She touched it and a small thrill passed through her. She closed her eyes and thought of the cocks that had pierced her and re-experienced the rapturous orgasms that had been delivered to her. Devlin had told her that she could have two fingers of scotch before she went to bed and she sat in her living room chair sipping it. Her eyes drifted up to the overhead cameras from time to time. She mulled over the incongruity of how safe she felt naked and collared in her apartment with unknown eyes watching over her.

She had lived through a hellacious weekend, interspersed with long, boring periods of being bound and isolated, and fervent bouts of fucking and terrifying, brutal punishments. A feeling of despair flowed through her as she thought of a full year of such weekends, 51 more. For despite her new found longing to be owned and possessed, she carried no desire to be whipped and beaten. Although, if pressed, she would admit its necessity to secure rigid compliance with Devlin's rules. For there was no sense in being his if she did not follow his rules religiously. That was the whole point. She had surrendered to his will and abandoned her own.

It had to get better, she thought. She would be good, obey every rule. Devlin would reward her, either personally or through his intermediaries, with exhilarating rounds of sex. She remembered Devlin's kiss before she left and how wonderful, accepted and owned she felt. As she sipped her scotch she re-experienced his thick cock between her lips.

After a while, having finished her scotch, she dozed off. She awoke to the sounds of her bedroom modem beeping. She had ten minutes to get ready for bed. She hurried off to the bathroom and took care of her essentials. She was up on her bed with ample time to spare. She knelt with her legs spread, facing the camera, and gave herself a wondrous, thrilling climax for Devlin's benefit, her mind swimming through the recalled experience of his cock inside her. When she was done, she took off her high heels and stockings, got under the covers and was asleep within a minute.

CHAPTER EIGHT

Like most things in life, Anna's duties to Devlin quickly settled more or less into a routine. Monday, she didn't hear from him at all, although she had to undergo another Sapphic session with her trainer, Cathy, at the gym. Tuesday, no Devlin and Cathy let her go after her workout. Both nights, Anna carefully followed Devlin's instructions at home.

Wednesday night was the Board meeting. Devlin insisted that Esther be invited so that she could be introduced to the Board members. They were all pleasantly surprised at her efficiency and skills as she gave them a report on placements she had made for the girls and her contacts with Ms. Schopenhauer of the Eastside Bank and Trust. Anna pitched the new position to be funded by the grant from the bank and, as per Devlin's instructions, told them about Ms. Harper whom she had already selected for the job. After the meeting, after all the Board members had left, Devlin took her into her office, locked her door, and fucked her on her desk.

Thursday, she had another round of pussylicking with Cathy at the gym. This time they formed a 69, with Cathy on top. Friday night it was back to Devlin's mansion.

Much of the time that she spent at Devlin's was 'dead' time, either locked in her little fourth floor room or, increasingly as time went on, in her cage. Devlin would use her, or not, as the impulse struck him. Saturday afternoons were usually reserved for Carlos. Sundays, Devlin always had one or more guests over for football or some other sport and Anna would serve them and they would fuck her, have her suck them off, or both. When there were more than two or three, the blond haired maid, Eva, or another one, a chestnut haired, West Indian beauty named Sharon, would help out. Sunday nights almost always ended in a delicious, elegant dinner with Devlin, a fuck in his room and a blow job in the foyer before she got dressed to leave.

More and more of her regulation came under the auspices of Mrs. Leopold. She ruled over Anna like a concentration camp kapo, punishing her harshly for the slightest infraction or hesitation in complying with an order, or sometimes for no reason at all. When Devlin was not around, or if he was busy, Anna ate her meals in the kitchen from a large, chipped ceramic bowl on the floor. Mrs. Leopold always preferred to have Anna's hands hoisted high up her back and locked to her collar. The two elderly female cooks would watch her, exchanging witty remarks in a foreign language that Anna thought might be Dutch or Flemish. When she was done, Mrs. Leopold would bring her back to her room, manipulate her to orgasm and leave her there chained to the bed. She always placed the hood over her head.

On a few of the Saturday nights, Devlin had her dress up and took her to the club for dinner. Anna was always impressed by the silent, obsequious women who served there, either in the bar, dressed in their short, revealing cocktail dresses, or in the dining room, wearing long, full skirts and low cut, tight blouses. They all wore leather collars and bracelets with the club's logo, the triskelion, on them embossed in gold. Anna had no illusions that they were there for purely decorative reasons. For some reason that she could not define, Anna always gave a little shiver as she passed the doorway to the nightclub, The Blue Cantina. Devlin never took her inside and never mentioned it to her.

She did see Elaine again, the young woman who had helped her buy her new clothes and get all made up the way Devlin liked her that first weekend. The first time was at the club. The tall, thin, black haired beauty was having dinner with one of the members. She was laughing with him, her hand in his lap when Anna and Devlin entered the dining room. She gave Anna a nod of recognition. Anna and Devlin ate with a dark haired man, in his late thirties, who Devlin introduced as James Farber, a local high powered lawyer. He was wearing the club's distinctive ring. He was with a very quiet, shy girl of about twenty, with long light brown hair collected in a ponytail. She was wearing a very daring dress that displayed most of her fine breasts and was quite a few inches above her knees. Anna couldn't help casting surreptitious glances at the handsome man and wondering when she would be made available to him. As they were leaving, Anna saw the man take the clearly unhappy girl up the stairs where there were bedrooms available to the members.

The next time she saw Elaine was at Devlin's mansion a week or so later. She was present in the sun room that Saturday morning when Anna was wheeled down in her cage so that Devlin could feed her her breakfast. Anna was shamed to be seen by Elaine this way. She was seated in one of Devlin's easy chairs dressed in a silk kimono covered with colorful flowers. It was clear that she had spent the night with Devlin. She and Devlin ignored her as they discussed a dinner party they were going to attend together that night. When Vincent brought her tray containing her breakfast, Devlin had Elaine feed her. She was kind and solicitous as she spooned her her oatmeal, petting her head and kissing her. Anna cried with shame as she fed her. Afterwards, Devlin offered to let Elaine go back to her room and fuck her. Elaine gleefully agreed.

Anna was filled with remorse and shame as Vincent wheeled her to her fourth floor room, Elaine following. She was freed from her cage once they were in her room and Vincent ordered her to the bed. He closed the door and locked it behind him. Elaine shucked off her kimono and crawled up on the bed next to Anna who was kneeling there, waiting for her.

Elaine's body was beautiful. She had round, firm breasts, not too big, but just the right proportion for her slender frame. Her skin was soft and shiny. Her belly tapered enticingly to her denuded loins. What Anna saw there surprised her. Just above her pudenda, was tattooed a florid, bright blue 'D', not unlike the letters embossed on Anna's leather bracelets. It was surrounded by equally bright blue flourishes. Elaine saw her looking at it and blanched. Anna had surmised that Devlin had some hold on the young, somewhat dissolute girl. Now she knew it for sure. And she understood that Devlin's suggestion to her to come up here and fuck Anna was not a suggestion at all, but an order.

Anna's sessions with her trainer had taught her that her aversion to girl on girl sex had been a foolish prejudice. But there was still something masculine about the hard bodied trainer, almost butch. She was forceful and ordered Anna to assume certain positions or to perform certain acts at her whim. As the unquestionably feminine Elaine knelt before her on the bed, her eyes softened, her look alluring, Anna knew that this would be something else.

She was still wearing the gag that had been on her in the cage and her hands were still bound behind her. Elaine crept nearer to her, stroked her face lovingly and then reached behind her head to loosen the belt that secured the gag. When she had pulled the gag free, she pressed her lips and her body onto Anna's. Their mouths opened together and they shared a deep, soulful kiss. Elaine's soft, light hands wandered down her hips and thighs while their tongues mingled and danced. Anna's loins began to burn.

Elaine's hands found their way to Anna's locked wrists. Their lips still married, their breasts pushed together exchanging their bodies' heat, she freed the clasps that kept them joined. Anna immediately wrapped her arms around her lover's body, pressing her body tightly against her. Elaine did the same. Their moans and sighs of lust intermingled as their passions grew. Elaine brought her down to the bed and they lay there, side by side, facing each other, exploring their breasts and bellies. When Elaine's hand found her smooth, hairless quim, Anna sighed and spread her legs. She found Elaine's slit too and they worried each other's pussies as they kissed and groaned their delight.

Finally, Anna took the lead. She pushed the younger woman to her back and insinuated herself between her thighs. She pushed their pussies together, grinding her hips, elevating her passions. While Elaine writhed and squirmed beneath her. slowly, she lowered herself, kissing her lover's neck then her chest and then subsuming her alert, rigid nipples in her mouth, one by one, suckling on them hungrily, causing Elaine to moan loudly. Then, her hands still in possession of Elaine's ripe breasts, she lowered herself further, kissing her belly, running her tongue into the gap of her belly button, washing the flesh marred by the elegantly designed letter that denoted her as Devlin's property.

When her lips found Elaine's pussy, Elaine spread her legs widely and placed her hands on Anna's head.

"Oh, yes! "Oh, yes! Oh, yes!" she sighed as Anna's tongue enflamed her. Her pussy's musky scent and the taste of her tart discharges made Anna swoon with lust. She probed deeply into Elaine's chamber with her tongue, lapping up her moisture, running her tongue upwards until it breeched the confines of her canal and alit on her stiffened love button. Elaine's writhing became extreme. Her thighs clamped around Anna's head. Her grip on her hair became tight. Anna flicked her tongue again and again on the little nubbin, alternating with long languid suckles. Her arms were wrapped around Elaine's thin, trim, tapered thighs, holding her mouth firmly against her sex. As her lusts grew higher and higher and her climax approached, Elaine's groans grew louder and her hips shifted and grinded against Anna's mouth as if trying to evade the tortuously pleasurable sensations.

When Elaine came, she shouted her ecstasy throughout the room. Her back arched and her body writhed wildly. "Oh! Oh! Oh! Oh!" she yelled. And finally, "Ohhhhhh-hhhhhhhhh!" as her orgasm crested and began a slow, pleasure filled winding down.

She lay there, relishing her post orgasmic bliss as Anna continued to lick and kiss lightly her puffy, blood filled labia. She did not linger, however. She quickly had Anna on her back and pushed her head between her thighs. Anna gasped as her lips took hold of her clit and sucked at it relentlessly. She too groaned and sighed as the well experienced woman delighted her quim. Her hands wandered over her belly and thighs, making her skin trill with excitement. When Anna was on the brink of her orgasm, her back arched and her legs spread wide, she relented her assault on her pussy, making Anna release a groan of frustration. Elaine shifted her attentions to Anna's plump, heavy breasts, suckling her nipples, massaging their bulk, her belly pressed against hers. And then, once Anna's lusts began to build high again, she lowered her head and began licking and stroking her vibrating pussy with her tongue and lips.

Howling with pleasure, Anna came hard as Elaine's mouth continued to excite her. She gripped the woman's hair tightly in her fingers and thrust her hips up at her. She groaned loudly as her climax reached its apogee and then issued a low, satisfied moan as the convulsions of her crevasse slowed and finally came to rest.

The two women lay in each other's arms for a long time. They kissed and stroked each other lovingly. Anna was dying to know more about the hold that Devlin had over the girl, but knew that the ever present camera in the upper corner of the room, the same camera which had captured their enthusiastic fucking, would record her answer, if she gave one, condemning her, Anna was sure, to a terrible punishment.

After a while, their lusts renewed. This time, Elaine had Anna come up to her knees. She shifted herself until she was behind her and took hold of her breasts. Anna was facing the camera and she knew that Elaine was displaying her caresses and Anna's reactions for the benefit of the unknown audience. While one hand found her pussy and began to play with it, the other drifted up and down her body, playing with her full, passion hardened breasts, caressing her taut belly, kissing her neck. Anna had her knees spread wide and raised herself up so that Elaine could have full access to her quim.

She closed her eyes and let her body and mind enjoy the woman's display of her lusts, her hands rubbing the insides of her own thighs. By this time, it didn't matter to her that her paroxysms of pleasure were recorded. They had already been recorded dozens of times, both here, in this room and back at her apartment. It was too late to be coy about that now. Elaine made her come twice before she released her, forcing loud moans and ecstatic exclamations from her.

Anna was about to turn and return the woman's favor when she heard Vincent's footsteps coming up the stairs. Elaine heard it too and the women exchanged a deep, satisfied kiss with each other, knowing that they would soon part. Vincent unlocked the door and ordered Elaine to adorn herself with her robe. He made Anna lie face down on the bed, affixed her wrists together, gagged and hooded her and left.

After that, from time to time, Devlin had Anna brought to his bed while Elaine was there and had them fuck for his enjoyment. When his voyeuristic pleasures were satisfied, he fucked Anna and sent her back to her room.

It was in the third week that she got a call at the office from Harrington. He told her that he wanted her to come by his office that evening after her workout. Anna knew what it was for. She tried to call Devlin and ask for guidance. She couldn't reach him. He had said that she had a duty to obey anyone who showed her the ring. Although Devlin had told her that he had the ring, Harrington hadn't actually shown it to her. Therefore, maybe she didn't have permission, or the obligation, to let him fuck her. Devlin's orders were always so literal. In the end, she decided to go with Devlin's specific instruction. She never wanted to get a beating for fucking someone without permission again. So she didn't go.

That night, at her apartment, when Devlin spoke to her over the modem, she told him and he replied that she was a good girl who followed instructions. Her good decision availed her nothing however. That Saturday, Harrington showed up at the mansion. Devlin had the naked and bound Anna show him up to her room. He beat her and fucked her brutally. When he was done, he made a point of showing her his ring.

Wednesday nights seemed to be reserved for parties. Devlin brought her to this or that affair, mostly charitable or political fundraisers. He always had her pull up her skirt and take his cock in her mouth while they drove there, finishing him off when they had arrived, using his hand to excite her. About a month after her slavery had begun, they went to a party at an elegant estate north of the city, in the exclusive Regency District. That night, in the car on the way there, Devlin presented Anna with a gold necklace. It had as its pendant the same golden triskelion with the diamond in the middle that was on Devlin's ring. He told her that from now on, she should wear it all the time.

The host served a luxurious buffet. Dozens of the rich and refined of the city were there, the mayor, some of the councilmen, bankers, lawyers, and more. Beautiful, languorously dressed women roamed the elegantly appointed rooms. Anna had a wonderful time, encouraged by Devlin who forced three scotches down her shortly after they arrived.

Anna was taken somewhat aback though, when, in the middle of the party, one of the male guests, a middle aged construction magnate whose picture she had seen in the papers, after commenting on her beautiful necklace, showed her his ring. He took her to an upstairs bedroom, made her undress and fucked her on the bed for an hour. She tried to deny her passion, but the heavy set man made her come repeatedly with his thick cock. When he slipped his cock into her rear opening, Anna groaned so loudly that he covered her mouth with his hand while he fucked her there. The abrasion of his cock across the delicate ring made Anna moan and groan and thrust her hips back at him madly as she came. He released her finally, thanking her for her favors, and helped her dress. When she returned to the party, she was dazed and unhappy. Devlin took note and made her drink two more scotches.

That night, when he took her to her apartment, instead of dropping her off, he accompanied her in. She stripped as soon as she entered and put on her collar. Devlin fucked her on her bed, her very own bed, smashing any idea she might have had that it was an island of refuge from him. After that, on those Wednesdays that they went out, he always came in afterwards and used her. She served him with the devotion of an acolyte. When he left, he always reminded her of her obligation to masturbate in front of the camera before she went to sleep.

Anna was surprised at how easily she had slipped into her role as Devlin's whore. At first, fucking all the strange men repelled her and made her ashamed. But as their number mounted, she began to think of them as so many extensions of her master, Devlin. He was like a god who came to her in his many forms. He started having his friends come up directly to her room on the fourth floor where she would be naked and bound on her bed, stored away until wanted for use. She served them fervently. Only once did one of them complain. She hadn't been feeling well and lagged in her performance. Devlin had Vincent take her to the punishment room and whip her savagely. It never happened again.

Her daily workouts were really getting her in shape. Anna reveled in her now tight, fit body. Her energy levels were way up and, at then end of each session, she was more than willing to go off to the 'stretching' room if her trainer ordered her to. Cathy didn't always take her there, but she did it at least once a week. One day, she handed her over to another trainer for her workout, saying she had to leave early and that Anna was to do everything he said. He was a blond haired, broad shouldered, well muscled Adonis, a bit younger than Anna. He worked her out hard and then took her to the 'stretching room,' where he fucked her. After that, the two of them took turns training her.

Harrington began a habit of calling her during the day and ordering her to come over to his office. The first time, he called about 10 o'clock. She had to run across town at lunchtime and go up to his private sanctum. She gave him a blow job while he was sitting in his chair overlooking the city beneath him. He had made her undo the bodice of her dress and her breasts were out, her hands behind her back. Just after she finished, his secretary came storming in with some important document he had to sign that a courier was waiting for. Anna was still on her knees in the process of putting her breasts away. The secretary gave her a stern, cold look. Anna blushed with shame. She scurried out as fast as she could. After that, whenever she came to service him, his secretary gave her a dour stare. Anna didn't like it, but there was nothing she could do about it.

Devlin also demanded her attention frequently during the work week. Carlos would come by the office with the limousine and take her to Devlin's office. His standing order was for her to undress as soon as she came in. He would fuck her on the floor or the couch or while leaning over his desk. Sometimes, he would have her stand around naked afterwards while he made phone calls or dictated letters. Anna would stand with her hands behind her back, her legs spread, his jism leaking down her thighs. Devlin made no effort to hide their activities from his secretary who was instructed never to knock. More than once, Devlin was in the process of plowing her or having her suck his cock when the pretty, young girl came in. She would always stand by until Devlin was done and never interrupted him. Anna would leave the office deeply shamed, but wondering if Devlin had the same kind of hold over his secretary as he did her.

More and more of the Center's executive duties had to be delegated to Esther. The new girl, Ms. Harper, settled in perfectly and she and Esther worked closely together.

It was in her tenth week that one of the men finally showed up at the door to her apartment. She had been glad to be home after a stressful day. It was a Tuesday and she knew that Wednesday night she would be going out with Devlin. She was looking forward to a long, hot bath. She was standing in her bathroom, naked and collared, as required, wearing her stockings and sandals, just starting to run the water, when the modem in the living room gave out three distinct beeps. She shut off the water and ran into the living room, glancing up resentfully at the camera there. Just the week before, Devlin had instituted a new rule. He had provided her with a gag and a pair of bracelets that she was to adorn herself with before she got into the cage. The bracelets had a latch on them so that she could connect them behind her back once she was in the cage by clicking them together. There was a little receiver connected to the latches that would spring them open when the signal came to open the cage.

And he had announced that he had purchased the building and moved the other tenants out. Now there would be no one to object to her screaming and shouting with pain if he decided to beat her. This fact was of no comfort to Anna.

Obediently, she crawled backwards into the cage, the gag in her mouth. She closed the door and brought her hands behind her, clicking the bracelets together. Then she looked up anxiously at the camera through the bars of the cage. She couldn't see Devlin, of course, but she always imagined him behind it, looking back at her.

Nothing happened. She began to fret about whether she had broken some rule. There were so many and she had received the painful, dehabilitating blast from her collar often. Devlin had made rules about her posture, the little resentful looks she gave the cameras. She was forbidden to cross her legs, a rule she was constantly forgetting about. He made her eat her meals on the floor like a dog, her hands behind her back, and god help her if she didn't eat it all or took too long or was too messy. She drank from a little bowl. She had to fold her clothes neatly and just so and had to clean up after herself thoroughly. He took away all of her books and her computer and she would be forced to sit around all night with nothing to do but watch TV or contemplate her embondment to him. He dictated the shows she watched. There were no news or educational shows, only game shows, reality shows and situation comedies.

Some nights he forced her to watch videos sent to her over the modem taken of her at the mansion being fucked by Carlos or one of the guests, or of her being fucked there in her apartment by Devlin. He made her clean constantly, something she was not proficient at and she received quite a few blasts of her collar or spent quite a few hours in her cage as a result of a failed inspection. She spent long hours with her nose in a corner of the room, her hands pressed behind her back, or on her bed, on her hands and knees, her legs spread, presenting her twin portals to the camera, just to enforce his dominion over her. From time to time, for this infraction or that, he took away her right to use the furniture and she had to spend her time in her apartment on the floor except for those reasons she had to stand such as taking a shower, getting dressed or cooking her food. But if she stood too long, lingering on her feet, 'Zap!' the next second she would be on the floor writhing in pain.

From time to time she received the signal to get in her cage and there was no reason for it except, perhaps, to remind her of her subservience. It always worked.

This seemed to be one of those occasions. Although she knew that eventually she would be liberated, she immediately experienced the familiar feeling of powerlessness, of abjectivity, that was the key to Devlin's domination of her. She was his to rule as he pleased. Her wants and desires meant nothing. Being a strictly confined prisoner in her own apartment was a stark and undeniable reminder of all that. Just the thought of being his prisoner, on whom everything was imposed and nothing was asked, was enough to make her pussy begin to moisten. It was moistening now as she awaited Devlin's pleasure.

About a half hour had passed when she heard a key in the lock to the door of her apartment. She turned to look, expecting either Devlin or Carlos stepping in. Her heart began to pound in her chest when she saw that it was neither of them. It was a man she had never met before. He was tall and slender, but carried himself with obvious strength. His features were Asian and he was wearing a dark blue suit. His hair was black and trimmed neatly. He looked to Anna to be in his mid forties. He was carrying a small travel bag, like he expected to stay the night.

Anna's heart sank when she realized that yet another safety zone had been breached. Devlin had fucked her in her apartment quite a few times by now, even stopping off once or twice after he had been out someplace else just to have her suck him off or to fuck her. But no one else. She realized that with her triskelion pendant on her necklace, something which all the women at the center thought very pretty, she could be plucked out of a crowd by anyone who recognized it and had one of the rings. It hadn't happened yet, except at that one party. But now a man had come to claim his rights with her right in her own apartment.

A lump formed in her throat when she thought of the possibility that the man expected to fuck her but wasn't wearing a ring. She looked at his hand as he placed the travel bag on the floor by the door. The ring sparkled on his right hand. Anna breathed a sigh of relief.

The man looked at her coldly. He crouched down by the cage and peered at her. Anna peered back, feeling like an exhibit on display at the zoo. She shifted her body inside the cage nervously. Already she was imagining his cock plowing the furrow between her thighs, or, perhaps, her lips around his cock. He looked strong and very masculine.

He said nothing to her. After he had satisfied himself, he stood and took a look around the apartment. He opened and shut the kitchen cabinets and when he found her liquor, took out the bottle of premier gin. He found a glass and some ice and poured himself a generous portion. He sipped it while looking down at her.

He then went off to inspect her bedroom. She heard him opening and shutting her closet, going through the drawers of her dresser. He came out within a minute and completed his inspection of her living area. Devlin had Carlos one afternoon, while she was at work, mount several whips and crops decoratively upon her living room wall. She gazed at them with horror when she came home and found them there. They were mounted just above the modem that was used to control her collar and the other electronics in the apartment and just below the camera which she gazed up at when Devlin summoned her. They were in her view whenever he talked to her, reminding her of his power to cause her pain. They were there, "in case they're needed," Devlin had told her, although he hadn't had the occasion yet.

The man removed a three foot long, thick riding crop from the display. He examined it closely, as if inspecting the maker's handiwork, swished it two or three times through the air, looking at Anna all the while, and then replaced it. He took a long, deep swig of his drink.

It was then he noticed the living room closet in which Anna kept the cage. He opened it. He was slightly behind Anna and to her left and she could see him if she stretched her neck and peered at him from the corner of her eye. He looked at the space where the cage had come from and then at the cage. Then he looked back. A sign of understanding came over his face. Leaving the closet door open, he went to Anna's small bookcase and placed his drink down on it. Turning back to Anna, he took hold of her cage and rolled it back into the closet.

Anna whined with the realization that she was to be stored away in a small, dark place, something Devlin did to her only to punish her. She began to panic. "….eeeeee …onnnn!" she tried to beg through her gag. The man did not respond to her plea. When the cage was lodged inside, he closed the closet door, rendering Anna into a terrifying darkness.

She shivered and whined in her cage, closed her eyes to try and blot out the darkness which surrounded her, to imagine away the walls and door which kept her so closely confined. She could hear him moving around outside. The refrigerator door opened and closed. A few moments later, she heard the microwave go off. Devlin kept her fridge well stocked with the one dish meals he dictated she should eat. They were top of the line diet cuisine. Anna ate only what she had been allotted each night and she often sat in a corner hungering for some cookies or a bowl of ice cream. Even some crackers would be nice, but they were all forbidden to her.

When the microwave beeped, she heard him open the door and then, shortly thereafter, the kitchen drawers opening and closing as if he were searching for silverware. She heard the scrape of one of her dinette's chairs as he apparently sat down to eat.

Anna realized that a significant change had just occurred in her relationship to her apartment. She had thought of it as hers, her dominion, even as her mastery of it was eroded by Devlin's domination. But it had still been hers. In a matter of a few minutes, that had changed. She was no longer the possessor of her apartment. Now she was merely an amenity of it. She could be stored away when not in use just like an iron or a broom. She had never felt more like a 'thing'. That was what she had been reduced to. Less even than a pet, who you would never lock up in a cage and put in a closet.

After a while, she heard the chair scrape again and the door under the kitchen sink being opened where the package for the meal could be discarded. She heard the faucet running as if the man were diligently washing off his fork and knife. Another closet opened and there was a clink of glass, as if the man were pouring himself another drink, a surmise confirmed when she heard the sound of the freezer being opened and closed again and the sound of tinkling ice.

His footsteps crossed the room and entered her bedroom. She could not hear what he was doing in there until she heard the sound of the shower. While the water was getting warm, the man came out to the living room and then returned to the bedroom. Anna theorized that he had retrieved his travel bag where his toiletries were undoubtedly located.

He spent a long time in the shower. Anna recalled her intent to have a nice long bath and a dismal pall came over her. She hadn't even eaten dinner! Her stomach growled. She shifted and squirmed in her cage. Her fear of the darkness around her made her shiver. "Please let me out! Please!" she kept murmuring in her mind. She knew that when he eventually did, it would be her turn to be used and useful, a process that would probably involve the whip he had admired. She trembled when she thought of it.

Eventually, the shower shut off. There was a long delay. Finally, she heard his steps, now lighter without his shoes, approach her prison. Her stomach turned over as she anticipated his handling of her. He had a coldness that portended severity and harshness.

The door opened and light came pouring into Anna's chamber. She looked up at the man dolefully. He pulled the cage out of the closet to the middle of the living room. He was wearing a dark blue, wraparound, terrycloth covering around his hips that went down to the middle of his thigh and nothing else. His hair was still wet although it looked like it had been combed. There was no hair on his chest and his muscles were well defined. His thighs were sturdy looking. His cock made a bulge under his wrap. He took a long look at her and then crouched down in front of the cage. He released its lock and opened the door. He stood, saying nothing. Instead, he snapped his fingers and motioned for her to emerge.

Up to a moment ago, Anna's cage had been her prison. It instantly turned into a place of refuge, which she, at the man's orders, was being forced to abandon. As soon as she was out, she would be subject to whatever he wanted to do with her. The thought made her shiver as she slowly edged herself forward in the cage.   Once she was out, the man rolled the cage back into the closet and closed the door. Anna stayed kneeling, not having been given any other instructions. The man came back and signaled her to rise with another snap of his fingers and a motion of his hand, the right hand, the one wearing the ring which made her his slave.

He took a while to examine her more closely. He felt her breasts, weighing them in his hands, flicking his thumb over her nipples to make them harden and rise. Going behind her, he ran his hand over her posterior. When he came back around front, her passed his hand over her firm belly, making her shiver and then pushed at her thighs until she opened them widely. He crouched down and inspected her crevasse, pulling aside her love lips, exposing her moistening hole and the pinkish tissue around it.

Standing, he reached behind her head and released her gag. Once he had tossed it aside onto one of her chairs, he made a careful inspection of her face, as if examining it for defects. He pushed her jaw down, forcing her to open her mouth and inserted two thick fingers. Anna understood that she was to suckle them and she began slipping her head back and forth, keeping a tight purchase on them with her lips, washing them with her tongue. Her eyes remained glued to the cold, slate colored eyes of her guest. They displayed no emotion, but only, perhaps, a hint of satisfaction at her performance.

Anna trembled when he went to release her wrists. Her fears of what was next was confirmed when he took her by the arm and led her into the bedroom. He pointed to the bed and she dutifully crawled upon it. She turned to him on her knees, her legs spread, her arms crossed behind her. She was still wearing her stockings and high heeled sandals. He motioned her to take them off. Anna kicked her sandals off of her feet and then sat on the bed removing her stockings. She cast a sidelong glance at the man and saw that his cock had risen, forming a tent under his wrap. When she was back on her knees in position, he undid the wrap and let it fall to the floor. His thick cock was hard and pointed slightly upwards. He crawled up on the bed and pushed her to her back.

He fucked her long and hard. He was not violent or brutal, but firm and brusque. He never said a word. He made her suck his cock for a long time, first on her knees between his thighs and then on her back, him over her reversed, lapping at her pussy. He pushed his cock deeply into her throat, leaving it there for long periods while he suckled her clit or lapped his tongue between her enflamed labia. He made her come twice and then exploded in her throat, discharging himself deep within her.

His cock didn't soften. He made her get up on her knees and he fucked her from behind, slowly, drawing his cock out almost its full length and then plunging it back inside, making her moan. He pushed her to her back again and fucked her long and hard that way, her knees raised high, pressing against her breasts. He fucked her sideways and then made her get on top, using her deep sheath to stroke his length.

All the time, Anna's lusts were run off the page. She was delirious with pleasure. It went on so long and with such intensity, that she felt like she had been whisked off to another dimension where she would spend eternity fucking. She had come twice more by the time that he was ready to come again. He took a dollop of lubricant from the tube that Devlin required her now to keep on top of her bedside table and, after making her kneel on the bed, her forehead on the mattress, greased her rear portal. She groaned with pleasure as he penetrated her. He rogered her there a long time, using long, languorous strokes. They eventually began to increase in tempo. He gripped her hips hard with his hands. When he came, he pounded hard against the back of her thighs, groaning loudly and sending Anna into another paroxysm of bliss.

Afterwards, his forces exhausted, he lay down with her on the bed. He silently stroked and petted her, kissing her from time to time as if they were lovers. After a while, he made her get back up on her knees again, her legs spread wide, her head down, while he went into the bathroom and cleaned off his cock. She heard him go into the living room and get himself another drink. A cell phone snapped open and he made a call to someone. He spoke in short, clipped phrases, in Japanese or maybe Korean, Anna thought. His voice was deep and authoritative. When he was finished with the call, she heard him bring a chair into the bedroom just opposite the bed. He sat there a long time, contemplating her twin holes so blatantly displayed. Anna could feel his eyes boring into her. After a while, he went back into the living room. Anna sneaked a look at him over her shoulder when he came back. He was holding the riding crop he had examined earlier that evening. Anna whined as he took up a position behind her. She drove her mouth into the mattress to suppress her inevitable screams of pain.

The first stroke, which landed across her proffered hindquarters, burned horribly, but she was able to suppress her yearning to howl. The second stroke seemed even harder. This time she screamed into the mattress, her voice emerging from it as a high pitched moan. The third and the fourth were just as bad, producing similar results. After the fifth one struck, she commenced a baleful sobbing.

Apparently that was enough to stoke his fires. He climbed back on the bed and, slipping his cock into her still moistened slit from behind, fucked her again, giving her long leisurely strokes. Her pussy clenched with pleasure when he discharged himself there, celebrating the throbbing, spasming tool inside of her.

Afterwards, he made her get up and get ready for bed. Once she had peed and completed her ablutions, he brought her back to the bed where he regagged her and, after making her lie on her belly, bound her wrists together again behind her. He used the bathroom himself. Shutting the lights, he laid down next to her, to her right, and pulled the covers up over them. He was asleep within a minute.

Anna lay awake, helplessly bound and gagged, reexperiencing the evening's combination of thrilling pain and delight, wondering who this strange man was. It had been a long time since she slept in the same bed as a man. His heat exuded from his body. He drew deep, heavy breaths, his aroma was distinctly masculine. And, to her surprise after being used so callously, it was comforting. She was asleep soon after.

In the morning, he was up at or near the break of day. He took a shower while Anna remained bound and gagged on the bed. When he was done and dressed, he allowed her to use the bathroom to relieve herself and had her suck his cock to completion on her knees in her living room, her hands locked behind her. Before he left, he reinstalled her gag and placed her back in her cage, just as he had found her. Devlin, or whoever was minding her, released her an hour or so later so that she could get ready for work. While Anna ate her breakfast, thanking God for the sustenance, and later when she used the bathroom to take her shower and put on her makeup, she noted that the man had left her apartment punctiliously neat, as if he had never been there at all.

CHAPTER NINE

That night, when Anna came home from work, she found a new alteration to her apartment. A chain had been installed in the middle of her living room, running down from the ceiling. She saw it as soon as she came in and, disturbed by its presence, wandered unhappily into the middle of the living room, forgetting to take her clothes off for about twenty seconds while she stared at it. It could only be for one thing: whippings! Her throat got thick and her stomach turned over. And then, suddenly, she remembered her duty. She quickly shucked off her clothes and installed the circlet of shiny, golden steel around her throat. She had just started to slip her feet into her high heeled sandals when the modem began to whirr. "Oh n...!" she started to yell. The shock came before she could get the rest of the syllable out. She screamed and fell to the floor in agony.

She was still sobbing when she heard the tones that required her to display herself before the camera. She quickly rose to her knees and scooted herself into place. She looked behind her and saw that her clothes were still scattered around the room. She had clear instructions to hang them up the moment she took them off. She whined as she realized that she had earned another punishment. And she wasn't wearing her sandals! She hadn't had time to put them on. If she got up now to do it, she wouldn't be in place in time. She was between the devil and the deep blue sea. There was nothing to do though but place her hands behind her back, spread her knees and look up at the camera. As she did, she could not ignore the array of whips mounted there.

It took several minutes for Devlin's voice to emerge from the modem.

"That was very naughty, Anna," he said. "And I see that you haven't hung up your clothes or put on your sandals. That's very bad. It seems like you're falling into bad habits. That will have to be corrected."

Anna sniffled, realizing that Devlin never bluffed when it came to punishments. She steadied herself, trying to prepare for another jolt from her collar.

"Go and pick up your clothes, Anna, and hang them up. Then put on your sandals and get back into your position."

She nodded her obedience and rose from the floor. She took the skirt and blouse into the bedroom and hung them up in the closet. Already hanging there were the outfits she had been dictated to wear for the rest of the week, including a long, rose colored gown for tonight with a pair of matching shoes and a small purse. Dolefully, she went back into the living room, slipped on her sandals and sank to her knees.

"That's a good girl, Anna," Devlin said. "I see that you have noticed the new addition to your apartment. It comes with a new set of instructions. You see, I watched your visitor last night when he whipped you and I realized that there was no mounting for a proper whipping in your apartment. What's the use of having the whips if there's no facility for using them?"

It was a question. Anna needed to answer it even though her blood was running cold.

"There's none, Mr. Devlin," she replied unhappily.

"That's right! There's none. And so I had Carlos come by today and install the chain."

Devlin paused to let the information sink in. He had said there were to be new instructions. What were they going to be?

"I want you to put on your bracelets and install your gag, Anna. Then I will tell you what to do."

She jumped up to obey. They were in a special box Devlin had supplied next to her bed. She ran in and got them and installed them on her body. The bracelets locked shut. They were irremovable unless given the proper signal from the modem. She returned to the middle of the living room and fell to her knees. She knew that she had to listen carefully to what he said, lest she make a mistake and earn more pain.

"Very good, Anna," he told her. "Now, I want you to stand and lock your bracelets to the end of the chain."

Anna moved to the middle of the room. She was just able to lock the bracelets to the chain by standing on the tips of her toes. Her arms were stretched high above her head, rendering her body defenseless. A few seconds after she had locked herself into place, the modem buzzed and the lock from the chain sprung free. She was afraid to lower her hands.

Devlin noted her obedience. "Good girl, Anna. You remained in position. Too bad you didn't remember your duties when you came in. Now I want you to lock your bracelets in again. I'm going to free them and I want you to lock them again. Keep doing it until I tell you to stop."

Wondering what the callous man was up to, Anna kept locking her wrists to the chain again and again until it became almost rote. Finally, Devlin interrupted her.

"Okay, then," he sad. "Now I want you to do it with your eyes closed. Just keep doing it until I tell you to stop."

Anna fumbled with the lock for about ten seconds before she was able to figure out how to lock her wrists to the chain without looking. She did it again and again until she got it down pat.

"Now, Anna, go into the kitchen area. There's a small box there. Open it and bring what you find back with you."

She scurried over to her kitchenette. There was a plain, brown box on the counter. It was sealed with brown packing tape and she had to get a knife out of the drawer to slit it open. She placed the knife down on the counter and opened the box. She saw a thick, black hood. There was a draw string by the opening. Anna felt a foreboding about what it was for. There was also a wide band of black spandex. She scurried back to the living area holding them.

"You forgot to put the knife away, Anna," Devlin said. Anna looked back into the kitchen. The modem whirred and she gasped. She was on the floor a second later, writhing in pain. She sobbed in misery. The pain that the collar produced flowed through her entire body. It made her stomach feel sick and her joints ache.

"Okay, now, Anna," Devlin's voice said. "Get back up. Go put the knife away. And please don't make any more mistakes."

Unhappily, Anna rose to her feet. She stumbled into the kitchen and put the knife back in the drawer. Then she returned to the living area, stepped under the chain and awaited instructions. Tears were streaming down her face.

"Okay, now," Devlin continued. "The spandex band goes around your head. Put it on so that it covers the tip of your nose to the middle of your forehead."

Placing the hood on the floor by her feet, Anna pulled the spandex band open so that she could fit it over her head. She placed her head into the opening and pulled the band down over her face. Then she pulled it back so that it caught the back of her head. She had to strain to get it open enough, but, with some effort, she was able to do it.

Her vision was totally blocked. Moreover, her features, except for her lips, were totally obscured by the black band. But her lips were already covered by the leather shield of the gag in her mouth. The band covered the tops of her ears, pressing them against her head. The diamond studs, though, the emblems of her enslavement, would be easily visible.

"Put the hood on now and draw the string tight around your neck," Devlin commanded.

Anna complied. She crouched down, feeling for the hood. When she found it, she rose and pulled it over her head. She tightened it around her neck.

"Now lock your bracelets to the chain."

She raised her wrists and easily locked them in. Devlin let her hang there for a few seconds. Her feet began to ache almost right away.

"When you hear this tone," Devlin instructed her, "you are to get yourself into this position." A long, deep tone came from the modem. It repeated itself three times. "You will have 30 seconds, so you'll have to be quick."

Anna agreed. She would have to be quick. Putting on the bracelets and gag would eat up ten or so seconds all by itself. Then she had 20 seconds to get to the living area, put on the spandex blindfold and hood and lock herself up. It would be a close run thing, especially if she were in the tub or using the toilet or even eating when the command came. She would have to put everything away first.

"Okay, Anna," Devlin stated, "I want you to wait right where you are. It's a little after six now and I'll be at your apartment about 7:30. That should give you plenty of time to contemplate the need to be obedient. And when I get there, I'm going to have Carlos come in and beat you. He's been begging me for a chance for the longest time. This is a good opportunity to satisfy his desire. See you in about an hour and a half."

He signed off.

Anna cried quietly. All around was black. She imagined what she must look like: a confined prisoner with a hood instead of a face, devoid of all personality except that conveyed by her desirable parts. Her available, desirable parts. Again, for the second night, she had been deprived of her dinner. She hadn't even had a chance to pee when she came in. "An hour and a half!" she screamed in her mind. Her feet were already aching beyond her endurance.

And she was going to be beaten. Her body shuddered as she anticipated the awful pain she would suffer. She pulled desperately at her bonds. "Maybe if I get loose I can get away," she thought miserably. She knew that she could not take much more of Devlin's governance. She had tried, god knows she had tried. But it was too hard. She couldn't do it. She wanted to be good, wanted his approval, needed it. But she knew she could never satisfy him.

And look what she had become! Last night a man who had never even said a word to her, had come to her apartment and used her as rudely as one might a street whore. And she had loved it! He had driven her way past her limits. She tried to remember a time when she chose who she slept with, when no one had he right to beat her. She couldn't bring up the paradigm for that former person's life. How had she then ignored the burning in her loins? How had she ever developed her self integrity? Could she find her way back there? No, not naked, hooded and bound in her very own rooms. Not while the very sound of Devlin's voice struck a chord so deeply buried in her psyche that it was primordial.

It had begun as a mission to save the center. The center was saved. How would she save her soul?

As she stood in the enforced darkness she realized that, for tonight at least, her function had changed again. Last night, she had been like an appliance one took out when you desired it. Tonight she was more in the way of a decoration. "Come inside and see the beautiful, naked woman, the woman with no face. Enjoy a drink on the house while she struggles and cries in a desperate attempt to relieve her suffering."

The men would come. She would be the first thing they saw when they came in, her naked, distended body, her entombed head. The ambiance would be established right away. Here you can do anything that you wanted. On her you can impose anything.

She had wondered why Devlin had made her install both the blindfold and the hood. The hood by itself blocked all light. It would make her seem less than fully human when the men came in to use her. When they whipped her, they would hear her muffled cries and screams of pain, but not be distracted from their pleasures by the sight of her anguished face. And for her, the idea that they were Devlin's avatars would be reinforced, as she would not see theirs.

And then it occurred to her. With the blindfold on, the men would be able to remove her hood and use her mouth without granting her sight or revealing more of her humanity than was absolutely necessary.

Anna was fighting off her sobs when the door finally opened. The pain in her feet was excruciating and she had to pee very badly. Her heart began to beat wildly. Two men had come in. One was Devlin. She could sense him, identify his walk anywhere. And the other was Carlos.

"Hello, Anna," Devlin said merrily. "Sorry we're a little late. There was a lot of traffic." Anna quailed as the men approached her. A hand, Devlin's hand, took hold of a breast. Due to her posture, it was stretched flat against her chest.

"You're looking much better from your workouts, Anna," Devlin continued. "But you've lost some weight in your breasts. We'll have to have that taken care of. They were so luscious before."

She heard Carlos removing one of the whips from the display. She sobbed in fear.

As Devlin walked into the kitchen area, opening up a cabinet to get himself a drink, Carlos approached her and dragged the ends of the multi thronged whip over her chest and belly. Anna whined.

When Devlin returned, she felt him insert a bowl between her thighs. "You have to pee first, Anna," he said. "We don't want any messes on the floor."

Dutifully and, to her great relief, she filled the bowl with her water. When Devlin removed it, he wiped her with a little tissue. She heard him go into the bathroom and empty the bowl in the toilet. He came back.

"Now, I want you to make this quick, Carlos," Devlin said. "We are going to be late as it is. I'm going to limit you to ten strokes, so make sure that they're good ones."

"No problem, Mr. Devlin," she heard Carlos answer. It was a voice she knew well, gruff and without a hint of kindness in it.

She heard the sound of Devlin clipping off the end of one of his cigars and lighting it. The room filled with the masculine smell. "Go ahead," he said. "Don't wait for me. Just make sure you keep it below the breasts. Her dress is rather low cut and we don't want to embarrass her at the party."

"Yes, Mr. Devlin," Carlos answered.

Anna sensed Carlos's arm being pulled back. Her whole body cringed. A second later, the thongs of the whip made a sharp slapping sound as they collided with her defenseless belly. Anna's body jerked and she let out a wail. The next blow landed on her rear cheeks. She had heard Carlos grunt as he applied it, obviously complying with Devlin's instructions. Fire erupted across her buttocks and she screeched in pain. He whipped her again and again. He walked the whip up her legs and back down again. He struck her belly several times. He did her back and rear. Her whole body felt like it had been dipped in a virulent hot sauce. She moaned and wailed and danced on the tip of her toes, crying inconsolably.

When Carlos was finished, she was a blubbering mess. Her body burned intently. She thanked god that Devlin had told him to lay off her breasts. The worse thing though was not the beating. It was where it was happening. Now she would never come into the apartment without remembering the whipping she got here, the first of what she assumed would be many.

Carlos released her from her chain. She fell to the floor.

"Come on, get up, Anna," Devlin said. "You've got to be ready in ten minutes. I want you all prettied up. There's someone I want you to meet."

Anna's wrists were still locked together. She heard the whirring of the modem and the lock popped open as did the lock to her gag. She pulled the hood and then the spandex blindfold off of her head and scrambled to her feet. She knew that Devlin meant it when he said ten minutes. He would allow her not a second more.

"I'll take those," Devlin said as Anna stripped herself of her confinements. That would save her some time. She ran into the bathroom and looked in the mirror. Her face was all streaked from her crying. She washed it quickly, applied some powder and refreshed her lipstick. She cast off her shoes and adorned herself with the dark red stockings that came with the gown, being careful to toss the ones she took off into the bin there for that purpose. She took the gown off the rack and then remembered her perfume. She hustled into the bathroom and adorned herself with it and then ran right out.

She pulled the gown over her head and shimmied into it. It had a neckline that barely covered her areolas, but was high in the back to hide her reddened skin. It went down well below her knees. She zippered the dress up her back as she slipped into the dark red high heels. She rushed back into the bathroom and quickly ran a brush through her hair. Devlin had been keeping it relatively short and it only took a few strokes to get it into place. She watched herself in the mirror. One could hardly tell that a few moments ago she was wailing and screaming at the end of a chain. Her diamond studs twinkled as did the gold of the necklace she wore at all times, the one with the triskelion pendant.

She just made it in time. She stood there with the little red purse in her hands behind her back as Devlin checked his watch. 'Good girl, Anna," he told her. He got up and they left.

As soon as they got in the back seat of the limousine, Anna shimmied her gown up to around her waist and placed her hands behind her back. She was still experiencing the dismal unhappiness which followed all of her whippings, an unhappiness which struck down deep in her soul. She had been Devlin's slave for almost three months. It was unsettling how low she had fallen in that brief time, so low that she would accept Devlin's right to give her to callous, anonymous men, men who would whip her and fuck her, use her brutally, and in her very own home. Her eyes welled up with tears. What was happening to her? Why didn't she rebel, run away? Why did she meekly accept whatever Devlin doled out to her?

Devlin looked over and saw that Anna was crying. His face softened. "Come here, Anna," he said to her, his voice mellow and comforting.

Anna sniffled and edged herself over to where Devlin sat, keeping her hands behind her. Devlin put his large, heavy arm around her and drew her into him.

"There, there, now, Anna. You looked beautiful tonight when I came into your apartment. So vulnerable and so available. You're my little whore, aren't you?"

"Y-yes, Mr. Devlin," Anna murmured.

"I want you to say it, Anna. Tell me that you're my little whore."

Anna's lips trembled. She hated herself for saying it, but she did. "I'm your little whore, Mr. Devlin," she replied.

"And I can do anything I want with you."

"And you can do anything you want with me," she repeated. Her voice was thick and tremulous.

"That was the deal, wasn't it, Anna? Wasn't that the deal?

"Y-yes, Mr. Devlin," Anna answered lowly, her voice just above a whisper.

"I kept my part of the deal, didn't I, Anna?"

"Y-yes Mr. Devlin."

"Then, you have to keep yours, don't you?"

"Y-yes, Mr. Devlin," Anna said back.

He turned her so she was facing him and stroked the side of her face with his hand. "You're such a good girl, Anna. You've turned into a wonderful whore. And I can tell that you like it when the men fuck you. You scream and moan like a whirlwind when you come. Tell me the truth, Anna, you like it when the men fuck you, don't you?"

It was such a strange feeling. Devlin was stroking her and hugging her so tenderly. It felt so good. It made her want to please him in every way she could. And yet, the words he was saying, making her say, pierced her, made her body sour with despondency. Yes, this was the deal she had made. Yes the men brought her pleasure when they fucked her. Yes, she had become a fine, little whore. But did she like it when the men fucked her? She liked what it did to her body, brought her pleasure beyond her wildest imaginings, but the fact of being used so callously, without a single concession to her right to self determination, repelled her. It made her feel scurrilous and dirty. Just like she used to feel. But that was just the point. It brought her back to a place she had left long ago, a place that now seemed safe and terrible all at the same time. She no longer had to conceal her inner sluttishness, fight off her feelings of inadequacy and vulnerability. Being used so callously, being forced to spread her legs, open her mouth, present her rear to these demanding, ruthless men was a thrill so intense it almost made her faint. So, did she like it? Yes, to her utter damnation, she liked it a lot.

"Y-yes, Mr. Devlin," she finally eked out. Her tears started to flow.

"Now, now, Anna, you don't want to have to ride in the trunk do you?"

A knife pierced Anna's belly. "No, Mr. Devlin, please don't!" she spat out desperately.

"Then you'll have to stop your crying. Can you do that, Anna?"

"Y-yes, Mr. Devlin." She did her best to hold back her tears.

"It pleases me to make you available to my friends. You do want to please me, don't you, Anna?

She could feel his warm body next to her. His heavy arm was hugging her shoulder. His free hand was stroking her face almost lovingly. A deep void opened in her, one only Mr. Devlin could fill.

"Yes, Mr. Devlin," she answered.

"Then you'll do as you're told, won't you, Anna?"

She felt tears building up in her again. She was desperately trying to hold them back. Yes! Yes! She would do as she was told! Anything! She would do anything, just to feel his arm around her and to hear from him the magic words.

"Y-yes, Mr. Devlin," she replied. She saw a smile break out on his face.

"That's a good girl, Anna," he replied. "You're a very good girl."

Those were the magic words. Words that she would do anything to hear from him, experience any indignity, tolerate any condition, suffer any pain. She grinned back, knowing that she was lost. He leaned forward and took her lips in his. She felt his tongue press between them and she opened her mouth to receive it. He kissed her deeply, hugging her to him. A flood of happiness suffused her. He was using her. He was possessing her. He was fulfilling her.

His hand drifted down from her face and slipped into the bodice of her gown, cupping her breast and giving it a strong, but gentle squeeze. She reveled in the sensation. Her hands, still obediently crossed behind her, clasped into little fists. Her loins moistened and she could feel the fire there beginning to burn.

He brought his lips back for a moment. "Take out my cock and stroke it, Anna," he said, his voice low and impassioned.

As he renewed his assault on her mouth, she reached out her hand and took hold of the fly to his pants. She pulled it down and the reached in through the hole in his shorts, rummaging for his cock. It was already stiffened and she was just able to guide it through the hole. Once it was out, she commenced a series of soft, steady strokes.

It wasn't often that he had her handle his cock except for the purposes of guiding it to her mouth. It felt hot and thick and long. It was as rigid as steel. She had felt it penetrate her so many times. She longed for it, pined for it. She felt privileged to be able to have such knowing, direct contact with it. Her eyes were closed as Devlin continued to kiss her and she imagined the image of it circled by her hand, its round, pinkish red helmet, the little slit through which his essence poured. She could feel its irregular, throbbing veins with her fingers, veins she had explored so many times with her tongue.

The car was speeding through the night. Anna could feel the hum of the tires on the road beneath them. There was a gentle rocking that was mesmerizing. His tongue was probing her mouth, exploring every corner, washing along hers. She felt like she was at the apogee of her existence.

He broke again. "Suck my cock, Anna," he whispered softly. He released her breast as she released his cock. She placed her hand behind her back to join the other and maneuvered herself so that she could lean over him. She subsumed the head of his prick between her pulsing lips and slid them down the meaty, rock hard column.

She suckled him long and slow as he liked it. She played with the fat head with her tongue and then fastened her lips around it, tickling the little slit with her oral appendage. She pushed her head down as far as it would go, letting it pop into her throat and holding it there as long as she could, letting him enjoy her hot moisture and tender tissues along the length of him.

She felt the car slow and pull over as if to a curb. Devlin's hand was on her naked buttocks, stroking them, delving from time to time down the valley between her rear cheeks and terminating on the slit between her spread thighs. She continued her ministrations to his manhood, knowing that he would tell her when he was ready to come.

It did not take long. His breathing got heavy as the car idled. He groaned. "Okay, Anna," he rasped. "Make me come. Now!"

In obedience, she accelerated the strokes of his prick with her mouth. Her tongue washed it wildly. She kept her lips held tightly against it. He gave out a deep, hearty groan and she felt his tool begin to jerk and throb. His cum washed against the back of her mouth and she swallowed it dutifully, happily. His hand and taken hold of her pussy from behind and he was sliding two thick fingers in and out of her burning canal. She moaned with pleasure, both at the physical sensations he was bringing her and at the psychic excitement she experienced each time he discharged himself within her.

Her pussy was still burning, yearning for completion, when he eased his fingers out and ordered her to raise her head. She made sure, as she withdrew her lips, that she consumed every drop of his salty discharge. At his instructions, she replaced his cock in his shorts and zipped him up. When she was done, he stroked her head, thanking her for the blowjob and telling her what a good girl she was. She beamed back at him in deepest gratitude.

"Pull your dress down, Anna," he told her.

The limousine pulled up a shirt distance and stopped again. When they emerged from the limousine, Anna saw that they were in front of the city's principal art museum. The front was lit up like a Hollywood premiere. A long, wide red carpet let up to the large, ornately decorated front doors. A silver haired man and his fur wrapped salt and pepper haired female companion were walking up the carpet ahead of them.

As soon as Devlin and Anna started to walk up the carpet, another long, black limousine pulled up behind them.

The foyer to the museum was a cavernous space, 200' long and 100' wide. The ceiling was at least 30' high. The floor was of a swirling green and white marble. The walls were covered with frescoes reminiscent of a Roman temple. A long line of elegantly dressed, beautiful people waited patiently to be allowed past the entrance booth. Anna saw Devlin pull two gilt edged invitations out of his jacket pocket. He was dressed in a finely tailored, black tuxedo with a ruffled shirt and a large, silk bow tie. Anna tip toed along silently as the line progressed.

"It's a fundraiser for the museum, Anna," Devlin told her. "My consortium has donated a somewhat obscure Caravaggio and I'll be presenting it tonight. I want you by my side during the ceremony. Until then, feel free to wander and enjoy the exhibits."

Anna nodded at him. When they got to the entrance booth, the sweet looking, college aged girl, with a long, chestnut colored ponytail, and wearing a prim, red and blue patterned dress, smiled at them. "Hello, Mr. Devlin," she said, her smile getting just a bit wider. Anna sensed that if Devlin had asked for her phone number, she would have given it readily.

"This is Anna Addunizio from the Center for Young Women," Devlin told her. She nodded and searched in a little box for a nametag. She located it and handed it to Devlin along with his own, as if anyone needed to know who he was. Anna pinned it to the front of her bodice. They walked past the entrance desk and into the museum proper.

Two pretty girls were handing out programs. The pamphlet announced the gift from "The Devlin Group" and had a color rendition of the painting that was being donated. It was an Italian landscape, showing a light blue sky with long, diaphanous clouds stretched out over head. Below it was a fruitful field with a dozen or so gaily dressed peasants working it. The girls, in unison, said, "Good evening, Mr. Devlin," smiling.

"If you only knew," Anna thought as they passed them.

Devlin and Anna separated. Before they did, he told her to enjoy herself, to have some champagne and *hors d'oeuvres*. A waiter was carrying a tray of champagne and Anna took one. She was surprised at how quickly she drank it and looked for another. The next waiter had a tray of puffed, cheese filled pastries. Anna took two and wolfed them down. She had had no dinner. The next tray that was carried by had large prawns skewered on long, multicolored, plastic sticks. Anna took two of those too.

She wandered around the galleries, eating as much as she could and drinking as much champagne as she could get her hands on. She walked into the American gallery. The first room contained early 19th century paintings. She admired the large, dark landscapes of the Hudson River School. Nature was monumentally depicted and the people were almost uniformly small. The next room took her into the later part of the century, with small, more civilized landscapes and scenes from rural American life.

The brochure said that the ceremony was at 10. It was a little after 9, and she had plenty of time to wander. She felt relaxed, calm, pleased with herself. She knew that when the night was over, Devlin would take her back to her apartment and fuck her. Her loins, still tingling from his tantalizing stroking of them in the car, gave her a little twitch as she thought about it.

She had passed through the rooms displaying early 20th century art, the beginnings of modernism, when a tall man with long black hair approached her. He had a long face with a prominent, aristocratic nose. He looked to be in his early forties. Like Devlin, he was wearing an elegant, black tuxedo.

Anna was looking at a painting of a nude woman by an artist named Robert Henri, of what was called the Spartacist School. It was softly focused, almost impressionistic. The woman had short, dark hair and was seated, facing the painter at a half angle. It showed her from just above her loins. Anna thought it was a beautiful picture. The woman's expression was disdainful, impertinent. Her lips were pursed, but closed. She had a working girl's face, not elegant, but handsome and, to an extent, primitive. Her skin was a dark cream color mixed with hints of green, red and gray.

"You like her?" the man asked. His voice was light and pleasant.

"I think she's beautiful," Anna replied.

"I think she looks a lot like you," the man said.

Anna knew a come on when she heard one. She was polite nonetheless. "Thank you," she replied. She turned and got her first good look at the man. He had an ironic smile. His skin was dark, a little yellowish. The name tag said that his name was Walter Perigourd from Perigourd Industries. French, Anna thought. He had a glass of champagne in his hand. As he raised it to his lips, Anna trembled. She saw the triskelion ring on his finger.

"You're very welcome, Anna," he said as he took a brief glance at her name tag. "And I'd bet that her breasts are not as nice as yours," the man continued. Anna's mind went to the necklace around her throat and the pendant that advertised her as available to all who wore the ring. Her throat constricted. She wanted to answer the man, perhaps make her excuses before he ordered her to go with him, but she couldn't get anything out.

There were other people in the room, young and old, all attired in their formal best. He wouldn't make her take them out here, would he? Her orders were to do everything that anyone wearing the ring said. She would have to do it or face terrible punishment. Her hands had become sweaty and her heart was thumping in her chest.

"I know a place where you can show them to me," he told her. "Come with me." He proffered her his hand. The one that wore the ring. He placed the empty champagne glass on a waiter's tray as he passed. Anna let him lead her. There was nothing else she could do. Her stomach was turning over a mile a minute. They left the American gallery and ascended to the second floor. There were sculptures to the left and early American artifacts to the right. There were fewer people up here, but no where that she could show him her breasts where they wouldn't be seen.

At the end of the corridor was a narrow elevator. The man led her into it and he closed the door. He pushed the button and it went up. Anna watched the floors go by, 3, 4 and then 5. She could feel his eyes peering at her, scouring her body, her breasts, her hips, her lips. It opened on the 6th. They exited the elevator. They were in the middle of a display of beautiful ceramics. He took her hand again and led her down the hall. Her high heels clicked on the stone floor, making an echo. They entered a darkened room with a placard mounted on a stand that said, 'Closed to the Public.' He took her in through the first room and into the second. There were long, empty, glass display cases and abandoned looking hooks on the walls.

When they reached the end, he turned to her. The light was dim and his features seemed even darker than before. The expression on his face had gone from amiable to hungry.

"All right, what are you waiting for? Let me see your tits!" he said sharply.

Anna suppressed a whine and reached behind her. She lowered the zipper on her dress to the small of her back and then slipped her breasts free of the strapless bodice. He took them in his hands immediately.

"Ahhhhhh, yes," he murmured as he manipulated them. He flicked their nipples with his thumbs. Anna was trembling. Her stomach was sour and she was sweating. Her hands were behind her back. His hands were boney and strong. His touch was harsh and groping. What was he going to make her do?

"Yes, I think I was right," he said, staring down at her. "Your tits are prettier than hers. You're Miles Devlin's whore, aren't you?"

Anna was surprised at the question. Were there other girls like her floating around who belonged to other people? She had never seen a necklace like hers on anyone, but, then again, she hadn't really looked. Did Devlin take strange women off of the street and fuck them? She hesitated to answer. He gripped her nipples and squeezed them harshly, making her moan. Her voice resounded through the empty room.

"I asked you a question, cunt!" he snarled.

"Yes! Yes!" Anna blurted out. "Please let go! Please!" she whined.

"That's, 'Yes, sir,' to you, bitch," he growled. He squeezed her nipples even harder.

"Yes, sir! Yes, sir!" Anna cried. "Ohhhhhhhhhh!"

"I'll have to have him lend you to me for a week or so. We could have a lot of fun! You'll learn some better manners!"

Anna moaned as he released her teats. They throbbed with pain.

"Okay, let's see the rest of you," the man said.

Anna issued a little sob as she dutifully lowered the zipper to her dress the rest of the way. She pushed her gown down over her hips and then stepped out of it. The man ripped it from her hands and threw it away to the side, far out of reach.

He took hold of the hair at the back of her head and brought her to her toes. "Nice," he said. "And you have a pretty little cunt. Spread your legs."

Anna slipped her feet apart. She had to stand on her toes to ease the pain from his grip on her hair. His hand covered her pudenda, stroking it. "Nice," he repeated. He insinuated a finger between her love lips and burrowed it into her without waiting for her lubrication. She flinched in pain. He drew it back and forth until thankfully, her juices started to flow in self defense. When it could move back and forth with ease, he removed his finger and drew it to his nose. He took a whiff. "Mmmmmmmmmmmmm," he hummed. "Delicious. I'm definitely going to have to get to know you better. Here," he said, proffering his finger to her. "Open your mouth."

He pushed it inside. Anna knew what to do; she closed her lips around his finger and suckled it. Her taste was on it.

He pulled out his finger and wiped it on her breast. "Get on your knees," he told her.

Anna obediently sunk to her knees on the cold, stone floor. "Take out my prick and suck it," he ordered.

Shamed, afraid that someone would come by and see them, Anna hurriedly zipped down the man's fly and brought out his cock. It was rubbery and not yet fully hard. She placed her mouth on it. It tasted of sweat and male musk.

It quickly grew to full stature in her mouth. She kept her hands behind her back as per Devlin's standard instructions. Her slurps and moans as she worked his cock echoed through the room. The man kept a firm grip on her head, forcing her to slow her efforts. "Play with your pussy," he told her. "Don't let me come until you do."

Anna shifted her right hand to her quim. She began stroking it earnestly. She tried to think of things that made her feel sexy. She imagined it was Devlin's cock. She had sucked it less than an hour ago. In a way, it was his cock. She was obeying his orders. She was being a good girl. She just wished that the man didn't have to be so cruel and mean.

It didn't take long for her pussy to get excited. Devlin had had it on near boil a short while ago. Her mouth slipped back and forth over the cock as she played with her clit, rubbing it in circles, pressing down hard. She dipped her finger into her sluice and gathered some moisture, spreading it over her love button, making it slip and slide under her finger. She issued a whine as she felt the tingle spread through her body.

All of a sudden, there was a voice. It was deep and masculine. "Hey!" it yelled. "Is anyone in there?"

Anna froze in terror. Walter held her head fast against his belly. Then Anna heard footsteps. They came closer and closer. Walter pulled her further into the shadows. The footsteps stopped; a beam of light entered the room, flitting back and forth. They were in a corner and Walter jammed them up against the wall, behind a display case. The light danced past them and along the wall behind them. Anna thought desperately of her gown on the floor in the middle of the room. If the man saw it they would be caught. She couldn't think of anything worse now than being thrown out of the museum for lewdness. She was sure Devlin would punish her for it, even though it wasn't her fault. She was so frightened that she started to shake. The man gripped her hair tighter. His cock was deep in her throat and she was beginning to choke from loss of air. She had been unprepared to have his meat rudely thrust in to its hilt. She pressed her hands against Walter's thighs in a desperate effort to free herself.

"Is anyone in there?" the voice inquired again. Anna felt like screaming. She began to feel faint. The light played around the room one more time and then went off. She could hear the footsteps receding. The man eased her face from his belly until his cock was free of her throat. Anna took a deep breath through her nose, making a loud snorting sound.

"Shut the fuck up!" the man hissed.

Tears were flowing down Anna's face. All she wanted was to get away from this cruel man. She quaked at the thought that Devlin might lend her to him.

The footsteps were gone. "All right," the man said churlishly. "Let's get back to work."

Anna suckled and kissed and licked the man's cock. She played with her pussy fervently. There was something about their near escape that had fueled her lusts. She couldn't help it. The thought of shame and degradation appalled her, but it also made her passions launch. There was just something so right about it.

Soon she was moaning and groaning as her pussy got hotter and hotter. She could feel her juices rising. She worked the man's cock assiduously making him groan in pleasure. Suddenly, as if it had been struck by lightning, her pussy exploded. She issued a loud groan. Walter began pumping his cock into her mouth. Shortly, he gave out a loud moan and his cock began to spurt and throb within her. His discharge was copious and Anna had a hard time swallowing it all. The fact that her pussy was issuing powerful, ecstatic contractions didn't help.

When his orgasm was done winding down, Walter drew his cock from her mouth. "Not bad, Anna," he told her. "We definitely have to do this again." He stepped away from her, leaving her on her knees. He picked up her gown. "I think I'll keep this as a souvenir," he told her as he turned to the exit.

"Oh, please, no!" Anna cried. "Please don't do that! Please!" she got up from her knees and started to follow him. He was striding purposely to the elevator. As he got closer and closer, Anna became more and more desperate. He couldn't leave her like this! He couldn't!"

"Please, sir, please!" she whispered lowly again and again. Her high heels clickety clacked on the stone floor as she tried to keep up with him. She was terrified that the guard might hear them and come back. She wanted to tear her gown from his hands, but she was afraid of what he might do. He pressed the elevator button and she heard it coming up from a lower floor. As it drew near, her panic went off the scale. She fell to her knees and placed her hands around his legs.

"Please don't take my dress! Please, sir, please! What will I do? You can't leave me like this! I'll do anything you say! Please!"

The elevator reached their floor and Walter slid the manual door open. He grabbed her hair at the back of her head and yanked it hard, making her release his legs. Then he pushed her over with his foot. She fell to the floor. Before she had time to get up, the door closed, Walter on the other side of it.

"Ohhhhhhhhhhhh!" Anna moaned. She didn't know how anyone could be so cruel. She had done what he said! She had obeyed him in everything! Why did he do this? Why? She started to sob. She was laying on the floor and she buried her face in her arms. What was she going to do? What would Devlin do when he found out?

Suddenly, the door opened again. Her dress came flying out of it. She heard the man release a loud laugh. The door closed again and the elevator was gone.

Anna quickly came to her feet. She knew that there was only a short time before the ceremony. Devlin would kill her if she wasn't there. She had left her purse in the room where they had been. She rushed back to get it and then stepped hurriedly into her gown. She pulled it back up over her hips and pulled the zipper up. She ran back to the elevator. She pressed the button but didn't hear it move. Panicked, she wondered whether Walter had pressed the lock button downstairs. She looked quickly both ways. There was an exit sign near a door. She dashed to it and hurried down the stairs, taking two at a time.

When she got to the second floor, she stopped for a moment, out of breath. Reaching into her purse, she pulled out a brush and ran it through her hair several times. After she put it away, she pushed open the door to the gallery. A middle aged couple was standing there looking at a Vermeer. Their eyes went wide when they saw her. She nodded at them, smiling politely and strode past them. She was just going down the stairs to the first floor when she heard a bell ringing. The ceremony was about to start. She was late.

The crowd formed a large semi-circle around the draped painting. The distinguished looking men and women of the museum's board of trustees were gathered around it along with the executive director, a svelte, blond woman who looked to be in her mid-forties. She wore an elegant gown of purple and red and was wearing dark maroon high heels. Her hair was shoulder length with a slight upturn at the ends. Her face was long with clean lines, a face that might have belonged to a fashion model in her earlier years. Her breasts, too, were fashion model sized, tea cup sized bumps high on her chest. She was smiling and standing next to Devlin. Anna squeezed herself through the crowd until she was at the front of it. Devlin saw her, and with a slight frown for her tardiness, motioned her to join him.

Anna stepped up to the line of dignitaries. The woman gave her a long look, like she was measuring her. Devlin introduced her.

"Anna, I would like you to meet Dolores Newcastle. She's the director of the museum." Anna smiled at her, wondering if the woman could detect up close her recent sexual escapade. Her pussy still felt squishy and moist and she had the taste of Walter Perigourd's cum in her mouth.

Ms. Newcomb extended her long, boney hand. "Nice to meet you, Anna," she said. "Mr. Devlin has told me all about you."

Anna extended her hand tentatively. Had he told her all about her? All? She hoped not. But then she saw the triskelion ring on her finger and she knew that she did mean all. An empty place opened in her belly.

Was this the person that Devlin had said he wanted her to meet tonight? She desperately hoped that it wasn't. Cathy still played her domination games with her at least once a week after her workouts, and she had had a few more lovemaking sessions with Elaine, but she sensed a certain cruelty in this woman that frightened her. She wouldn't want to be loaned out to her for a weekend, that was for sure.

Standing next to Ms. Newcastle was a tall, thin man dressed in a fashionable tuxedo like all the other men. He looked about 40 too. He was handsome, if a little boyish looking. He had light brown hair that was a little longer than it needed to be. He had an American flag pin in his lapel. His name tag said that he was County Commissioner Peter Everhardt. Anna knew the name. He sat on the committee that decided on the County's charitable grants every year, including the over a million dollars a year given to the Center. He would be a good person to know. Anna looked quickly at his hands. There was a golden wedding band on one finger, but nothing else. He was safe. Hopefully, this is who Devlin was referring to. He introduced her.

Everhardt extended his hand. His grip was firm, but pleasant. His hand was warm. He seemed to approve of Anna's appearance since he gave her body a strong, not quite surreptitious look. He had a nice smile, not like a politician's at all.

"My pleasure, Ms. Addunizio," he said. "I've heard wonderful things about your program and especially about you. You deserve a lot of credit for what you've accomplished."

"Have you ever been to the facility?" Devlin interjected.

"No, I can't say that I have," he replied.

"I'm sure that Anna would be willing to give you the cook's tour. Wouldn't you, Anna?"

"Oh, yes," Anna said just a little too enthusiastically. "I'd love to."

"That would be wonderful," Everhardt replied.

"How about next week?" Devlin suggested.

"I'm not sure, I'd have to check my calendar." Everhardt said.

"Anna will make herself available any day, any time," Devlin stated.

"That's terrific," Everhardt answered. "I'm going to be the chair of our social services committee this year and I'm trying to get to know all of our grantees better. I'll have my secretary call tomorrow."

"That would be fine," Anna gushed. She looked away from Everhardt and blushed. "I'm acting just like a teenager," she thought.

Ms. Newcomb signaled one of the museum staff to blink the overhead lights. When they had blinked twice, the crowd, which had been murmuring like a mountain stream, began to come to silence. Ms. Newcomb clapped her hands loudly twice and the crowd quieted.

There was a microphone on a stand and Ms. Newcomb moved up to it. She welcomed all the guests in a firm but pleasant voice. She went on and on about Devlin's generosity and the generosity of the guests who had shelled out quite a pretty penny for the tickets. She made a pitch for their corporate donors program and then told a little joke which the audience appreciated. Then she introduced Everhardt.

The Councilman told his joke, evoking more laughter, and then paid his obligatory commendation of Devlin's largess. He then gave a short speech about corporate responsibility and how important it was to the county and the city. He spoke of the importance of art and of the museum's young artists' program funded by the County. Anna was surprised at how well spoken he was. He seemed to be speaking off the cuff without any prepared remarks, but he hit all his points confidently and without hesitation. Best of all, he seemed earnest, like he believed what he was saying and was not just another politician pressing for publicity and votes.

Devlin got up to say a few words. He was eloquent as he spoke of the importance of art to the community and how happy he was that he was able to give this gift. Anna was not surprised that he was able to hold the audience spellbound.

Then came the great unveiling. The lights were dim-med and a spotlight shown on the painting. Devlin and Ms. Newcastle shared the duties of removing the red velvet covering. The crowd burst into applause. Anna gasped as she looked at it. It was the same painting as in the brochure, but, then again, it wasn't. The colors were so much brighter, so much more alive. The brush strokes were graceful. The little people, so far away, seemed so lifelike even though it was clear that they were created by only a few very delicate strokes of the brush.

After a few obligatory publicity shots, ones that Devlin insisted Anna stand in on, the party continued. A long line of people assembled to get a better look at the painting. Anna spent some time talking to Everhardt about the Center and how it got started. He talked a little about his dedication to the more unfortunate of the community. He seemed so earnest that Anna believed him.

Ultimately, he was called away, but he renewed his promise to visit. Anna drifted among the paintings, hoping that no one else with a ring, such as Ms. Newcastle, would sweep her away again. Ms. Newcastle did make a point of talking to her. Anna shifted her feet uncomfortably as she complemented her on her wonderful figure and pretty face. She promised that they would get to know each other better. A chill went down Anna's spine.

Finally, the crowd began to thin out. Anna was looking forward to a good hard fuck from Devlin at her apartment. He saw her and came over, putting his arm through hers in a proprietary manner. Anna's pussy began to get warm. She knew that as soon as they got into the car he would go to work on her.

They strolled past one of the trustees, a broad shouldered, gray haired man who looked like he was in his early sixties.

He smiled when he saw Devlin and called out to him. Anna felt a sense of foreboding as she looked at his hand and saw the ring. Devlin introduced them. Anna's hand trembled as she shook his. "Andrew Convery, Midstate Investments," it said on his lapel. He and Devlin had a brief conversation. When it was over, Devlin offered to let him have Anna for the night. Convery broke out into a smile and accepted.

"Do me a favor, though," Devlin added. "She was late for the unveiling ceremony and needs to be punished." The man assured Devlin that he would fulfill his request with pleasure.

CHAPTER TEN

Convery's driver let her off at her apartment a little after 8 the
next morning. He had fucked and abused her into the wee
hours in a special room in the basement of his mansion.
Anna's body bore a dozen new, angry red stripes from his
whip. He had left her in the room all night standing spread-
eagled, her wrists and ankles tied off to columns on either side
of her. In the morning, his servant, a middle aged black
woman, led her up to the ground floor of the house where he
had her suck his cock one more time before she left.

She stripped and put on her collar as soon as she stepped
into her apartment. She took a cold shower to try and revive
herself. Her new wounds stung. After her shower, she lay
down on the bed to rest for a second. She awoke two hours
later to the beeping of the modem in the living room. When
she was kneeling before the camera her arms crossed behind
her, Devlin came on the speaker and admonished her for
being late. He told her to get dressed right away and report to
work. Her punishment could wait until tonight.

After that, two or three nights per week, Anna would be
summoned to the chain in the middle of her living room to
prepare herself to receive guests. There were only a few who
could resist giving her body a few blows with the whip before
using her on her bed. She never saw who they were, although
they used her mouth just as much as her other entrances.
Some of the voices became familiar as did the ways that she
was used, confirming her belief that some of the men were
repeat customers.

Sometimes two men came together. Once there was three.
They laughed and kidded each other like frat boys while they
used her. She could hear them drinking and smell their cigars.
Devlin had stocked her apartment with some frozen *hor*

d'oeuvres and Anna could hear them cook them up in the microwave and eat them. They were for guests only, Devlin had made clear, and Anna was not permitted to deviate from her strict diet. With one exception. She now drank at each meal a dietary concoction that Devlin had told her contained a formula that would increase her breast size. It came in little 7 oz. containers and she kept a host of them at the center so she could drink them at lunch time and in her refrigerator at home for consumption at breakfast and dinner. Anna didn't know what was in it, but it seemed to work as her breasts grew a few inches in circumference, way beyond her original size. It seemed to affect her libido too as she seemed lately to be always yearning for sexual release.

The men kept her busy until very late. By the time the third one had used her, the first one was ready again. They used all of her orifices. They whipped her too, with the flogger, making her whole body an angry red. She was left hooded and hogtied on her bed, Devlin having added ankle bracelets to her regalia. The modem didn't release her until the morning.

After the third week, Devlin added another feature to her bondage, a spreader bar. As per his instructions, she applied it to her ankles before finishing off her other confinements. Now when the men came in, her legs would be spread widely for their convenience. Few of them could resist manually or orally bringing her to climax as she was, or whipping her pussy before commencing the rest of the night's activities.

On the few nights when the men didn't come, Anna would spend it in trepidation that they would.

The Asian man came back several times. For him, Anna was always required to get in her cage. He would shove her in the closet while he took his shower and ate a meal and then he would use her, fucking her long and hard as he had the first night. He never said a word to her, communicating his wants by grunts and gestures. He always spent the night.

She did get to give Everhardt a tour of the Center. With Devlin's permission, she had lunch with him a few days later. She began to see him at more of the Wednesday night functions and he always talked to her. Anna liked him and was attracted to him. It was ironic that she was available to all these other men but she could not make a pass at the one man, besides Devlin and the Asian man, who made her lusts start to rise each time she saw him. She was conscious of the repugnance he would certainly hold for her if he really knew what she was. After she talked to him at parties, she always wandered off morosely knowing that there could never be any connection between them. She also worried that he would see her getting picked off at one of these affairs by one or more of the ring owners, which seemed to be happening more and more often. If there was no place at the party to use her, they often took her out to their limousines and used her there. Or, with Devlin's permission, took her to a motel for a couple of hours or home for the night.

Between Cathy, her trainer, and Elaine, her erstwhile lover, Anna's skill at fucking and sucking were increased considerably. Cathy had added Kegel exercises to her regimen. She would make Anna stand with her legs spread and try to keep a slim dildo she had slipped up her quim from falling to the mat. When she failed, she was beaten by her trainer's whippy stick. When she succeeded, she was given a resounding orgasm as a reward and the standard by which she would be measured, either by time or by weights added to the dildo, or both, would be increased. She would practice assiduously all week to try and avoid her beating, exercising those muscles several times every day. Eventually, they became quite strong. Her orgasms and the pleasure her pussy could bring to a cock were drastically increased.

Elaine patiently educated her in the arts of pleasuring a man and spent hours maintaining her at the edge of sexual completion, thereby deepening and making more intense her passions. Anna had never known her body was capable of such explosions of lust. Between what Cathy and Elaine had taught her, Devlin was impressed and started fucking her face to face, rather than just from behind, or allowed her to fuck him from up top, where she could better display the lessons her female lovers had taught her.

One Wednesday night, it was in the beginning of the fifth month of her captivity, as he was getting dressed and preparing to leave her apartment after their night out, Devlin began to query her about Everhardt. Did she like him? Did he like her? Did she want to fuck him? Anna, now used to total and complete honesty with her master, knowing that there was nothing she could hide from him for long, said yes. She was sitting on the corner of her bed, her wrists bound behind her, naked but for her stockings and sandals. They had had a long, steamy session and she was limp and tired. Devlin caressed a breast and told her that he thought that maybe she should have a break from her harsh regimen. That maybe he would let her have an affair with the man, if she wanted it. The only restrictions were that she would continue to serve him as he needed her and she would keep him apprised as to all the developments between them. He would ease off on the whippings so that she wouldn't be all marked up when she finally managed to bed him.

Anna agreed to the conditions enthusiastically.

A few days later, she was on the phone with Everhardt and she maneuvered their discussion of possibly having lunch to having a drink together after work. It had been Devlin's idea on how to finally spark the sexual relationship. He chose for Anna a fancy, secluded bar on the outskirts of town. It was a real cheaters place with high backed booths and a dim ambiance. A piano player filled the room with soft, mellow jazz.

That night, they had their first kiss. It started in the parking lot next to her car where they were saying goodbye. It ended in his car with the driver's seat down and her sucking his cock.

He called her again the next day and invited her out to dinner. Devlin had anticipated his move and instructed her to suggest a restaurant just beyond the outskirts of the city. The restaurant was appurtenant to a motel. They ended up in one of the rooms and fucked like teenagers for several hours.

Anna was elated. It was the first time in a long time that she had gotten to choose her sexual partner, even though it was with Devlin's permission and with his guidance. Fucking him was heaven. She sighed with joy when his cock slipped along the soft membranes of her inner coosh, filling her. After each bout, they lay entwined for a long time, stroking and petting each other.

On the third night they spent at the motel, they always went to the same motel and used the same room, he told her that he was falling in love with her. Anna cried when he said this, knowing that for her, for the next six months at least, the time remaining on her contract, love was out of the question. When she told Devlin, he laughed and asked her whether she was falling in love with him too. She told him that she was.

Their affair went on for the better part of six weeks. They had met at their special place at least a dozen times. He was a little reserved at first, unlike Anna's usual sexual partners who used her callously any way they wanted, but Anna soon had his libido loosened and, with her encouragement, he was using her mouth and her ass as much as he used her pussy. Anna could tell that he had never used a woman before with such freedom. As for her, she passionately used all of the skills and techniques she had learned over the months to heighten his sexual pleasure. When she deep throated him, he groaned and writhed on the bed. He had been reticent, at first, to suck her pussy, but soon he was insisting at licking her to a tumultuous orgasm at least once every time they got together, to Anna's great delight.

True to Devlin's word, the visitations from the strange men dwindled to a trickle. The Asian man, however, made regular, bi-weekly visits. Anna surmised that he had business in the area and that he flew in once every other week or so to take care of it. Even he forbore beating her, except for the flogger, which he used to turn her rear cheeks or breasts a bright red.

Devlin had insisted that Anna maintain her regular weekends with him. On this particular Friday night, about six weeks after her affair with Everhardt had begun, Anna was standing by the door to his office, outfitted by Mrs. Leopold in the regular manner, her hands fastened up behind her on her back chained to her collar, naked except for her stockings and high heels, her gag in her mouth. She stood there for a long time. She had seen Devlin's limo in the parking lot and all of his other cars, so she assumed that he was there in his office. It didn't matter to her how long she waited. Someone would come by to use her eventually or Vincent would send her up to her room.

After about a half hour, she heard a car pull up outside. A minute or so later, the doorbell to the mansion rang. Vincent appeared and strolled slowly across the foyer to answer it. Anna speculated that one of Devlin's friends had come by to use her. Her stomach became a bit uneasy as she never knew whether her 'customer' would abuse her or not.

Vincent opened the door. To Anna's horror, Peter Everhardt stepped in. Anna wanted to run and hide, but she knew she would suffer an awful punishment if she did. In any case, it was too late. Peter had seen her. It was spring now and he wore no overcoat, just his regular business suit. Vincent brought him to the door to Devlin's office. Peter gave her a cold, hard stare and then Vincent led him in.

Anna stood there crying and sobbing as she awaited the next development. The only good thing in her life in the last six months had been smashed to pieces in an instant. What would he think of her now? It was easy to figure that out. He would think that she was a slut and a whore, which, after all, she was. She was filled with bitter remorse at the thought that their idyllic interludes would certainly be at an end. Devlin, in his nefarious way, had been stringing them along like a puppet master. She should have known, she thought unhappily. He never did anything nice for her without an ulterior motive.

About fifteen minutes later, the door to Devlin's office opened. Vincent emerged and, taking hold of her arm, began to escort her in. She struggled with him for a moment, desperately wanting to avoid any closer contact with her now former lover. He just gripped her arm all the harder and pulled her after him.

Everhardt was sitting in front of Devlin's desk. He had a dour, defeated look on his face. Before him, spread all over the desk, were a number of 8x10" glossy photos. Anna saw right away what they were. They were pictures of them taken from outside and inside their motel room. In one, she had Peter's cock in her mouth and he was grimacing with pleasure. In another, he was fucking her from behind, a look of extreme enjoyment on his face. There looked to be two dozen photos. Peter was holding one in his hand. They were clasped into a deep, soulful kiss, both of them naked, kneeling on the bed.

"Good evening, Anna," Devlin said, a hint of irony and amusement in his voice. "You know Mr. Everhardt here so there's no need for introductions. Mr. Everhardt was going over my collection of photos memorializing your trysts. I thought he might like to have them as keepsakes of your love affair."

"That's enough of that, Devlin," Everhardt spat out. "I've agreed to your terms, what more do you want?"

Devlin did not respond directly to Everhardt, but continued to address himself to Anna. "You see, Mr. Everhardt is the swing vote on a new project that myself and a few friends are in the process of developing. It involves the use of County land and Mr. Everhardt was assiduous in maintaining that we are getting the land at less than market value. I'm afraid he's right. It is quite a steal. Now, of course, he's agreed to change his tune. The vote is this week and he will suddenly announce his change of position before it's taken."

So that's what it was, Anna thought miserably. She had been used as bait to bring Peter into Devlin's evil orbit. He had fallen for her hook, line and sinker. If the newspapers got a hold of the story of his affair with the director of a social service agency under his committee's purview, they would have a field day. Not to mention what his wife might do. His political career would be over.

Peter was giving her a hateful stare. Anna, who had been naked with him more than a dozen times, now was shamed at her nudity before him. She was clearly some deviant, an agent of Devlin's power. He would think that all of her passion had been feigned, that she had ruthlessly used her body to entrap him. He would never believe that she hadn't known that Devlin's agents were taking pictures. She was the one, after all, who had suggested the situs of their trysts. Everhardt was not a wealthy man and he had had to use his County expense account to pay for the room. That would be another damning detail. He could get indicted.

"What's the sense of all this," Everhardt demanded. His voice was strained. Anna wasn't sure what was hurting him more, being under Devlin's power or her betrayal of him.

"My dear fellow," Devlin oozed. "You do not yet understand the full nature of our arrangement. I wouldn't think of asking for your cooperation without a quid pro quo. And I'm not referring to my suppression of these pictures. That goes without saying. I'm going to propose you as a full member of our little club. I'm sure your unhappiness will be assuaged when you learn of all the benefits this will bring you.

With your popularity, and the financial assistance of our club members, you will be a shoe-in for County executive next fall. And after that, who knows, the State Senate, Governor? You'll make your fortune and have the benefit of free use of our club's amenities, of which Anna is just one. There are dozens of beautiful women who will be at your beck and call, refusing you nothing, giving you their all. There's nothing like having a beautiful woman at the end of your whip or sucking your cock on her knees."

Devlin paused to take a long toke of his cigar. "And then there's Anna. You can have her anytime you want. Here, at my mansion, or at her apartment. You can have her tonight. In fact, if you wish to punish her for her betrayal of you, Vincent will show you up to our punishment room where you can take out your pain on her body. And then you can fuck her in her room upstairs. She'll be most cooperative, I can assure you."

Everhardt became red in the face. His self control was about to boil over. His eyes burned into Anna's, conveying his fervid detestation of her, his bitter hatred. Anna shivered at the thought of what he might do to her. "Please, Peter! Please!" she screamed in her mind. "You've got to believe me! I didn't know! I didn't know!" Tears were streaming down her face. All she could emit from her gagged mouth was a dismal, unhappy whine.

"Yes," Everhardt said through his teeth. "I'd like nothing more than to whip this bitch raw. Since I'm in your power, Devlin, I might as well take advantage of the situation and get as much for the sale of my soul as possible. And revenge on this cunt is top on my list!"

Devlin laughed. "Of course it is," he said. "Vincent, why don't you escort Anna and Peter upstairs so they can have their fun together. And since he's a neophyte at this, give him all the assistance that he needs."

Vincent just nodded. Anna let out a wail. He attached a leash to the front of her gag and began to lead her from the room.

"And, Peter," Devlin interjected as the now bought and paid for County Commissioner was rising from his seat, "don't exhaust all your forces. When you're done with Anna, we'll have dinner at my club. There's a wonderful nightclub there, The Blue Cantina. You'll love it, I'm sure."

Everhart, his lips grimly pursed, nodded his agreement.

As they trudged up the stairs to the 4th floor, Anna was sobbing. Peter was climbing the stairs behind them and she could feel his hateful eyes on her naked buttocks. When they got to the punishment room, Vincent released her hands from her back and affixed them to the dangling chain overhead. Peter stood there glaring at her while Vincent went to the closet and retrieved a whip for him. It was a long, tapered steel crop. It would leave angry red lacerations wherever it fell.

Anna's body went sour and she cringed as Vincent handed it to her assailant. Peter looked at it, familiarizing himself with its weight and heft. Then he looked back at Anna. "This is going to be an extreme pleasure, Anna," he said bitterly. "I hope you don't expect me to hold anything back. I'm going to give you a lash for every lie that you told me, for every tender thought I foolishly had for you. I want to remember this night for a long time. I don't know what evil deal you have with Devlin, but it's time to pay for your betrayal of me."

Vincent removed Anna's gag. They were not used in the punishment room. Victims here got to scream and beg for mercy as much as they wanted.

"Pleeeeeeease, Peter! Pleeeeeeeeease! You've got to believe me! I didn't know! I swear to god, I didn't know! Pleeeeeease! Pleeeeeeeease!" she screamed.

"Why should I believe your lies now, Anna? That's what got me into trouble in the first place. All my life all I wanted was to be an honest public servant, to do what's right for the community, to oppose people like what you've just made me become!"

"Pleeeeeeease Peter! You've got to believe me! I'm in Devlin's power too! I had no choice!"

"Then you should have made a better deal, Anna," he replied coldly. He reared back the whip and delivered a vicious blow right across her breasts. Anna screamed in agony. He went at her again and again, laying the lash all over her body. Anna screamed and danced and begged for mercy. She sobbed and moaned and pleaded for forgiveness. She turned and twisted in her chains, the many images of them reflected on the mirrored walls, her anguished voice echoing off of them. She twisted and turned in her chains, trying to avoid the worst of Peter's blows, but he relentlessly pursued her, lashing her back, her rear, her thighs her belly and breasts again and again. Devlin and Vincent had whipped her here often, but theirs was a cool, deliberate punishment. Peter's efforts were fueled by rage and carried that much more emphasis. Anna felt like her body had been set afire. Her pain was made so much more worse by her dismal unhappiness at having turned Peter's love into hate.

Finally, Vincent brought an end to it. He caught Peter's stroke in mid air, taking hold of his arm. Peter's face was angrily red. His breathing was heavy. He had removed his jacket to administer her punishment and his shirt was drenched with his sweat. He took a step back to examine his handiwork. Anna hung virtually lifeless from the chain, her toes dragging on the floor, moaning and sobbing. Her body was covered with a latticework of fierce, red lines from her knees to her neck. Blood was oozing in several places. Vincent gave Peter a glass of water to drink. He downed it quickly, not taking his eyes off of his victim. When Vincent released Anna's wrists from the chain, she fell to the floor.

He let her lie there a time, while she recovered her breath. Then he forced her to her feet and affixed her wrists to the front of her collar. He led her and Peter to her room across the hall and closed the door behind them. Peter used her brutally for more than an hour, slapping her cruelly when she was slow to respond, fucking her ass, twisting and turning her nipples, clenching her pussy's lips hard until she screamed in pain, jamming his long, thick cock down her throat until she choked. When he finally arose from her, his body was smeared with the blood from her wounds.

Vincent came by later and applied a soothing salve to her body. He had her drink a large cupful of a soporific potion. Then he chained her to the bed for the night, hooded and gagged.

* * * * * * * * * * * * * *

The beating and violent rape she underwent at Peter's hands marked the commencement of a steep decline in what little was left of Anna's independence and self esteem and a sharp acceleration of her decline into absolute submission. Two weeks after their confrontation was Peter's formal induction into the club and Anna served as the fulcrum of the lusts of the participants in the ceremony. She was hooded and gagged through most of it, her ears filled with wax lest she hear the words of the devilish ritual. Each one of the twelve men present took turns beating and fucking her, with Peter leading the way. At the end, her hood was removed and she tearfully sucked off all the men in turn, with Peter triumphantly last.

Every week, at least once, it seemed, thereafter, Peter visited Anna at her apartment after work, or sometimes in the afternoons when he could get away. Carlos would drive her there. He always rabidly abused her. Two days after Peter's induction ceremony, on Monday afternoon, Devlin had Carlos drive her to a tattoo parlor where his emblem, the blue, florid 'D', was etched into her lower belly, just above her mons, the same mark that Elaine wore. He had apparently been waiting until Everhardt had been reeled in. It would have been a difficult thing for Anna to explain the tattoo to him. Now, it made no difference. Anyone who used her knew she was Devlin's whore anyway.

The visits from the unknown men increased and Devlin started lending Anna out on weekends.

Her first weekend was when she was delivered to the country estate of Dolores Newcomb, the museum director. That Friday night, Ms. Newcomb showed her who was boss by beating her savagely. On Saturday afternoon, there was a party in her garden and Anna, dressed in only a tiny, pink, frilly skirt, pink garters and stockings and pink high heels, waited on the guests, all women of Ms. Newcomb's general age and social class. Her hair was tied back by a pretty, pink bow. The women all complemented Ms. Newcomb on Anna's beauty and compliance and remarked on the residual evidence of her beating of the night before.

After luncheon was served, before the coffee and desert, one of Ms. Newcomb's maids laid a blanket out on the grass amidst the circle of seated women. Ms. Newcomb's chauffer, a tall, broad shouldered, black man, fucked Anna on it while the women watched, using all of her orifices, making her scream alternatively with pleasure and pain, and coming in her three times. After, while the women were having dessert, Anna made the rounds on her knees, servicing each woman in her turn, licking and suckling at their pussies. Ms. Newcomb had her brought to her bed that night where she fucked her long and slow with a two headed, vibrating dildo.

Sunday morning, she was brought back to Devlin's where she underwent the normal end of weekend use.

The weekend she spent as Walter Perigourd's guest was two days of hell. She spent a weekend with Convery and his cruel, black maid, and others as well.

All during this time, Devlin kept a close watch on her. He varied her routines, added punishments, and continued to use her, although not as frequently as before. Still, when he held her in his arms, droning on about what a good girl she had been that day or that night, Anna would sob and melt into his arms, happy to have pleased him. The only other solace she received was when the Asian man stayed with her overnight at her apartment. Not only did his presence mean that no other men would come and use her that night, but she got to spend the entire night in bed with him, albeit gagged and bound. Just the sensation of his warm body next to her rendered her grateful for his presence.

One night, a Saturday, when Devlin had taken her out to the club for dinner, the *maitre'd* approached Devlin half way through their meal. It appeared that they were short of serving girls. Devlin smiled and volunteered Anna.

The *maitre'd* led her back though the kitchen to a dressing room. There she saw a long line of uniforms and dresses. He made her put on a long skirt and a tight, low cut blouse. He also adorned her with leather bracelets and a collar which were embossed in gold with the club's emblem, the triskelion.

Her duties in the dining room were simple. She carried out the tray of food for the customers and distributed the plates at the *maitre'd's* instructions. When the diners were finished, she cleared the table and prepared it for the next customers. Of her additional duties, she learned while Devlin was still drinking his coffee. At the table next to him were two members of the club, a young, thin man with a long, harrowing face and an older man with grey hair and distinguished features. Anna served the two men demitasses of espresso and snifters of brandy. When the brandy and coffee were done, the young man, who looked to Anna to be particularly cruel, took her hand and led her upstairs to the bedrooms. Devlin gave her a little smile of approval as she left. She had been right about the young man's cruel bent, as he whipped her with a thick riding crop, and then spilled himself in her trembling, unhappy mouth. Afterwards, after cleaning up, she was returned to the dining room by one of the club's stewards where she resumed her duties. She was taken to a bedroom twice more before the night was through where she was used thoroughly by both men.

When the kitchen closed, and that was very late, after 1 A.M., she was led back to the dressing room where she stripped and serviced the *maitre'd* with her mouth. She was taken then downstairs to the basement of the building where she was locked into a small cell with a single sized bed. Three of the staff members visited her there before the night was through. On Saturday, she served lunch in the dining room, garnering three more clients, one of them a woman, and was assigned to the bar for the evening. She dressed in a very brief cocktail dress, sans underwear, of course, and served drinks to the men and women at the tables. The customers were free to caress and stroke her as they pleased and she serviced a few of them on her knees. Two men, at different times, took her up to a room.

Sunday morning, she was returned to the mansion by Carlos, who then brought her to her room where he took his turn with her. She had dinner with Devlin that night, as usual, and, after they fucked in his bed, she cried in his arms while he soothed her.

She started spending more and more time at the club as a whore and less and less time at Devlin's mansion. Sometimes Carlos would come to her office in the late afternoon and take her there, returning her to her apartment that night when her duties were complete. On a number of occasions, they kept her there for several days. When she was finally able to get back to work, she would find that Devlin had made some excuse for her and that Esther had covered her duties.

In fact, Esther was doing practically all of her work now. It seemed that every day Devlin, or one of his cronies, would call her to come to their office for the morning or the afternoon. Sometimes, Devlin kept her at her apartment for the whole day for no apparent reason, or because one of his 'friends' wanted some morning or afternoon delight. At the Board meetings, Esther and Gail Harper, the other new staff member Devlin had foisted on her, had to assume the responsibility of presenting the reports to the Board. Anna hardly knew what was going on at the Center and would not have been able to answer any of the Boards' questions.

Anna knew that the other women who served at the club were also under some kind of devious control, as she was, but she was never able to be alone with any of them so that they could talk about it. At night, on the few occasions now that she slept over at Devlin's mansion, when she was locked in her 4th floor room, she would still hear the footsteps of other, unknown, prisoners, walking down the hall following Vincent's lead and on their way to Devlin's bedroom or back. Or she would hear fervent, anguished female screams and pleas emerging from the punishment room across the hall.

Despite her knowledge that other women were embonded to Devlin, or the club, or both, through some nefarious mechanism, the thought had ceased to bother her. What happened to other women were their look out. She had enough troubles of her own.

One night, a Friday, at Devlin's mansion, she was led to Devlin's bed at about eleven o'clock. She was surprised to see him in bed with two very young, blond girls. They looked so much alike they could have been twins or at least sisters. They were shapely and vivacious, and naked. One of them had been sucking Devlin's cock when she came in and rose up, wiping her lips with the back of her hand.

"Here she is," Devlin announced. The one girl squealed and rushed off the bed only to drag Anna back to it. Devlin released her wrists from her collar and the girls went to town on her, suckling her breasts, stroking her clit. It was as if

Devlin had promised her to them as their entertainment. One lay next to her, giving her deep soul kisses and playing with her breasts, while the other fucked her with a dildo strapped to her waist. In between bouts, Devlin laid out long lines of cocaine for both of them. Anna was shocked since it was the first time she had seen Devlin with drugs. There had never been any at any of his parties, not that she had seen. After doing two lines apiece, they made Anna kiss their pussies. They screamed and writhed when they came. And they played with her breasts and kissed her while Devlin fucked her from behind, making her groan with pleasure. Afterwards, Devlin rang for Vincent who took her back to her room.

In the morning, when Mrs. Leopold was taking Anna down to the kitchen for her breakfast, naked and bound as usual, her hands up behind her connected to her collar, Anna saw the two young girls again in the second floor hallway near the landing. They were both naked and locked into tiny cages on wheels, like the one that Anna was lodged in from time to time. Their hands were bound behind their backs and they were gagged. When they saw Anna, they began a cacophony of muffled pleas, their eyes conveying their desperation and the clear fact that their confinement was far from consensual. Anna looked away. Their fate was none of her concern.

She had just five weeks left on her contract. You might think that after all this while as a sex slave, and all the men she had had to fuck and suck, that her efforts would have begun to flag. Her fear of Devlin's punishments, however, kept her honest and she fucked each man or woman as earnestly and enthusiastically as the next, even when they were in rapid succession. And her level of sexual pleasure never waned either. The potion that she drank three times daily helped with that. She didn't come every time someone used her, but she almost always became aroused and yearned for completion. She had so many partners that she always came at least three or four times during the course of the day, not counting her evening performance before Devlin's camera.

Would Devlin let her go? What would normal life be like? How would she govern herself? Would she suffer a nervous breakdown now that all the pressure of losing the Center and serving as Devlin's whore would be gone? These are the questions that dogged her as her days of enslavement finally began to wane.

With all her time at the club, she still had never been inside the Blue Cantina or knew what was down there, although she had long surmised that there was sexual entertainment of one form or another. When the men entered or left, the loud music from inside would escape into the club's other environs. The men always emerged happy and sated and always entered with wild signs of eager anticipation on their faces.

Finally, one night, a Saturday, when she was coming downstairs after a coupling with one of the guests, one of the stewards came up to her and told her to follow him. They went down a set of stairs at the back of the building and into a dressing room. Anna could hear the loud music of the Blue Cantina on the opposite side of the door. The steward ordered her to strip off her dress and handed her a light blue thong and a pair of light blue stockings, telling her to put them on. When Anna was nude, she picked up the thong and began to put it on. It was cut high and had a narrow waistband with large frills on it. She saw that the front part, which covered her sex, had a slit in it. She im-agined that it was so that the men who she was apparently going to serve could make use of her pussy without removing the thong. She was close, but not exactly right.

Once she had replaced the red high heels she had been wearing with a pair of light blue ones that matched the thong and stockings, the steward took a look at her. "No, no, no," he muttered. He approached her and reached down to her loins.

He spread wide the slit in the front of the thong so that it framed her denuded love lips. "That's the way to wear it," he said.

Anna looked at herself in the wall length mirror near the dressing table. Her pussy was plainly visible, more than that, advertised, by the thong's configuration. Its lips were colored bright red from the gloss she had been trained to apply there. She had no doubt that one or more of the men would want to make use of it.

The steward explained to her carefully that she was to serve the customers drinks. Since the music was so loud, they would write their orders down on little pads. She was to collect them and bring them to the bartender. He would fill the orders and she was to bring them to the tables. If the men wanted to caress or play with her, or if they wanted her to suck their cocks, she should obey, but always return to work as soon as possible. The men probably wouldn't be too interested in her, he concluded, so she shouldn't worry too much about it.

He led her to a door. Anna could hear the music on the other side, steady, rhythmic music like at a disco. "Go ahead," the steward ordered. Anna pushed the door open and was met with a wall of sound. There were ten small tables like at a cocktail lounge. Several men in groups were huddled around them. In front of them was a stage. A beautiful, naked, young girl, wearing leather bracelets and a collar was dancing her heart out on it, swaying and grinding her hips lasciviously. On her belly was tattooed a large, scriptive '*D*' like she had seen on Elaine and which she now wore above her loins. The men all had their eyes pinned to her. The lights were dim, but Anna could see that the entire lounge was decorated in blue, from the tops of the tables to the walls and floor. There were little blue cocktail napkins and a blue neon sign behind the bar spelling out in italic letters, "The Blue Cantina". The bartender, who gave her a little nod, was wearing a blue vest and a blue bow tie.

Anna skirted the tables. A few of the men handed her written orders, none of them too complicated, a martini here, a scotch on the rocks here. While the girl danced through two more songs, Anna served the drinks. Anna watched from the girl from the corner of her eye. She had long, auburn hair and a shapely figure, was no more than 19 or 20. She performed a sexual act on herself. Her orgasm at the end seemed real enough. When she was done, she retreated quickly up the runway to a doorway.

A man who was big enough to be a bouncer, dressed in a blue t-shirt with the club's logo and the name of the nightclub written on it over the left breast, fastened her hands behind her back, installed a ball gag into her mouth and then opened the door. Once the girl had passed through it, another girl emerged, a blond with short hair, a bit slender, but extremely attractive. The bouncer released her arms from behind her back, removed the ball gag from her mouth and she hustled down to the stage where she immediately commenced her routine. Anna noticed that when the auburn haired girl went back stage, one of the men got up from his table, went to a door on the side of the stage, swiped a card in a slot near the door handle and went in. She had no doubt that the auburn haired girl had drawn a customer.

Anna continued her duties, more or less ignoring the girls on the stage and concentrating on her tasks. The music was so loud and the beat so monotonous that it drove all thoughts out of her mind. She would look up and glance at the girls occasionally, wondering where they came from and how they had ended up dancing at The Blue Cantina. They were all beautiful enough and appropriately skilled at being seductive, that they could have worked at any of the first class men's clubs in the city. Or a first class whorehouse for that matter.

She imagined that they got paid a lot to be dancers and whores under bondage conditions.

She suffered a few gropes here and there, nothing serious, and one man did ask her to suck his prick, but he got up and went backstage before she could get him to come. She was wiping a table down where the men had all left to go backstage when she glanced up at the stage. A thin girl with long, chestnut hair and beauteous breasts had come out. She looked nervous to Anna, like she had not been doing this for very long. She started with a slow dance, caressing her body, flitting her fingers in and out of her sexual orifice, rubbing her clit. It was when she closed her eyes, for some reason, that it hit her. The girl looked extremely familiar. When she turned her face into profile, Anna remembered.

It was Audrey! She had left the Center about four weeks ago. Anna had a distinct recollection of seeing her off. Ms. Schopenhauer from the bank had come to collect her. She had been recruited for a job down state and was extremely excited about it. There were smiles and kisses all around. What was she doing here?

Anna watched her carefully. There was no doubt of it, it was her. She could see her eyes flitting nervously about the room like she was afraid of not pleasing someone. The spotlights on the stage prevented her from peering out into the audience and seeing Anna. Anna served some more drinks while she was dancing and was able to get closer to the stage. She saw that there were fresh whip marks across her thighs and breasts. When her routine was finished, Anna watched her hustle back up the runway. Her lips were trembling when the bouncer restored her ball gag and Anna distinctly saw a tear rolling down her cheek. One of the men got up to go back stage.

Anna worked the rest of the night. She saw Audrey three more times. Each time she seemed more unhappy than the last. Once Anna started looking closely, none of the girls looked that happy. They all had false smiles and nervousness in their eyes. More than one had lash marks on her body.

The Blue Cantina closed around 3 A.M. Anna was allowed to shower and then brought to one of the cells where she spent the night and serviced several of the staff members who were just getting off duty. The next morning, she was back in the restaurant. Carlos came and got her to bring her back to the mansion after she had served lunch and a demanding female club member upstairs, who the steward referred to as Dr. Evans.

She said nothing about it to Devlin. How could she, with her suspicions and all. She had noticed on the monthly status reports that more and more of the girls were finding placements quickly while others lingered on. And the turnaround average was way down, meaning that some of the girls hardly spent any time at the Center. What was going on?

On Monday morning, after making sure that both Esther and Gail were out at meetings somewhere, she asked Phyllis to bring her Audrey's file. When she looked at her placement records it said that she had been hired as an intern in the communications department of a Midstate Investments office in a small town about 120 miles west of the city. That was Convery's company! Anna picked up the phone and called the contact number. A woman came on the line. After about ten minutes of dancing around and trying to get the name of someone who was in charge, the woman confessed that she was just an answering service and that she would have to take a message and have someone get back to her. Anna demurred.

The next thing she did was to search on line for the Midstate Investments branch office in that town. She could find nothing. She called the town's chamber of commerce. No luck there either. Then she called the company's headquarters and talked to a PR guy who told her that there was no branch office there.

A dark feeling came over Anna. Esther, Devlin's appointee, was in charge of all placements. Why was Audrey recruited for a job that didn't exist? She looked at her file. Her parents were deceased. She had been living with an abusive uncle, her only relative, when she ran away from home at 16. She had been picked up in a drug raid at a flop house in the poorer section of the city. She had been trading sex for drugs. She spent thirteen months in foster care and then came to the Center about two weeks after her 18th birthday. She had been there all of three months when the job with Midstate had come up. There was no contact name or number in the file for any friend or relative. No one would ever miss her.

She decided to have Phyllis bring the files for the last three months' placements. There were twelve. Seven of the girls had gone to local businesses and were living locally in subsidized apartments. Five of the girls had gone to placements outside the city. Two went to offices run by the bank and one to Midstate. One had allegedly been given a job at Perigourd Industries. The other went to a company she had never heard of. She checked those files. The oldest girl was nineteen. She had been at the Center for six months. She was the longest. The other girls were all at the Center for less time than that. All of the girls had come through foster homes and had been runaways from abusive families. None of them had had any contact with their families since they had run away from home. None of them would be missed. Their pictures were in the files and they were all very attractive. One of them looked like one of the girls who had been dancing at The Blue Cantina Saturday night.

Anna sat glumly staring into space for a long time. Devlin had used her. That was clear. The whole scheme had been to get her out of the way so that the Center could be trolled for prospective sex slaves. Those poor girls, she thought. How many had there been? It was almost eleven months since she had become Devlin's slave, eleven months since Esther had been hired. She remembered Esther's first placement, Wendy. The little red headed girl. Anna retrieved her file and called the bank branch where she was supposed to have gone to work. She spoke to the branch manager. Wendy didn't work there, had never worked there. She had been scheduled for a placement eleven months ago but had never shown up.

Anna burst into tears. She could still see the happy face of the bright, vivacious, young girl as she left that day. Little did she know that she was being sent to her doom. Where was she now? Did she spend time as a dancer at The Blue Cantina until somebody bought her and took her far away? She thought of the bondage dungeon in Convery's basement, where she had spent a night. Had Wendy done time there? The black woman who was Convery's servant thought nothing about leading a woman upstairs in chains. Was Wendy serving now in some private whorehouse, kept prisoner and obedient at the point of a whip?

When she stopped crying, she thought of the two blond girls who had been caged and ready for shipment at Devlin's a while ago. Anna had thought nothing of it, was too lost in her own captivity to care. Where were they sent and where had they come from? Now that she thought about it, there was something familiar about them.

Anna had Phyllis bring the files for the girls who had been rejected for placement at the Center within the last three months either because of drug or discipline problems, or because of a perceived lack of interest. They always kept a file on each girl in case she came back later or someone wanted to know why they were rejected. They also took a picture to help verify identification. She had seen the girls at Devlin's a couple of weeks ago. She looked through the files. It was one of the things that she normally did, check through the rejection files for quality control purposes. She had been falling down on the other aspects of her job, but this one she had kept up on.

Sure enough, three weeks ago, two sisters, Destiny and Brooks Murray, had been interviewed by Gail. They were 18 and 19, born 13 months apart. They had been recommended to a drug program as a condition of being admitted to the Center. They had both refused. They were working as go-go girls at a strip club downtown when they were picked up on a drug raid. They were originally from Florida and hadn't seen their parents since they were 16 and 17 respectively. They were released from the county jail on time served sentence a few days after Gail's interview, about the same time they showed up at Devlin's. Where were they now?

Anna felt horrified that she had seen the girls all bound and caged up and done nothing. She looked back at the file. It had a little orange tag. So did seven of the fourteen files from the last three months. Anna looked through them quickly. They were all attractive girls who wouldn't be missed. She still had Audrey's fie on her desk. That had an orange tag too. And so did the others she had picked out as likely candidates for Devlin's slavery scheme.

She left her office to go to the filing cabinets. She pulled open the drawer where the records for the last year were kept. There were twenty orange tags on girls who had come through the center and forty on the files of the girls who had been rejected for one reason or another. With the girls from the last three months, that meant that 70 girls had fallen into Devlin's clutches. Where had they all gone? Where were they now? How could Devlin dispose of 70 girls within 11 months? He had to be part of a vast conspiracy that probably reached clear across the country, maybe even internationally. Then she remembered the Asian man. He had come by like clockwork. She shuddered. That had to be it! They were being sold overseas!

Panic struck deep into Anna's psyche. If Devlin found out that she knew, it would spell her doom. He would probably make sure that she disappeared as well. What could she do?

The first thing she did was to put all the files back in the cabinet. She finished just in time as Esther and Gail walked in together. Anna gave them as friendly a hello as she could under the circumstances and rushed back to her office. The police. She had to call the police! It was 11 o'clock and she was scheduled to be at Harrington's office at 2. She had three hours to get the story in front of the right detective. If she was not at Harrington's by 2, Devlin was sure to find out and there would be hell to pay.

Her hand trembling, she picked up the telephone and called the central police station. She spoke to a dispatcher and told her that she needed to report a crime. After a few simple screening questions, she was directed to the detective bureau. She told the detective that she had information on a slave ring operating in the city and she was shunted off to sex crimes. The detective who took the call was named Daniels. He listened to her abbreviated version of the story and told her to come right down to the station immediately.

Detective Sergeant Daniels was about 45 or so and was typically phlegmatic as Anna's conception of a detective from TV. He was wearing wrinkled black slacks, scruffy black shoes and a white short sleeve shirt. His tie looked like he never untied it but slipped it off his head each night, slipping it on in the mornings when he went to work. His desk was covered with loose papers and used Styrofoam coffee cups. Anna conjectured that the only reason he was not smoking was because it was not allowed in the station.

He took her to a conference room, bringing with him a small spiral notebook. He took assiduous notes as Anna talked. She was embarrassed and shamed to tell the part about her own enslavement and broke into tears when she told him about the 70 young girls who had apparently been kidnapped and sold into slavery. He got her a cup of stale coffee while she recovered.

"So you say that this girl is at this place called The Blue Cantina right now as we speak?" he asked her in his raspy voice.

"Yes! Yes! Something's got to be done. She and another girl, I'm sure of it. At least them, maybe more."

"This is that millionaire's club out in Springdale?" he queried.

"Yes, I think it's in Springdale. I'm not sure. I've never driven there. I've always been in the back of Mr. Devlin's limousine."

"I know the place you're talking about," he said. "It's got those big lions or something at the gate."

"Yes! Yes! That's the place!"

"This Devlin's a pretty shady character," the detective commented. "He's got his fingers in a lot of pies. I know he's got connections in the police department so I've got to be very careful about this. I think that I should go directly to the State Attorney General's office. That may take some time."

"But you have to move fast!" Anna pleaded. "I think that they're selling the girls overseas. Audrey and the other girl could be gone any day. You've got to save them."

"I give you my word that I'll move on them tonight. I'll call the A.G.'s office as soon as you leave. What time can you get free?"

"I have to see one of Devlin's friends, Mr. Harrington of the Eastside Bank and Trust, at 2. He's a member of the club too."

Daniels whistled. "There's some high powered people in on this. I have to be sure that you're telling the truth."

Anna started to cry again. "You've got to believe me! Lives are at stake. Those poor girls, raped night after night! You don't know what it's like!"

"Listen, Anna," Detective Daniels interjected, "I've been on the sex crimes unit for ten years. I know what it does to women. I've seen it all, believe me. It's not pretty. But if we fuck this up, they're likely to empty the place out and we won't find any girls there at all, nor any hide or hair. Without proof, all you've got are suppositions."

"I know! I know!" Anna said.

"Okay. So are you available after 3 or so?"

"No. I've got to go to the gym at 4 or the trainer will tell Devlin. He might get suspicious. I'm usually done with my workout about 5:30. I can meet you wherever you want at 6."

"I think it's better if we wait until dark, say 8 o'clock. Then there'll be a whole lot of people there. We'll catch them all red handed. It'll give me more time to get my ducks in order. They'll probably send the State Police Tactical Squad. They can muster up 100 uniforms. This way we'll go inside, I'll confirm what you've told me and then I'll blow the whistle. The uniforms will storm the place. Not even a squeak will get past them."

"Okay," Anna murmured. Devlin would know something was wrong if she wasn't home by 6 o'clock. She would have to hide somewhere. She could dodge him for two hours. The idea of catching all those callous, cruel people with incriminating evidence was exciting.

"Where will I meet you?"

"Let's meet at 19:45, a quarter to 8 that is, about a half mile down the road south of the club," Daniels suggested. "We'll go in in my car. I'll be armed with a warrant and a Colt .45."

Anna nodded her agreement.

"And we'll pick up this Esther and Gail after work. I'll bet when they get downtown, once they find out they're facing 70 consecutive life sentences, they'll sing like canaries. We'll get this Schopenhauer broad too."

She made it to Harrington's office just in time. All the way there she was elated beyond imagining. Her ordeal was about to end. Some of the girls would be saved. Maybe, once their destination was known, the police overseas could track down the girls who had been sent there. She could only hope. She kicked herself for being so stupid. Why hadn't she seen it? It occurred to her that maybe the whole thing about Carol had been a set up. Maybe Carol had been kidnapped too! She prayed it wasn't true, but it made sense. Carol would have told Devlin all about her. He would have known about her past and how to exploit it. She had always had the sensation that Devlin was able to peer inside her brain and that would explain it.

All the time she had Harrington's cock in her mouth, she kept thinking that it would be the last time. She imagined him in handcuffs being led to the county jail, pleading guilty and being sent to prison. And Devlin too. She would have to resign the Center once the whole story got out, but that was a small price to pay to know that from now on the girls would be safe. She swallowed Harrington's cum dutifully although she felt like spitting it in his face.

Once she had put her top back on and left Harrington's office, she sped back to the Center. She did the best she could to act like everything was normal. Devlin called at 3:45 to let her know that they would be going to a party this coming Wednesday and that she should get her nails and hair done tomorrow. He had made an appointment for her at 11.

At the gym, Anna ran through her workouts. To her dismay, Cathy had her go back into the stretching room, as she called it, and made her lick her pussy for a long time and then licked her in return until she had three shattering orgasms. There was no question that she was going to miss the sex, especially the girl on girl stuff. "Maybe I can get something on with Elaine once she's out of Devlin's clutches," she thought. She had had enough cocks for a lifetime.

Anna went to a diner on the outskirts of the city to wait until it was time to meet Det. Daniels. She had a double cheeseburger, crispy fries and a vanilla milk shake. They were all wonderful. Yet she couldn't help having this ominous, foreboding feeling. She had been Devlin's slave for almost a year and had gotten to the point where she didn't make a single move without his express permission. To be disobeying him by not going directly to her apartment after her training at the gym seemed like she was rebelling against God. It would take a long time, she knew, before she was able to get rid of that feeling.

When she arrived at the rendezvous, Daniels was sitting in his car, a dirty looking, golden brown GTO. She parked behind him, then got out and opened his passenger door. She sat down next to him. Her heart was beating wildly. Her stomach was in a knot and her hands were sweating. Her whole body was trembling.

"You ready?" Daniels asked her.

She nodded. "But where are all the other policemen?" she asked nervously.

"We couldn't very well have them lined up and down the road, could we?" he replied. "Don't worry, when I send the signal, they'll be there."

"Okay," Anna answered meekly.

Daniels started the car. It was a typical detective's car, messy and banged up but with a large engine that purred like a kitten. They turned into the entrance, between the two angry, stone lions and cruised up the driveway. When they got to the gate, Det. Daniels showed the guard his golden shield and a copy of the warrant. The guard opened the gate and let them in.

Daniels stopped the car in front of the entrance. The car valet, dressed in eighteenth century servant's livery, tried to take the keys from him to park the car, but Daniels just snatched them away from him. The doorman opened the door. Anna stepped over the threshold with great trepidation. The last time she had been here, two days ago, she had been a slave. It was hard to forget. As they walked down the hallway to The Blue Cantina, her heart was pounding. They passed several wide eyed men who Anna was sure had fucked her one time or another.

He swung open the large carved door with the club's evil insignia and the name of the nightclub on it emblazoned on it in bright blue letters. The music came out blaring at them immediately. They walked down the stairs. The club was empty. There was no bartender, no bouncer, no customers. The door to the backstage was locked. Daniels looked at Anna quizzically. He leaned over and put his mouth to her ear. "Where are the cells you were talking about!" he screamed over the music. Anna pointed to the door to the dressing room.

When they passed into the dressing room, the sound of the music reduced to tolerable levels. Anna led Daniels through the door to the hallway. She was pretty sure this was the way. It took a couple twists and turns and they came to a doorway that looked familiar. Anna pushed it open and strode through. She was right. There was the long line of cells. There was the open central area where the guards usually hung out and the girls were made to strip before they went to their cells for the night. There were four of the guards, big, bulky fellows, wearing Blue Cantina t-shirts. And there, to Anna's shocked surprise, was Devlin.

He smiled. "Hello, Anna," he said.

CHAPTER ELEVEN

Anna turned as if to run, but Daniels was blocking the door. She tried to run to the other exit down the hall, but two of the guards got in her way. Stupefied with fear, she stumbled back to the center of the room. Devlin was sitting in one of the guard's chairs, smoking a cigar. The guards closed around her. Anna fell to her knees and let out a loud, plaintive wail. She bent her head to the floor and began to sob. It couldn't be true! It couldn't! But it was. She was trapped and at Devlin's total mercy. She knew she would get none.

"Good work, Daniels," she heard Devlin say. "Why don't you come back later tonight? You can fuck her if you want."

"Thanks, Mr. Devlin," Daniels replied. "I might just do that. First I have to follow up on this missing persons report about one Anna Addunizio. Seems she just ran off without telling a soul." He laughed and Devlin did too.

Anna heard the door shut behind her. It had the sound of the knell of doom. She knew she was lost, utterly, irretrievably lost. And she faced a storm of punishment. Her insides began to twist and turn. Suddenly, she raised her head and vomited her wonderful dinner all over the floor.

"That's nasty, Anna," Devlin said, humored at her distress. "All that fatty food. Your system can't handle all that after the diet you've been on, Anna. I could have told you that. We had you followed of course. But don't worry, you'll be well taken care of." He nodded to the guards.

They sprang into action. Two of them grabbed her by the arms while the other two began tearing off her clothes. She struggled valiantly, but was no match for them.

"No! No! You bastards! You fucking bastards!" she yelled out. They had her blouse off of her in a moment. Her bare breasts swung to and fro while they tore at her skirt and pulled it down over her hips. She was nude underneath, underwear being a thing of the long ago past. They pushed her down to the floor on her belly, carefully avoiding the puddle of vomit and fastened a pair of leather bracelets on her wrists. She strained mightily to avoid her hands being brought behind her back, but they quickly had them joined there. A collar was fastened around her neck.

She was still screaming invectives against them, and Devlin too, even though she knew that she would pay for them dearly later. One of the men pulled at her hair, lifting her head from the floor and a gag was shoved between her lips. She jammed her teeth closed firmly, but one of the men took hold of her cheeks just above her jaws and squeezed them mightily. Anna screamed in pain, or tried to. Once she opened her mouth, the gag slipped right in. She felt it being buckled behind her head. The men pulled her to her feet.

Devlin was still sitting in his chair calmly smoking his cigar. Anna was sobbing and crying, fear passing through her like a fierce, electrical current. Two of the guards were holding her firmly by her arms. She stopped struggling, knowing that it was futile.

"It certainly took you a long time to figure things out, Anna," Devlin said. "I wouldn't have pegged you for being so stupid. I guess all that cock you were getting went right to your brain." He laughed. "I have to admit though that once you did suss it out, you took all the right steps. You were cool as a cucumber when I talked to you this afternoon. That shows character. I've always admired you for that, Anna, believe it or not. You've got real character and that's rare in this world. It's too bad that you'll probably never get a chance to show it again."

Anna's heart sank. She realized that Devlin would never let her see the outside of the club. She had heard what Daniels had said. The plans for her disappearance had already been laid. They even had her car. She had driven it here for them.

"You see, Anna, I knew that the game was up with you about a quarter after 10 this morning. Phyllis, your receptionist, called me as soon as you asked for those files. You didn't know that she was working for me? That's too bad. It seems that she has a little brother in state prison at Phillipsburg. I hear it's the toughest prison in the state. Gangs and all that. He's just a little white kid sent up for dealing acid at a Dead concert last year. That's heavy duty stuff. Just a little bit puts you into the big time. He got a 15 year sentence. My people up there could make the place hell for him or give him some cushy trustee's job. Phyllis decided the latter was better and so she started spying on you."

"Phyllis!" Anna exclaimed inside. How could she do this? The one person she had relied on as absolutely trustworthy. It seemed that Devlin could corrupt anyone.

"You never did see the camera I had installed in your office. I watched you sneak those cookies and candy bars from time to time. It wasn't worth punishing you for since I didn't want you to know about the camera. I made up for it in other ways though."

Devlin took a long drag on his cigar. He blew out a long plume of light grayish smoke.

A bitter hatred for him infused her. All those girls! And now it would go on and on! Esther would certainly be made the new Director. Gail would move up to her slot and, she was sure, Devlin would have someone ready to take Gail's. The depredations would continue, maybe for years! Anna felt a surge of energy. She pulled at the iron like grips on her arms and tried to rush at Devlin, kicking at him. She released a loud, angry roar from behind her gag.

"That's the spirit, Anna," Devlin said, laughing. "That's one of the reasons I like you. But we can't have you acting out like that." He reached into the pocket of his suit and pulled out a small electronic gadget. He looked at it for a second, flicked a switch and aimed it at her. A second later, her collar sent out a paralyzing, excruciating shock to her whole system. She screamed in pain and twisted and turned in the arms of her captors. If they had not been holding her, she would have fallen to the floor.

When she had recovered, she broke out into sobs. She looked at Devlin dolefully. He held all the cards.

"Please don't make me do that again, Anna," he told her. "Rebellion serves no useful purpose here. It's so easily quashed."

Anna had to concede the point.

"You've probably guessed by now that the whole Carol thing was a setup. She's still here, you know. The third cell down, on your left. I kept her around in case I needed any more information about you. Unlike you, she really has a low threshold for pain. She told me anything I wanted to know. She's been useful here too. You can't know how hard it is for the staff members to keep their dicks in their pants during working hours. All those beautiful girls going around spreading their legs and opening their mouths, displaying their tits. She was a great help in that department, although her enthusiasm did pale from time to time. But that was easily corrected."

"Carol!" Anna thought. "Poor Carol! What would become of her now?"

It seemed that Devlin was reading her mind.

"We'll ship her out now, now that she's served her purpose. You too, I'm afraid. We can't take the chance of you getting loose and maybe telling the real police. Not that you'd find any in this town." He laughed again.

"I'm really going to miss you, Anna," he continued. "It was so sweet to have you crying in my arms. But your time was almost up and you would have been in the same predicament you are in now in a week or two anyway." He stood up.

"They're going to take you to your cell now, Anna. I'd be very cooperative if I were you. It's going to take a little while to arrange things so you'll be spending a few more days with us. Be a good little girl and fuck like a bunny. If you don't show the proper enthusiasm, I'm afraid you will have to suffer needlessly. And don't worry. I'm not going to punish you for what you tried to do. Your new life will be punishment enough. And I'll see you before you go. I promise."

Devlin nodded to the guards. They dragged her down the hall and into one of the cells. They chained her securely to the bed, hooded her and left.

Anna cried and cried. She cried for herself and the terrible predicament she was in. She cried for all those poor girls. She cried for the Center, her Center, the one she had worked so hard to make a success. And she cried for all the abuse and shameful acts she had underwent, all for nothing, all as a dupe to Devlin's malevolent scheme.

She had been bound and gagged before, even locked in confined spaces, awaiting punishment or use. But this was different. Here she was a real prisoner. She had always had the idea, what she now knew was just an illusion, that the time would come when she would be free once again, free to live the life that she chose.

That was not the case now. She was on a one way trip to oblivion which would end only with an anonymous death. No one would come by later to release her and let her drive home. She would not get up tomorrow morning and drive to the Center, assume her alter ego, make phone calls, talk to her friends, comfort and counsel the young girls just struggling to get an honest shake in the world. She would not make a single solitary decision, take a single, solitary action, for the rest of her life unless at the behest or with the permission of a master.

Her body would never be hers again and she would never again have the right to deny anyone access to it.

No one who cared anything about her knew where she was. And those people who did care about her, her friends, she had spent the last year pushing them away. Her erratic behavior would be cover enough for her disappearance. Maybe Devlin would pull the same old gag about the stolen money. He had her undated note. He could have Esther forge a check in her name, drop it in her account and then have the money disappear. Harrington would be real helpful in that department. She wondered whether he knew as she was sucking his cock earlier that she was destined for the dungeon like cells of the club today. He probably did and, as she was thinking of him wearing a prison outfit, he was thinking of her naked and bound on the very bed she lay on now. Clearly, it was his vision of the future that prevailed.

A guard came in about an hour after she had been chained to the bed. He removed her hood. She blinked in the bright light. If he expected that she would cooperate any more in her rape and abuse, he and Devlin had another thing coming, she thought. Then she saw the long, cylindrical object in his hand. Her legs were spread wide and he placed the end just inside her love lips. Desperately, Anna tried to shift her hips to avoid it. A second later a fierce shock erupted from its end. It made Anna's body jump on the bed. He pussy absorbed the energy of the electrical pulse and spread it through her body, a pain that raged through her down to the minutest follicle on her head.

"Mmmmmmmmmmmmmmmm!" Anna moaned dismally. Her eyes became as wide as saucers as the man poked the end of the cattle prod in her vagina again.

"…eeeeeeeeeee…! ….ooooooooooo!" she screamed through her gag. The cylinder spat out another jolting shock. It felt like a horse had kicked her right in her quim. She screamed as her body writhed and twisted on the bed.

She was crying uncontrollably when the man unchained her from the bed. Her wrists were confined to a ring in the front of her collar. He pointed the cattle prod to a place on the floor in front of him. Anna knelt there obediently. When he took out his cock, she subsumed it into her mouth and sucked it with devoted passion.

That was the end of her rebellion. She fucked all comers with all the energy she could muster. Daniels came by that night and they took her to a bigger room down the hall with a bigger bed and a whipping post so he could have his fun with her. Several times she was hooded and bound and escorted to one of the upstairs bedrooms where she served one of the members who wanted to have a last fling with her. Harrington fucked her there as did Perigourd who, to Anna's surprise, was uncharacteristically solicitous. That woman, Dr. Evans, had her twice there. It seemed somehow to Anna that she knew everything about her, all of her triggers. She was demanding, cold and cruel.

Devlin had her sent up for his benefit for one last thrill. He had Carol sent up at the same time and she and Anna had a tearful reunion before Devlin made them perform for him. He sent Carol away first, fucked Anna a long time, around the horn, her mouth, her pussy and her ass, and then held her while she cried and cried in his arms. Anna was near hysterics when the steward came to bring her back to her cell. She begged and pleaded with Devlin desperately to spare her. She cried and sobbed and promised never to tell a soul, to be his slave for life, to do anything he wanted. He just smiled and patted her head as the steward locked her wrists behind her back and then gagged her. He pulled the hood over her head, sealing off her tear filled eyes. It took two of the stewards to carry her to her cell. When they got her there, one of the guards was waiting and he fucked her on her little bed before leaving her there hog tied and hooded to sob in dismal mourning.

It was hard for Anna to say how long she was held a prisoner in the basement of the club. There was no day and night in her little cell and her meals, always eaten from a bowl on the floor, seemed haphazard and random. There was a toilet, a steel one like they have in real prison cells. Her wrists were generally kept locked to the front of her collar and a chain ran from the back of her collar to the head of her bed. The shower was down the hall and she would be brought out alone once in a while and washed there. She never saw any of the other girls and she didn't see Carol again. Unlike her room on the 4th floor of Devlin's mansion, she could not hear anyone coming and going outside her cell, the isolation and silence, other than her own occasional sobs and pleas for mercy, was complete.

The chains that bound her and the heavy steel door that sealed her in were implacable, remorseless, invincible, just like the callous men who continued to use her. She often thought of the incongruity of being reduced to living in a 12' by 12' underground space, when there was an entire world out there of free people just a mile or so from where she lay. They were all ignorant of the terrible things being done in their midst. It was a world she had once inhabited but now was as far away from her as she was from the moon. She knew that she would never see it again.

Her time was spent in either dull, emotionless acceptance of her lot or in deep fear and tearful dismay as to what her future portended. She knew that she lacked power to affect her destiny in any way. She was in the possession of conscienceless, evil people. The thought of the unfairness and cruelty of what they were doing to her and to the innocent young girls of the Center darkened her heart and soured her belly.

Finally, one day, they came for her. She knew it as soon as the cell door opened. She was half sitting, half lying on her bed, gagged, her wrists confined to her collar. There were three of them, all wearing the Blue Cantina t-shirt, all muscular and broad shouldered, all bigger and stronger than her.

She struggled nonetheless. Within seconds though, one of them had given her an injection in her rear. The other men held her down until she became torpid and listless. One of the men went out of her cell and returned with a padded wooden platform on wheels. She was brought over to it and forced to kneel down. Her hands were locked behind her back and her ankles to rings in the platform. A chain was attached to the ring on her collar and pulled through a ring in the front of the padded platform. Her neck was pulled down until her breasts touched her thighs.

The men wheeled her out of her cell and down the hall. Anna's awareness of what was going on around her was dim at best. The men took her through a door and down another hall. At the end was a large room. There were several closed crates there. The chain on her neck was loosened and she felt her head pulled up. Through her fog she detected her former master and his Asian friend.

Devlin patted her face. "Come awake! Come awake, Anna!" he said. "It's time to say goodbye!"

Anna came to attention. She saw the crates around the room, saw the sides and top of another one laying against the wall and presumed they were for her. It was the end of the line. The utter hopelessness and unfairness of her predicament passed through her like a sudden illness and she began to cry.

"There, there, Anna," Devlin said. "I have good news for you. Taketo here has taken a personal interest in you. He intends to keep you for himself for the foreseeable future. Serve him well and who knows, he might keep you out of the general stream of commerce for a year or so.

"The place you're going to is called Aguna Island. It's a tiny island, no more than 2 or 3 square miles, about 35 miles northeast of the island of Okinawa in the East China Sea.

The Yakuza organizations have a pretty good deal with the government. The government doesn't inquire about what goes on there and the people in power get a nice piece of change every month. It's a clearing house for all kinds of contraband, including, I'm afraid, the girls from the Center. We get a pretty good buck for them. They either stay on the island as entertainment like you will be, or are shipped off to buyers throughout East Asia, even as far away as the Middle East. There's quite a market."

He pointed to one of the sealed crates. "Your friend Carol, here, I'm sad to tell you, has already been purchased. Her crate won't even leave the airport. There'll be a plane waiting for her and away she'll go. This one over here is Audrey, the girl you were so worried about. And these two over here are Destiny and Brooks. You remember them. They're going to be a great matched pair for somebody."

Devlin turned back to look at Anna. "Like I said, there's quite a market. That's why eventually Gail will be taking over as Director and Esther will be starting up a new branch of the Center down in the state capital. From there, who knows? Maybe we can franchise the idea all over the States. Pussy may become a cash crop!"

He laughed. Anna did not feel like laughing. She could barely keep her eyes open. She struggled to cast one more vile aspersion on Devlin's ancestors and him personally, but it emerged from her gag as a mere mumble. She saw Devlin give the guards next to her a nod.

The gag was unbuckled from behind her head and a type of gas mask was placed on in its stead. While the men started to assemble the sides of her crate, Devlin continued to talk to her, like he was truly sorry to see her go and couldn't tear himself away. He came close and began to stroke her head, like he was saying goodbye to a favorite pet. "The mask is for the air tank that will be installed on the top of your crate. In a minute or so, you'll be given another shot. This one will slow your heart and metabolism rate down almost to a dead stop. It's top secret stuff from the military, but we have found a connection for it. There'll be enough air in your tank for 36 hours, believe it or not."

Three sides of Anna's crate were installed and the guard was waiting to install the front. Anna looked up. Her new master, Taketo, was standing next to her old one, Devlin. Well, in the end, what difference did it make? Her fate had been decided many years ago.

"Goodbye, Anna," Devlin said. "I won't forget you."

Anna felt the chain that led to her collar being pulled down. Her head was lowered until her breasts were touching her knees once more. She felt a jab in her neck and the sensation of something being pumped into her. A few moments later, just as the front of the crate was being added on, her mind started to shut down. Her body felt like it was wandering away from her. She was losing sensation all over. She didn't notice it when the top was applied to the crate. It was two feet high and contained her air tank. Her hose was connected and the top screwed in, sealing her in place.

The men quickly rolled the seven crates to the elevator where they were brought up to the ground floor. They began loading the crates on the Blue Cantina van and securing them in place. Taketo turned, said something in Japanese to Devlin, bowing slightly and shook his hand. Devlin just smiled. He took out a cigar and clipped its end while the men finished loading the truck. By the time they were all on, it was lit and he had taken a big puff.

The doors to the van shut. The driver and his assistant got in. The engine fired up and it pulled away, Taketo in his limousine right behind it.

"Goodbye, Anna," Devlin thought. "It was fun while it lasted." He took another puff of his cigar. And then he remembered. That woman was coming by tonight, Sheila, the one with the gambling problem. She was a real looker from her pictures, long, wavy, chestnut colored hair, about 24 or 25, large breasts and delightful curves. Seems she was into a local bookie for over 250 large, a quarter of a million dollars. Of course, he had laid out the credit to her at Devlin's instructions and the bets had all been covered so that no one was really out of pocket. But she didn't know that. All she knew was that Bubba had shown up at her door and convinced her that she had to find a way to pay or she would be buried in a 55 gallon drum out in the woods somewhere.

Somehow, someone had given her the idea that Devlin might help her. Well, he just might.

* * * * * * * * * * * * * * *

Six months later, Anna was kneeling on a tan *tatami* mat in the front room of an elegant Japanese style house overlooking the East China Sea, gazing out the large picture window. It was near sunset and red rays of light were flooding the horizon. The sea was roiling from a storm passing several hundred miles to the west, crashing loudly onto the rough rocks some 200' below. She was naked, as she had been constantly since her life began here. Her hair was longer now; Taketo liked her to keep it in a ponytail. A thin chain led from a ring in her outer labia to a ring in the floor. It was just long enough to allow her to reach the amenities if the need struck, but not long enough for her to leave the room.

Taketo would be coming home today. She could see out the window the road on which he would be driving and she was peering intently down it, seeking the first sign of his coming. He had been away for the last four days on his bi-weekly trip back to the States to obtain merchandise. Anna had spent them in the main resort, being used by the wealthy Chinese, Japanese and Korean patrons, and down in the training rooms helping to break in some of the new girls. It had been rough for her in the beginning too. Taketo had helped her to understand that her new status was permanent and that she shouldn't waste her time and energy in fruitless fantasies of rescue or liberation.

She didn't mind serving in the main resort, as long as they kept on bringing her back here to her master. The fact that they had meant he would be arriving soon.

He would be pleased. Fuko had almost completed the tattoo of the design Taketo had drawn for her breasts. It was a nearly naked, beautiful, reclining courtesan. She lay across her chest, her legs spread around Anna's right breast, her nipple serving as the clit of her vulva. Her arms were reaching out, circling Anna's left breast, proffering it to the observer. She was smiling lasciviously and wearing a colorful kimono that was open and revealing all of her considerable charms.

Fuko was about half done now. Much of the work on her back was completed as well as up and down the front of her thighs. The old artisan had a smattering of English and he gave her to know that Taketo would not be bothering to adorn her with his personal designs unless he meant to keep her for a very long time. That suited Anna. Taketo was polite and considerate, not mean at all, not usually, and he fulfilled her every physical need. He was stricter and harsher than Devlin had ever been, but that was only right if she were to remember her place as his slave and her duty to keep pleasing him. And she did so want to please him. Later tonight he would have his friends come over so she could entertain them. Woe betide her if she failed one iota in her duty.

She saw the headlights of a car approaching. Her heart began to beat wildly and her stomach began to flutter. Her pussy clenched at the thought of being used by him. Soon. He would be here soon.

The end.